NOWHERE TO RUN

(A Harley Cole FBI Suspense Thriller—Book 3)

Kate Bold

Kate Bold

Bestselling author Kate Bold is author of the ALEXA CHASE SUSPENSE THRILLER series, comprising six books (and counting); the ASHLEY HOPE SUSPENSE THRILLER series, comprising six books (and counting); the CAMILLE GRACE FBI SUSPENSE THRILLER series, comprising five books (and counting); and the HARLEY COLE FBI SUSPENSE THRILLER series, comprising five books (and counting).

An avid reader and lifelong fan of the mystery and thriller genres, Kate loves to hear from you, so please feel free to visit www.kateboldauthor.com to learn more and stay in touch.

Copyright © 2022 by Kate Bold. All rights reserved. Except as permitted under the U.S. Copyright Act of 1976, no part of this publication may be reproduced, distributed or transmitted in any form or by any means, or stored in a database or retrieval system, without the prior permission of the author. This ebook is licensed for your personal enjoyment only. This ebook may not be re-sold or given away to other people. If you would like to share this book with another person, please purchase an additional copy for each recipient. If you're reading this book and did not purchase it, or it was not purchased for your use only, then please return it and purchase your own copy. Thank you for respecting the hard work of this author. This is a work of fiction. Names, characters, businesses, organizations, places, events, and incidents either are the product of the author's imagination or are used fictionally. Any resemblance to actual persons, living or dead, is entirely coincidental. Jacket image Copyright Galyna Andrushko, used under license from Shutterstock.com.
ISBN: 978-1-0943-3005-1

BOOKS BY KATE BOLD

ALEXA CHASE SUSPENSE THRILLER
THE KILLING GAME (Book #1)
THE KILLING TIDE (Book #2)
THE KILLING HOUR (Book #3)
THE KILLING POINT (Book #4)
THE KILLING FOG (Book #5)
THE KILLING PLACE (Book #6)

ASHLEY HOPE SUSPENSE THRILLER
LET ME GO (Book #1)
LET ME OUT (Book #2)
LET ME LIVE (Book #3)
LET ME BREATHE (Book #4)
LET ME FORGET (Book #5)
LET ME ESCAPE (Book #6)

CAMILLE GRACE FBI SUSPENSE THRILLER
NOT ME (Book #1)
NOT NOW (Book #2)
NOT WELL (Book #3)
NOT HER (Book #4)
NOT NORMAL (Book #5)

HARLEY COLE FBI SUSPENSE THRILLER
NOWHERE SAFE (Book #1)
NOWHERE LEFT (Book #2)
NOWHERE TO RUN (Book #3)
NOWHERE LIKE THIS (Book #4)
NOWHERE GIRL (Book #5)

PROLOGUE

Spencer leaned against the tour boat's metal railing and stared into the cavern growing larger along the shoreline. There was something menacing about the way the cavern rose from the earth like a greedy mouth, eager to swallow them whole. If the Rio Grande rose a little higher, he wondered, would it fill the cavern? Or did the cavern keep going deeper and deeper into the earth, like a stomach that could never be sated?

Something smooth and cold pressed against Spencer's elbow, startling him.

"Come on, have another," Jordan Armstrong said, lofting a beer. He was sweating in the early morning heat, which was just beginning to penetrate the blanket of cool air that had covered the river during the night. There was a riotous gleam in his eye, the kind that usually signaled he was going to lead Spencer into some kind of trouble.

The bachelor party on the river had been Jordan's idea. It had also been Jordan's idea to bring along Ed Mullins and Jaylen Ware, both of whom had been in Spencer's dorm back at the University of Claxton. All four had graduated five years earlier, each with plans for conquering the world.

What happened to us? Spencer wondered, glancing toward Ed and Jaylen, who were engaged in a sidebar about the pros and cons of cryptocurrency. *When did we get so old?* It seemed like just a few months earlier they had been making plans to get Mr. Reynolds's Kawasaki onto the roof of the gymnasium. Life had been fun then and full of excitement.

Now? Well, now life was about responsibility—bills, IRAs, water cooler politics, and of course, planning the wedding, a task that was never finished. When did it all change?

Pondering these thoughts, his gaze continued past his friends to the group of people filling the rest of the pontoon boat, strangers with whom Spencer had exchanged no more than a few polite lines of conversation. At the far end, piloting the boat, was their tour guide

1

Colin Sharpton—a bronzed, bearded statue of a man straight from antiquity.

It was not Sharpton who caught Spencer's eye, however, but rather the passenger beside the tour guide—a young woman about Spencer's age wearing a crop top and swim shorts. There was a pleasant sprinkling of freckles across the bridge of her nose, and Spencer couldn't help noticing the tone of her abs—a striking contrast to the flab his fiancée Sandra had recently put on.

The woman caught him looking and smiled. He glanced away, feeling guilty for the comparison, and reached into his pocket for the wedding band he had recently started carrying with him everywhere he went—as if by constantly reminding himself of his decision he might finally make peace with it. He found only his phone, which was supposed to be waterproof for up to half an hour, and remembered he had left the ring at home rather than risk losing it in the river. He felt the ring's presence, nonetheless.

"It's your last chance to live a little," Jordan was saying, pushing the beer against Spencer's white polo. "As soon as Sandra gets you in her clutches, your life will be nothing but folding fitted sheets and endless agonizing about whether the end table should go on the left side of the couch or the right. And then if you have *kids*…"

Jordan turned to include Ed, the only one of the four who had kids of his own—probably the only one who had ever changed a diaper, Spencer supposed. Ed, however, was too absorbed by his conversation with Jaylen to notice Jordan, so Spencer was spared the lecture on the pitfalls of parenting.

"Look," Jordan continued, stifling a burp, "all I'm saying is you don't want to look back a year from now and regret the things you didn't do, okay? There's a golden age that dawns in every man's life when he sets out from his parents' house to make his own fortune, and it ends when a beautiful woman convinces him to beat his sword into a plowshare."

Spencer arched an eyebrow, impressed by the metaphor. "Come up with that one yourself?"

"Ancient History, 101." Jordan waved his hand, dismissing the thought. "The point is, there's no going back."

Spencer turned his body toward him, still clutching the rail with his right hand. His eyes wanted to drift to the freckled girl—he felt an urgent need to see if she was watching him—but he forced himself to keep his attention on Jordan.

2

"No," he said, "the point is, you're drunk. You're supposed to be helping me have a good time, not telling me why I'm making a huge mistake."

Jordan placed his hand on Spencer's shoulder. Before he could offer whatever defense he had prepared, however, the engine died and Sharpton dropped the anchor over the side. The gleaming metal plopped into the water and vanished.

"This is as far as we go," Sharpton said in a voice of cheerful command. "Anyone who wants to see the cavern: stow your beers, grab a life jacket, and hop on into the drink."

Spencer slipped out of his flip-flops, tossed them into the compartment beneath one of the seats, and stood on the edge of the boat like a condemned man before a pirate's plank. He stared at the impenetrable darkness of the cavern and had the odd sense he was looking into his future—a murky, unknowable mystery. Was it a mystery worth exploring, or would it really be as bleak as Jordan suggested—a life where his only escape became the office and every vacation involved packing the stroller with every item a child could possibly need?

"Come on, already!" Jordan said, giving him a nudge. Spencer's feet slipped off the edge of the boat and the water rose to meet him, a sheet of glass shattering beneath his knees. The water was cooler than he had expected, and he felt a pleasant shiver course through his body.

You gotta stop thinking about it, he told himself. *What will be, will be. That's all there is to it. Just enjoy your freedom while you can.*

There was a shout from the boat. Spencer pivoted just in time to get hit by an explosion of water as Ed cannonballed into the river. Several others joined him in rapid succession, and before Spencer knew it, he was being left behind.

Knuckling the water from his eyes, Spencer leaned forward and kicked his feet as he swam toward the cavern. Something soft and slippery brushed against his toes. Then he touched sand, and he pushed upward, rising into a chorus of laughter.

"Swims like a duck!" Jordan pronounced, slapping Spencer on the shoulder. Spencer looked around at the grinning faces, feeling a bit like an explorer washed up on an island inhabited by an undiscovered species of monkeys.

Just go along, he told himself. *Pretend you're having fun, and it just might happen for real.*

Doing his best to live in the moment, Spencer raised both fists. Ed and Jaylen cheered. A genuine smile pulled at the corners of Spencer's face—and then he saw the freckled girl staring at him from the opposite side of the pool, her sapphire eyes gleaming with an intensity that seemed almost feral.

Spencer, to his own surprise, stared right back. With a sly smile, the girl dropped her eyes and turned, moving toward a dead space along the cavern wall where the golden lines of the water's reflection did not dance. She gave him one more look over her tanned shoulder and winked. Then she disappeared inside the tunnel.

Spencer stared after her, unsure what to do. Was it an invitation, an offer? Or had he mistaken her? She might have been blinking away a drop of water, for all he knew. He would feel mighty foolish, creeping up on her while she attended her personal business.

"A cavern like this would have taken thousands of years to form," Sharpton was saying, one foot perched on a lump of mineral that had dropped down from the ceiling. He looked like a conquistador—all he needed was the crested helmet to complete the image.

Spencer was not listening. He was still staring after the girl, puzzled by her disappearance.

A hand rocked his shoulder.

"Look," Jordan said, pointing to where he had scratched a crude version of tic-tac-toe on the wall with a stone. "An Indian hieroglyphic."

Jaylen started to explain that "hieroglyphic" wasn't the right word, but Spencer ignored them.

Maybe Jordan is right. Maybe this really is my last hurrah, my last chance to live life on my own terms, beholden to no one.

And if that was true, what better time to take some risks? He wasn't getting any younger, and this was probably the least tethered he would be for a long time, given Sandra's hints about popping out babies as quickly as they could make them.

Yes, if he was going to do something a little crazy, if he was going to prove to himself that he wasn't selling his man card right along with his singleness, this was the time. As for opportunity, she was waiting for him on the other side of the cavern, somewhere in that dark passage.

Leaving Jaylen and Jordan to their discussion, Spencer cut across the pool to the tunnel on the far side. He half expected someone to challenge him and ask what he was doing, but nobody said a word.

4

They were engrossed in their own worlds. When he looked back, no one was looking in his direction.

She might have gotten lost, he thought, feeling a sudden need to justify his own actions. *Sandra would understand I was just trying to help.*

Yes, that was all he was doing—helping someone out. It was a humanitarian mission. And if the person he was helping just happened to be young, fit, and beautiful, who was he to discriminate?

And if something more should happen, if she should want to show her gratitude…well, it wasn't really cheating until they were married, was it? He wasn't looking for a relationship, after all. He just needed some…adventure. Something a settled, married life couldn't offer.

He knew he was using Jordan's logic—a shaky proposition under any circumstances—but he did not care. The truth was he had been playing it safe all his life, the only kid in the group wearing a helmet while he rode his bicycle. That was why he had continued working at his dad's company for the past five years even though it felt like a dead end, why he had agreed to marry the first girl his parents approved of, and why he had turned down Jordan's endless attempts to get him to invest in the stock market.

He was reasonable, careful, and sensible.

Sometimes, however, he just wanted to throw caution to the wind.

He tried to remember her name—he knew he had heard it at least once—but he was drawing a blank. She must have been waiting for him to make a move, but he hadn't. He was the dutiful husband-to-be, after all. He didn't fool around, just like he didn't try Jordan's mushrooms or drink more than he could handle. Heck, he didn't even go more than ten miles over the speed limit, even on the freeway.

Maybe just this once, however, he could experience how it felt to live without the training wheels, to just go for it and see what happened.

I'm really doing it, he thought with a thrill as he moved forward. *Boy, will I have a story to tell those guys.*

All he had to do was find the girl. But how hard could that be? It was a tunnel, for goodness' sake.

As he moved deeper into the darkness and the voices faded behind him, however, he began to worry he might get lost. It was difficult to keep track of his progress, and he felt the wall twisting beside him, corkscrewing downward as if the cavern were a portal into the underworld.

"Hello?" he called, feeling foolish at the tentative sound of his own voice. "Are you back here?"

No answer. Where was she?

"I didn't catch your name," he said into the darkness, trying to steady his voice. Above the undercurrent of fear lay a trembling anticipation, a sense of unknown possibilities that filled his head like a drug. He imagined how it would feel to touch this girl's skin in the darkness—just the two of them deep in the cavern, their hushed whispers close in the confined space.

"I'm Jordan," he continued, running his fingertips along the slick wall as he inched forward. He almost said, *I'm about to get married,* which had become almost automatic, as if it were an integral part of his identity, but he stopped himself in time.

He paused to listen. As he waited for a response, a sulfurous, rotten odor reached his nostrils, like the time he returned from vacation to find he had left a carton of empty chicken eggs on the counter, the albumen congealed and stinking.

Bat guano, he thought with a shiver. *There could be hundreds, maybe even thousands of bats, nesting back here. I'll have to be careful I don't spook them.*

Yes, it made sense there might be bats nesting in a cavern along the bank of the river. Only…why didn't he feel anything under his feet but smooth stone? And did bat guano really smell so much like…like…well, like dead fish washed ashore, bloating in the sun?

He reached into his pocket, remembering his phone.

"I'm going to turn a light on, okay? It's just too dark."

He hoped this wouldn't ruin the moment. There was something appealing about a tryst in the dark, but that appeal would quickly disappear if he bruised his knee walking into a wall.

He pulled out his phone and turned on the flashlight, revealing a small, oval chamber hollowed out by untold years. The light gleamed off four golden shapes sprawled across the floor.

Spencer's heart jumped. He felt suddenly as if he were in some Egyptian museum, staring into the reenactment of a tomb for Pharaohs. Whether these were wrapped in gold or made of solid gold, Spencer could not tell. If it was the latter, they might be worth tens of millions of dollars.

This could be the greatest archaeological discovery of the decade, he thought, burning with excitement. Dimly, in the back of his head, he

6

wondered what mummies would be doing in a cavern along the Rio Grande, but he ignored the question. The answer would come in time.

I need to tell the others! he thought. As he turned around to execute this plan, however, it occurred to him how foolish he would feel if he brought everyone back to the cavern with him only to discover these were props of some kind, mannequins staged there for a movie. He would never live it down.

No, he needed to know this was the real deal *before* he told anyone. Besides, if these had been left here hundreds or even thousands of years earlier, they would be no more than skeletons. What was so frightening about a skeleton?

But if they're just skeletons, why do they smell so bad?

Again, he ignored his doubts. He wasn't going to go back and hear Jordan tell him he'd been too scared to get a good look at the bodies himself. He was a man, and he was going to act like one.

Steeling himself, he squatted down beside the nearest body. From the feet to the neck, the body was tightly wrapped in a gold blanket that crinkled when Spencer touched it. The face, however, was different. The gold seemed to be painted on, covering everything except the slits of the eyes and mouth and the holes of the nostrils. The gold had cracked as it dried, revealing spider lines of skin beneath.

Skin, Spencer repeated with an inward groan. *No, it couldn't be. The skin should have been long gone by then, unless…*

Drawn by an irresistible curiosity, he reached one questing finger toward the cheek and pressed. He felt the bloated flesh sink against bone. Then, as if triggered by Spencer's touch, the lips began to quiver, the painted flesh peeling apart as an enormous blowfly wriggled out.

Spencer jumped back with a choked cry, striking his shoulder against the wall.

It can't be, he told himself, rubbing his aching shoulder. *You're just imagining things, hallucinating. This has to be a practical joke somehow.*

Yes, that was it! Jordan had decided to play a prank on him, and somehow, he had convinced the freckled girl to go along with it. It was an elaborate trick, sure, but a trick nonetheless, and as soon as Jordan explained it to him, everything would make sense.

"Real funny!" he said aloud, shining the light toward the far side of the chamber. "Joke's over, so come on out!"

No answer came but a chorus of laughter from the main room of the cavern, distorted by distance so that it sounded ominous, like laughter from a grave.

I have to get out of here, he thought, growing desperate now. He had stayed too long.

He spun around, adrenaline now galloping through his veins, and nearly crashed into the girl with the freckles, who was staring in wide-eyed horror at the body behind Spencer. If a joke was being played here, she was not in on it.

Startled by the sight of the girl, Spencer staggered backward, tripping over the gold-wrapped body on the ground. He landed on the torso, and a breath of noxious, pent-up air billowed out through the fat lips and washed over Spencer's face.

He screamed.

CHAPTER ONE

FBI Agent Harley Cole tossed the legal pad aside and slouched back against the wall, stumped. Around her spread a sea of papers patterned with sticky notes, the contents of the file her father had passed on to her just a few days before. Somewhere in all those police reports and witness statements, amidst all the irrelevant details, lay some piece of evidence to help explain why Harley's younger sister, Kelly, had gone missing on a camping trip seventeen years before.

It has to be here somewhere, she thought. *I just need to keep looking.*

She had grown excited when she learned a homeless man had been found sleeping in his car near where Kelly went missing. The police had investigated him thoroughly, however, and found no indication he had anything to do with Kelly's disappearance. As for witnessing anything, he claimed to have heard nothing all night except crickets.

Still, Harley wasn't going to let herself get discouraged that easily. It took a peculiar kind of self-confidence for her to believe she could find something her father and a host of investigators had overlooked for nearly two decades, but she had one advantage all the others lacked. While her father had the determination to crack the case but not the investigative experience, and the investigators had the experience but not the determination of a grieving family member, Harley had both. She was both motivated and trained, which gave her the best odds of anyone to figure out what happened.

That was how she looked at it, anyway.

Then again, that didn't mean the best way to find those answers was to keep beating her head against the wall until she jarred something loose. This was going to take time, and as much as she wanted to sprint to the finish line, she needed to treat this like a marathon, and that meant recognizing she had needs.

Namely eating, sleeping, and otherwise behaving like a human being.

Sighing, she plucked the last fry from the carton at her elbow, dragged it around in the salt, and popped it into her mouth. She chased it down with a cold swallow of black coffee, then grimaced as she chewed a few grounds that must have overflowed the coffee filter.

Really living the high life, she mused.

Her phone lit up with a notification. She scooped it up eagerly, hoping it might be Bryce, her high school crush with whom she had recently reconnected. A moment later, she sagged back, disappointed to see it was merely an alert from her phone company saying an automatic payment had gone through.

It had been a full week since she had last seen Bryce, and he hadn't been responding to her texts since then. She assured herself he was just busy—caring for a hundred horses took a lot out of a man.

Still, she couldn't help questioning whether she had read too much into their previous conversations.

She read the last message she had sent: *Hey, just checking in. Haven't heard from you in a bit. Everything okay?*

She started to write a new message, something about how she was thinking of him, but then she deleted it, deciding it sounded desperate. The ball was in his court. She wasn't going to go begging on her hands and knees.

You knew it was too good to be true, a nagging voice told her. *Thinking you could rebound a month after divorcing Rob? A lot to ask, don't you think?*

Maybe it was a lot to ask, but she was a new girl in an old town, and she was still making it her home again after spending almost half her life on the East Coast. She needed all the help she could get.

He's stringing you along, the voice told her, and she thought of that band of white skin she had seen on Bryce's ring finger. Had he recently been divorced, or did he just like to play the field when his wife wasn't around? She didn't think Bryce was the kind of man who would step out on his wife. Then again, a lot had happened since high school. It was possible her former crush had changed just as much as she had.

Deciding she would need another cup of coffee to get any further through her father's notes, she scrambled to her feet and plucked the coffee mug off the carpet, swirling the last few sips around and watching the coffee grounds bob to the surface. Before she could leave the room, however, her phone buzzed.

Praying it wasn't going to be a waste of time, she stepped across the heap of papers, picked up the phone, and swiped right before the call went to voicemail.

"Hello?" she said, then held the phone away so she could read the name: Alex Newbury, the station chief of the FBI's Santa Fe field office—and her direct superior. She heard a garbled sound and held the phone to her face again.

"How are you, Agent Newbury?" she said.

"Another day in paradise," Newbury answered in his baritone voice. "How's the house coming along?"

Harley had been on leave for the past several days, settling into her new house and recovering from the adrenaline high of the Rasco case, an investigation that had nearly ended with her being eaten alive by a herd of feral pigs. That was the reason she had given Newbury for requesting time off, anyway. The truth was her purpose had a lot more to do with the file of papers her father had handed her than with any R and R. Kelly's case was the one she really wanted to solve.

"Better than expected," she said, gazing around at the unfurnished living room as she paced. "Starting to look a lot more like home." This was not exactly true, but she needed to say something.

"Glad to hear it. Some agents struggle when they're off the clock, have a hard time keeping themselves focused."

Newbury paused. Harley sensed an unspoken question in the silence.

"I find ways to keep myself busy," she said.

"Not too busy, I hope. I'm going to need you to come back."

Harley's heart sank. "Another homicide?"

"That's right."

"Can't the local PD handle it? It's not in our purview to investigate every killing in the state." The Bureau could assist the local police on investigations at their discretion, but they generally didn't get involved unless a federal crime was committed—a bank robber hitting banks across state lines, for instance, or a body found on Indian land.

Newbury sighed in a way that suggested he had more on his plate than he could stomach. "Listen, just get down here, okay? When you see the mummy with your own eyes, you'll understand."

Harley stopped pacing. "The *mummy*?"

"Wrapped in gold foil like King Tut. Do I have your attention now?"

Already Harley could feel the gears turning in her mind. That was all it took—a little curiosity, a little mystery, and she was off to the races. She couldn't help it.

Damn you, Newbury, she thought, though she wasn't really upset with him. She just didn't like being manipulated so easily.

"I'll be at the office in twenty minutes," she said, preparing herself mentally for the chaos she was about to go back into. Ordinarily she would have welcomed the chaos—she thrived in it, after all—but she couldn't help wishing for just a little more time off.

"Good," Newbury answered. "I have a feeling we're going to need all hands on board for this one."

Harley ended the call and let her hand drop as if the phone had suddenly doubled in weight. She glanced toward her office, thinking of the papers spread out across the floor—the papers that very well might contain the clues to understanding her sister's disappearance.

Those clues would have to wait for now. Harley had to go see about a mummy.

*

A cacophony of sound washed over Harley as she entered the Bureau's normally quiet field office in Santa Fe. Phones were ringing, agents in dress shirts and suspenders were talking in small groups with their hands on their hips, Newbury's secretary was racing about with a file of paperwork pressed against her bosom, and a TV was playing in an adjoining room.

Whatever was going on, it was *big*. Harley felt a flutter of excitement in her stomach.

Slipping into the break room, Harley turned up the volume on the TV. An African American woman in a sleeveless blouse was standing at the edge of a river, gesturing toward the mouth of a cavern roped off with yellow caution tape.

"The bodies were discovered by a tour boat that set out south along the Rio Grande earlier this morning," the reporter said. "If you look closely, you can actually see the tunnel leading to the chamber in which the bodies were found."

Here the feed switched to a camera showing a close-up of jagged walls glistening with moisture. The passage delved forward into darkness, then seemed to take a hard turn.

"Police have yet to offer any theories on how the bodies got there," the reporter continued, "as well as comment on the state of the bodies found. Are they recent killings, or is this an ancient burial site just now discovered? There is some speculation that—"

"Getting your information from the news stations now?" a voice behind Harley interrupted. She turned around to see Anthony Callaway, her partner on the Rasco and Navarro cases, filling the doorway with his broad frame.

At first glance, the two appeared to be opposites. Callaway was the big, folksy cowboy, always polite and never in a hurry. Harley, on the other hand, was the slim and trim Yankee, a firebrand who would stop at nothing to get results. But they had developed a hard-earned respect for one another over the course of their previous two investigations, and there was not another person in the world Harley would have rather worked alongside.

Harley gestured at the stubble on Callaway's jawline. "Is that just me, or are you getting a few grays?"

"About time I got credit for all my wisdom," he said. "Don't worry, you'll get there."

Callaway was Harley's senior by two years, a fact that he liked to remind her, as if he were always one step ahead on the path to wisdom and experience.

The TV droned on as a speleologist with spectacles that kept slipping down his nose talked about calcite deposits and carbonic acid.

Harley let out a deep sigh and looked at Callaway, waiting for him to speak. He stared back silently, a touch of curiosity in his emerald eyes.

"So?" Harley said. "You going to tell me how many bodies we're dealing with?"

He nodded, his face growing serious and professional. "Four. All female, it looks like. It's still early, and we're getting all our information from local PD. We haven't sent anyone down yet."

"Why not?"

"I was waiting for you."

"Just my luck," she murmured. "I ask for time off, and my boss calls me back to investigate a quadruple homicide."

"Come on, you were born for this. Besides..." He lowered his voice, leaning close enough for Harley to smell the cinnamon scent of his cologne. "Newbury trusts us to get shit done. That's why he gave the case to us, not someone else."

Harley stared at the TV, though she was not listening to it anymore. As much as she would have liked to be back at home studying her sister's file, this was her job—and she was damn good at it.

13

"Okay," she said, nodding as she mentally got herself in gear. "Tell me everything."

"There's the Harley I remember," Callaway said with a fleeting smile as he closed the door behind him. Then, locating the remote beside the microwave, he muted the TV and leaned back against the sink. His dress shirt rustled as he crossed his arms.

"They were found by some twenty-somethings on a boat tour," he said. "Bachelor party. But you probably know that much already."

"Have we identified any of the bodies?"

"One." Callaway paused, gazing at her steadily. She had a feeling she wasn't going to like what he was about to say.

"Does the name Daisy Ballard ring any bells for you?" he said.

She was about to say no, when suddenly she recalled a jingle she had heard on the radio a week or so ago as part of a politician's ad campaign. Harley was pretty sure the politician had been running for governor, and the song had been from an old family video of his daughter singing to him.

Harley's heart sank as she made the connection. "The governor's daughter, the one from the radio ad."

Callaway nodded. "Governor Trenton Eugene Ballard. He's getting an early start on his reelection bid this November. About two months ago, he filed a missing persons report for Daisy."

Harley cursed softly. She could already feel the pressure beginning to mount. Though every homicide was a crime, not every homicide was newsworthy. But the murder of a governor's daughter, especially alongside three other bodies? The press would eat it up. And Harley suspected it would not be long before the governor was breathing down their throats, demanding answers.

"He's no friend of law enforcement," Callaway continued. "He was a defense attorney before he became governor, and he made it abundantly clear on more than one occasion how low an opinion he has of us. Learning his daughter has been found dead after he reported her missing two months ago—I doubt it will improve his opinion."

She fished her keys from her pocket. "Then we'd better head over to that cavern and find some answers before we talk with him."

CHAPTER TWO

Harley parked at the edge of the dirt road overlooking the Rio Grande and stared at the trio of news vans, her mouth tightening. It was the very thing she had feared—a media circus, even before the agents had a chance to enter the crime scene. This was not going to be a quiet investigation but a public one.

"A day late and a dollar short," she said, watching a sandy-haired man with a camera over his shoulder stagger toward the stony descent that presumably led to the cavern. They were high above the river, which coursed with sluggish determination through a screen of trees, its underbelly showing here and there in jutting sandbars.

"Let's just hope they haven't cracked the case before we get down there," Callaway answered, flashing her a wink as he popped the latch on his door and shoved it open. He moved toward the trail with long, steady strides, his hands fitting casually in the pockets of his jeans with the thumbs exposed.

He turned back. "You coming?"

Harley leaned out the door as she switched into her trail running shoes. "Right behind you." She wasn't about to blister her feet by wearing flats over stony ground. She considered changing out of her blazer as well, but the day was still early enough that she did not think she would be too hot. Besides, the cavern ought to be cool.

After locking her Jeep, Harley joined Callaway and together they descended the rocky path, dislodging stones that bounced and pitched themselves into the golden water below. There was a pungent odor wafting off the river that would probably have been off-putting to someone unfamiliar with it. To Harley, however, it smelled like childhood kayaking trips on the river and fishing with her father on the banks.

At the bottom of the path, sectioned off by a strand of caution tape wound around a series of traffic cones, was the cavern, a glittering maw cut into the side of the cliff. A dozen or so people—the members of the boating party, Harley presumed—hunkered down against the far wall of the cavern, eating snacks and murmuring to one another, eyebrows pinched together in worry. The pontoon boat bobbed gently nearby.

The sandy-haired cameraman, who had just finished setting up his tripod, noticed the two agents and hurried toward them with the gawky gait of an adolescent still growing into his body.

"Alan Fielding, Sunny Day News," he rattled off, crab-walking so he could keep the camera pointed at their faces. "Can you tell me why the FBI is getting involved in this investigation?"

Shit, Harley thought. He must have seen one of their badges clipped to their belts. Either that or he had made an educated guess.

"No comment," she answered in an even voice, keeping her focus on the caution tape as if it were a finish line. All she had to do was get there, and Fielding would have no choice but to watch from a distance.

"I'll take that as confirmation the FBI is indeed joining this investigation," Fielding said, undeterred by Harley's brusque response. His foot caught on a stone, and he stumbled, barely managing to regain his balance. The misstep affected him as little as Harley's dismissal, however.

"We have a witness who claims there are multiple bodies in the back of that cavern," he continued, his speech accelerating as they neared the caution tape. "Can you clarify that number for us? And does this mean we have another serial killer on our hands?"

The reporter's words surprised Harley. The only "witness" Sunny Day News could have was one of the members of the tour boat, which meant someone was talking. Harley and Callaway needed to get a lid on this case as soon as possible, because one of the best ways to identify the perpetrator of a crime was to catch them sharing information only the perpetrator could know. If every detail of the case became general knowledge, this investigative tactic would no longer be an option.

"Do you have any advice for the general public?" Fielding pressed. They were only a few paces from the caution tape now. To Harley, the cavern might as well have been the Promised Land.

As Fielding shifted in front of her, forcing her to detour around him, she lost her patience. She stopped and stared directly into the dark lens of the camera.

"Yes," she said, "I do have some advice. Stop watching the news. It's bad for your health."

With that, she ducked beneath the tape and turned her back to the reporter, ignoring his follow-up question about why she didn't believe the public had a right to be informed.

16

"You shouldn't lose your cool like that," Callaway murmured, removing his sunglasses and peering around the cavern with his emerald eyes. A heavyset police officer with a caterpillar mustache and a slight limp moved toward them, a surgical mask hiding his neck.

"I can only take so much," Harley said to Callaway. "He's lucky I didn't chew him out."

"No, *you're* lucky you didn't," Callaway said. "That's the last thing we need—a clip like that going viral, making it sound like we think we know better than everyone else."

Angry as she was, Harley knew he was right. She would need to be more careful. It was too easy to take words out of context, and considering they already had a high-profile victim on their hands, there was no need to draw more attention to this case—or to the agents working it —than there already was.

"You must be the Feds I was told about," the officer said as he reached them. He stuck out a meaty hand. The brass name tag just above the officer's right breast pocket read "BULLOCK."

"Agents Cole and Callaway," Callaway said by way of introduction. "Where do things stand, Officer Bullock?"

Bullock's eyes scanned the camera crews as he spoke. "Well, we've got eleven frightened people who just had the shock of their lives. Officer Hessler and I—" he nodded toward a second officer on the far side of the cavern handing out bottles of water to the group huddled against the wall, "—have been taking witness statements, but there's not a lot to be said. None of them have been here before, not even the guide, and most of them didn't even see the bodies."

"Even so," Harley said, "someone's talking to the media. I don't know what you told them, but they need to understand this is a criminal investigation, and they risk charges by sharing what they know with the public."

Bullock sighed as if he had worried about this very thing. "I warned them, of course, but with this many people it's like trying to patch a sieve. Took all my energy just to keep them from disturbing the crime scene before the CSI got here."

This surprised Harley. "There's a CSI here already? Who is it?" First the press, now the CSI. Why did she feel like she'd been one of the last to know about the bodies?

"Angelina Brenner."

The name didn't mean anything to Harley. Callaway, however, seemed to recognize it.

17

"I know Angie," he said. "Worked with her a time or two." His face remained stoic as he said this, betraying no emotion at all.

Bullock nodded, a look of respect in his eyes. "Sharp as a scalpel, that one. Handle with care unless you want to get cut."

Harley, who could not relate with Bullock's description because she had never met Angelina, was still trying to figure out the order of events. She held a hand to her forehead and squinted her eyes.

"Wait a minute," she said. "Run through it again for me—how did everyone get here?"

Bullock didn't seem to mind backtracking. "The tour guide, they do these river tours, right? This morning they're out cruising the river, drinking beers, working on their sunburns. One of them kids sees this cave, has the bright idea it would be fun to poke around in there, and—" He turned, spotting another cameraman—this one older, with a salt-and-pepper beard and thick-framed glasses—as he pushed up against the caution tape.

"I'm going to need you to step back, sir!" Bullock said. "Away from the tape!"

The cameraman backpedaled, but he kept the camera focused on the trio.

"Animals," Bullock muttered, wiping sweat from his forehead with the crook of his arm. He jerked his head, indicating the two agents should follow him away from the cameraman.

"You were saying something about the people on the boat?" Harley said as they skirted the pool in the middle of the cavern. It was clear and deep, with a murky bottom through which pale fish drifted, lifeless one moment and darting so quickly the next moment that her eye almost couldn't follow them.

Bullock said, "So they go into this cave, right? Tour guide wants them all to stay at the entrance, liability reasons, yada-yada-yada, but two sneak off into a tunnel—looking to do a little exploring of their own, and not just to find petroglyphs, though there are some back there. Only instead of a tryst it becomes a threesome. A sixsome, if you will."

He looked at them and raised his eyebrows, apparently impressed with his own joke. When neither reacted, he cleared his throat with a hint of embarrassment and went on.

"So the tour guide, Sharpton, calls dispatch."

"And you were the first to respond?" Callaway said.

"CSI beat us to the punch."

"How did she get here so fast?" Harley asked.

"Keeps a scanner in her car. She was nearby, heard the report, and decided to drop in. As for the news crews..." He shrugged. "You got a bunch of scared people in there with cell phones, calling their families. Only a matter of time before word gets out."

Harley nodded, satisfied she had been brought up to speed. "I appreciate the explanation, officer. Mind showing us in?"

Bullock led them toward the back of the cavern, where a trail of glowsticks illuminated a narrow passage. As they moved through the luminescent darkness, an odor like spoiled eggs permeated the air. Harley coughed and covered her face.

"Oh, I almost forgot," Bullock said, pulling a package of surgical masks from his pocket. "You're going to want these. A couple of the bodies look—and smell—like they've been in there a good while. Whoever killed them, he's gotten away with it for a long time."

CHAPTER THREE

They rounded a corner and found themselves standing at the entrance to a small chamber perhaps twenty feet deep by twelve feet wide. The room was lit by a pair of halogen lamps set up in opposite corners, the light glinting off the golden skins of four bodies spaced equidistantly around the room.

The sight was surreal to Harley. It looked very much like a museum exhibit.

At the far end of the chamber, an African American woman with a bob haircut that revealed an understated earring on one ear, was frowning down at a pad of paper. The quick, lateral movements of the pencil suggested she was sketching.

"That's far enough," she said without looking up. "I'm still documenting the scene."

The trio stopped where they were.

"I've got good news for you, Angelina," Bullock said. "Uncle Sam brought you reinforcements."

Angelina looked up and studied them with a critical air. "Who's your friend, Tony?" she asked. There was a cool formality to her voice. It took Harley a moment to realize she was addressing Callaway. She knew his name was Anthony, but she had almost never heard him called Tony.

"This is Agent Harley Cole," Callaway said, clearing his throat uncomfortably. "My new partner."

"Well, could you please tell your new partner she's standing on possible trace evidence? The scene has already been disturbed enough by a bunch of gawking college grads. I don't need gawking agents in here too."

Harley moved her foot, taken aback by the woman's sharp tone. "If you think there are tracks," she said, "why haven't you documented them yet?"

"I'm getting to that," Angelina said without pausing her work. "I've already photographed the room from four different angles, moved the lights twice, and done a video walkthrough, but please, if you think you need to tell me how to do my job, proceed."

Harley raised her eyebrows at Callaway, wondering if this was how Angelina normally behaved. Callaway just lifted his hands and shrugged, as if to say he had no control over how Angelina acted.

Harley took another look around the room, this time noticing the unzipped bag at Angelina's feet. She could see several items poking out: a measuring tape, scissors, plastic gloves, and a stack of evidence bags. She had come prepared.

"You always carry your tools with you when you're off the clock?" she said.

Angelina snorted. "Off the clock? Is that a thing?" Then her tone changed as she answered the question, "I keep a go-bag in my vehicle at all times for situations like this."

Harley nodded, understanding. There was no harm in being ready for anything.

She dropped to a crouch beside the body nearest her. Several blowflies, fat with unplanted larvae, rose from the corpse and drifted about the room. Harley leaned close to study the corpse's face, which was covered by a golden mask, its perfection marred only by a series of spider line cracks. The cracks reminded her of the way mud dries in the sun, separating as the moisture evaporates. These cracks had not been formed by shrinkage, however, but by bloating.

The victim's hair, which was the delicate pale blonde of a sheaf of wheat, was pulled back from the scalp and tucked neatly behind the neck, almost entirely hidden from view. It was the only part of the woman that had not been turned to gold. From the neck down all the way to the feet, the body was wrapped in a thin, metallic blanket— almost like tinfoil, but less sturdy—with no visible seam, suggesting the seam was probably beneath the victim.

"What happened here?" she said, gesturing to the collar of the gold foil, which appeared to have been torn downward, revealing a triangle of the victim's naked chest—the right collarbone, the upper slope of the right breast, and the hollow at the base of the throat. There were faint scratches on the skin, as if someone had ripped the foil in one quick, careless motion.

"Oh, that?" Angelina said, shaking her head with an expression of annoyance. "Our good friend Spencer Newman thought it would be a good idea to double check that it wasn't, I don't know, a mannequin or something like that."

"He's the one who found the bodies," Bullock murmured behind them. Harley hadn't realized he was still there. As they all turned to look at him, he ducked his head sheepishly and retreated from the chamber.

"Who identified her?" Harley said.

"Officer Bullock. His daughter met Daisy at Albuquerque Academy."

"Rich school for a cop's daughter," Callaway murmured. "A lot more than I could afford back when I was walking the beat."

"That's because you always had holes in your pockets," Angelina said.

Callaway's face reddened, but he said nothing. Harley couldn't help wondering just how long these two had known one another—and what exactly had been the nature of their relationship. There was a clear tension between them, taut as an anchor cable.

Angelina flicked her bangs away from her eyes, held the sketch up to the light, and gave a self-satisfied nod. "There. That's a pretty good likeness."

Harley cleared her throat. "So this is, what, some killer's secret graveyard?"

"You have to dump the bodies somewhere, right?" Angelina said. "Might as well toss them in the back of a cavern. The only reason we found them was because a couple of hormonal twenty-somethings decided to have themselves a little fun."

"Wild age, isn't it?" Callaway murmured, almost to himself.

Harley rose, studying the other three bodies. They were all intact, painted and wrapped in exactly the same way as the first victim, except that Newman hadn't disturbed any of these. She found her eye drawn to the contours of the cavern floor. It rose and fell unevenly, creating shallow troughs, and it was in these troughs that the bodies had been laid.

"They weren't dumped here," she said as a newfound conviction rose in her.

Angelina sighed and planted her hands on her hips. "Excuse me?"

"Look how they're positioned," Harley continued. "The ground beneath them makes a natural cradle. The killer didn't just throw them back here—he set each one in place."

Angelina's face grew thoughtful as her eyes moved about the room. "Your new partner makes a good point," she said to Callaway.

Callaway did not answer. He was watching a carrion beetle trundle across the floor, its back teeming with mites that crawled about in all directions like sailors on a sinking vessel.

"Either of you seeing this?" he said, his tone a mixture of awe and revulsion.

"They do that," Angelina said, crossing her arms. "It's a symbiotic relationship. The mites get transportation so they can eat fly eggs, which in turn reduces the competition for the beetle's offspring."

Callaway raised his eyebrows at Harley, looking for a moment like a seven-year-old in a science museum. "Nature is wild."

"Anyway," Harley said, getting the conversation back on track as the mite-laden beetle disappeared in the hollow space between one of the victim's shoulders and head, "what have you learned so far about the victims?"

"Not a whole lot that you can't see at a glance," Angelina answered. "Four bodies, all women, various stages of decay. Your first victim—the one Newman stumbled across—is pretty fresh. The bruises on her throat suggest strangulation, though that's not an official diagnosis."

Harley's eyes darted to Daisy Ballard's body. Now that she looked more closely at the throat, she could see the bruises Angelina was talking about. She could almost make out the outline of an entire hand.

"Cause of death for the other three, though," Angelina continued, "is anyone's guess. If there were any bruises to begin with, the bodies have decomposed too much to identify them anymore."

"How old are they?" Harley said.

"The second one is already starting to liquify, which suggests at least a month. The third and fourth are in a much more advanced stage of decay." She shrugged. "You really need a medical examiner if you want to learn more than that. There's a lot of fluid trapped in that foil, and I'm not about to unwrap them and see how much."

Harley considered all the information she had learned so far. She pieced it together in her mind, searching for what was missing. The two main questions in a homicide investigation were cause of death and time of death, neither of which she would be able to establish on her own. These bodies were wrapped tightly, making it difficult to guess cause of death, and Harley had neither the training nor the tools to determine time of death.

In short, she was not going to learn much more about the bodies until they were transported to the morgue, where an ME—probably a forensic pathologist, in this case—would perform autopsies on the four cadavers. In the meantime, Harley would have to keep herself busy by investigating other details of the case.

"I hate to say it," Callaway said, blinking as if rousing himself from a nap, "but we need to speak with Governor Ballard before the press learn his daughter's identity. We don't need him hearing about this on the news."

"I'll be alright here," Angelina said. "My four new friends will keep me company."

Harley decided she liked the CSI's dry humor. She was a little rough around the edges, but so was Harley.

"Let us know if you find anything interesting," she said. "I'll give you my number."

"I have Tony's," Angelina replied automatically.

The room went silent for several moments. Harley felt that tension again, ratcheting tighter by the second.

"Alright, then," Harley said. She turned to Callaway. "What do you say we go talk to Governor Ballard?"

Callaway nodded, avoiding her eyes. "Sounds like a plan."

The CSI gave a noncommittal wave, and the two agents left the chamber.

"What was that all about?" Harley questioned as soon as they were out of earshot.

Callaway acted like he didn't understand. "What was what about?"

"The palpable tension between you two? Is she an old flame or what?"

Callaway's face remained impassive as they skirted the pool at the center of the cavern. He had a face of stone, like a sandstone cliff that can only be worn down by years of the wind's persistence.

"If I thought we needed to dredge up ancient history," he said, "I'd have told you already, okay?"

As much as she would have liked for him to be an open book, the truth was she had been reluctant to share her past with him at times, so it was only fair to give him some privacy about his own. She just hoped he would learn to trust her sooner or later.

A few moments passed in silence.

Callaway said, "Can't say I'm looking forward to seeing the governor. If he didn't dislike law enforcement before, he sure will now."

"You really think he'll blame us for this?" Harley asked.

Callaway gave a low, humorless laugh. "His daughter was missing for two months, and we weren't even the ones who found her. If he can pin this on us, he will."

CHAPTER FOUR

A team of security guards surrounded Harley and Callaway as they followed the governor's aide down the carpeted hall, which was lined with marble busts whose faces Harley did not recognize. Staring at the obvious signs of opulence, Harley had a hard time reconciling her surroundings with Ballard's campaign promise of embodying the role of a "public servant."

If this is how a servant lives, she thought, *what does that make the homeless?*

The aide, a small and trim man with an erect posture, led them to a wall of intricate wood paneling. Had there not been a protruding glass knob, Harley would not have realized there was a door.

The aide nodded at one of the security guards—a grizzled man with a salt-and-pepper beard and a nose that appeared to have been broken and never set right—and then walked back the way he had come.

"Now what?" Callaway said.

"Now," the guard answered, "we wait." He folded his hands behind his back and stuck out his chest, giving the door a fixed stare. From the other side of the door, Harley could hear the faint murmur of a man's voice interspersed with pauses—the radio interview the aide had mentioned, Harley supposed.

Callaway turned his head toward Harley without taking his eyes off the door. "So who gets the honor of breaking the news?" he murmured from the side of his mouth.

"Rock-paper-scissors?" she suggested, not about to volunteer for such an odious task.

He glanced at her, as if trying to measure how serious she was, and then grunted.

The door slid open, and they saw the governor—dressed in a white suit, his thinning hair combed neatly to the side—gesture with his left hand for them to enter while he rubbed his forehead with his right.

A young woman in a pencil skirt, who stood close to the governor's elbow, handed him a pill and a glass of orange juice. The governor threw the pill back, chased it with a hearty swallow of juice, and turned to face the agents.

"These local stations," he said, shaking his head as he leaned his weight against the edge of the desk. "We go over the questions in advance, and they still have to get a few curveballs in."

His eyes focused on the agents and one of his eyebrows rose to an imperious height. "I don't recall having a meeting with the FBI on my schedule."

"We apologize for the interruption," Callaway said. "But there's something very important we need to talk with you about."

"Is it a matter of national security? Another terrorist attack?"

"No, but—"

"Then I don't have time." The governor strode past them, adjusting his cuffs. "You'll have to schedule an appointment, just like everyone else. I have a cabinet meeting to attend."

Like metal filings drawn to a magnet, the team of security guards gathered around him as he left the office.

"It's about your daughter!" Harley said, raising her voice as the aide in the pencil skirt leaned close to murmur into the governor's ear.

Governor Ballard stopped abruptly as if he had reached the end of an invisible leash. He made a signal to the aide, who took a step back and went silent, staring at the floor.

"What about my daughter?" The governor's voice was flat and colorless, and Harley had a feeling he was closing his eyes, as if it might protect him from whatever he was about to hear.

Harley's voice softened with genuine sympathy. "We found her, Governor Ballard. I'm deeply sorry."

For the next few moments, the world seemed frozen in time. Nobody moved or said a word. There was no sound of traffic, no birdsong, no music. It was as if the world itself was taking a steadying breath.

Then the governor pivoted slowly toward them. His eyebrows were pinched together in an expression of pained interest.

"Leave us," he said.

The security team, along with the aide, drifted away like leaves scattered by a winter wind. The governor stepped back into his office and slid the door shut behind him, enclosing himself in the office with the two agents. He strode to the pair of tall windows overlooking the garden and drew the curtains. Then he let his arms drop, standing there with his back to Harley and Callaway again, as if seeing their faces would make the pain of their news worse.

"Tell me everything," he said in a haggard voice.

26

The two agents exchanged a worried glance. Harley had never met the governor before, so she had no way of predicting how he would react when he learned all the details. Then again, it was the nature of his job to deal with high-stress situations, and his daughter had been missing for two months. He must have known there was a good chance Daisy's story would not have a happy ending.

She cleared her throat. "We found her body in a cavern along the Rio Grande, along with three other bodies. We're still working on identifying the others."

Several moments passed in silence.

"What was she like?" Ballard said, his voice bleached of all feeling.

"Peaceful," Callaway said. "Like she was sleeping."

Harley thought of the bruises on Daisy's throat. There was nothing peaceful about strangulation, and it was a detail Ballard was certain to learn before long. But he didn't need all the details just yet. For now, he needed a chance to grieve—*after* sharing anything that might help them apprehend his daughter's killer.

The governor nodded, still facing the curtain. The silence lengthened again.

"Governor Ballard," Harley began, choosing her words carefully, "we know this is difficult. But if there's anything you can tell us about your daughter, anything at all…"

"Like I did two months ago?" There was an edge to his voice, thin and sharp as a razor. He turned around. His red-rimmed eyes burned with anger. "When Daisy went missing, I went to the police. I went to the Feds too. You know what you people told me?"

Harley waited.

"No evidence of a federal crime," he continued. "I told them it would be a federal crime if she was kidnapped and used to blackmail me, but they told me there was no sign of kidnapping." He shook his head bitterly. "Even suggested to me she was off seeing the world and just happened to have forgotten to check in with me. But people who go sightseeing don't usually wind up dead in caverns, do they?"

Neither of the agents answered. The skin around Harley's neck was getting hot, but she resisted the urge to adjust her collar.

"Governor Ballard," she started, "whatever stance the Bureau may have taken before, everything is different now. All Agent Callaway and I are concerned with is finding the person who killed your daughter and bringing them to justice."

"Of course. It's the dead you care about, not the living. Besides, like I said, I already spoke with you people." He moved around them and sat down heavily in the chair on the opposite side of the desk.

"That was two months ago," Harley said. "Have you learned anything new since then?"

Opening a drawer, Ballard pulled out a bottle of scotch and a tumbler and poured himself a glass. He didn't offer the agents a drink.

"Nothing I'm going to tell you," he said, knocking the glass back and pouring another. "I've already hired my own investigative team, people who actually know how to do their job. You're free to go."

Harley glanced at Callaway, taken aback by the governor's response. Never before had she been dismissed in such a way—by the victim's own father, no less. Then again, she couldn't blame him for hiring his own investigators after his daughter's disappearance.

"Whatever your investigators might have turned up," she said, "could prove extremely helpful to us."

The governor grunted and shook his head. It was clear he had no faith in the Bureau.

"They couldn't have been doing their job very well," Callaway said. "They didn't find your daughter."

The governor threw the second glass back. "So I'll hire new ones," he said. "But it won't be you."

Moving mechanically, as if more by obligation than will, he reached for the glass again. Before he could get his fingers around it, however, Callaway plucked it from his grip and set it aside.

Ballard glared at Callaway, his eyes burning with anger. "What the hell are you doing?"

"My job."

"Your job is to harass me?"

"My job is to find your daughter's killer, and if I have to get under your skin to do that, so be it."

The governor stared at him for a few moments as if he could not believe what he was hearing. Then he grunted and leaned back. He slid his hand beneath the edge of his desk, reaching, Harley supposed, for an alarm that would summon the security team.

"Before you do that," Callaway said quickly, "just know that if the killer gets away, you're going to be the one responsible. You'll have to live with the knowledge that you could have helped find him, and instead you sabotaged the investigation because you couldn't get past a petty grudge."

The door opened, and the guard with the broken nose advanced into the room, flanked by two other members of the governor's security detail. The guard's sharp eyes studied the scene.

"Is there a problem here?" he said.

Ballard did not answer. He went on staring at Callaway. Harley could only hope they had not pushed the governor too far, because if he kicked them out now, they would be up the creek without a paddle. Communication between different departments was difficult enough without the governor throwing his own team of PIs into the ring.

Finally, Ballard took a deep breath and tore his gaze from Callaway. "No problem, Ronnie," he said to the guard with the broken nose. "Hit the alarm by accident."

Ronnie stood his ground, still frowning at the two agents. "You sure, boss?"

Ballard nodded. "I'm sure. Everything's fine here."

"Roger that. I'll be in the next room if you need me."

"Thanks, Ronnie."

As the guards left, Harley let out a pent-up breath she hadn't known she was holding. Ballard leaned back and drummed his fingers on the desk, the belligerence now gone from his eyes. He looked tired.

"What do you want to know?" he said.

Callaway pulled a pad of paper and a pencil from his breast pocket.

Harley cleared her throat. "What was your daughter doing when she went missing?"

Ballard closed his eyes, frowning. "Daisy went to Columbia, studied political science so she could become a policy analyst. I thought it would give her a chance to learn how things work in the real world and to make a difference on issues she really cared about: homelessness, the state of public education, income inequality, those kinds of things."

He opened his eyes and blinked rapidly at the desk, as if shuffling through things to say. "Somewhere during her sophomore year, though, she got disillusioned about the whole thing. Her mother thinks it's a natural stage we all go through, but personally I think she fell in with the wrong crowd."

He paused. Harley had the impression there was a lot he was holding back—not out of a desire to deceive them, but to avoid the pain.

"Anyway," he continued, "she called me up one night—this was just about a year ago now, around the time summer break was about to begin—and she told me she needed some time to rethink things, decide if what she was doing was really best for her. I invited her to fly back for the summer, thinking I'd line up an internship for her somewhere and that would get her head back in the game, but that wasn't the kind of break she was looking for."

"What was she looking for?" Callaway said, pencil poised as he waited.

The governor lifted both his hands, palms upward. "Beats me. She wasn't thinking about her career, that's for sure. She wanted a gap year or two. Didn't have any plans about when she'd finish her degree."

"You said you thought she fell in with the wrong crowd," Harley said. "Did she mention any boyfriends, anyone who might have raised a red flag for you?"

Ballard shook his head. "My Daisy was careful when it came to boys. Besides, anyone she met out in New York, she left them when she came back, and it didn't sound like she was keeping in touch."

Sometimes you just need a fresh start, Harley mused, thinking she and Daisy had some things in common.

"Did she stay with you when she came back?" Callaway said.

Ballard laughed but did not smile. "I tried to convince her, but it was like she wanted nothing to do with me. She wanted 'freedom,' which for some reason meant cruising around in this little RV and sleeping beneath the stars."

He shook his head as if the idea was utterly beyond his understanding. "I could have put her on the fast track to career success and financial stability, but instead she chose to live like a hobo. I tried to warn her it was dangerous. There are all kinds of people out there, living on the fringes of society, and many of them will rob you just as soon as they'll chat about the weather."

Listening to the governor's words, Harley couldn't help thinking of her own sister Kelly, gone missing during a camping trip. Is that what Kelly had done? Trusted the wrong person?

"She was just so trusting," Ballard continued with a pained expression. "She'd go hiking alone, even in the dark, then come home and leave her door unlocked. It was like she was trying to prove how decent people were by giving them the opportunity to take advantage of her."

"What was her last known location?" Harley said.

"They found her RV in some no-name spot in the middle of the desert, off Route Twenty-Five. I'm not sure I'd even be able to find it again."

Ballard sat forward and rubbed his chin. "The hell of it is, I kept tabs on her—had Ronnie stick a GPS tracker under her RV so I'd know where she was. Then one day the tracker goes dead, so I send Ronnie out to look for it. He finds it on some wilderness trail, all beat to hell. Probably got torn off when she hit a rock. She really liked blazing her own path."

"Do you still have the tracker?" Callaway said.

The governor opened the bottom left drawer of the desk and pulled out a black rectangle about four inches long. The plastic was cracked, exposing the circuit board inside.

Harley's heart sank at the sight, but she tried not to show her disappointment. How in the world were they going to learn anything from that?

"My PI team didn't have any luck getting it to work," Ballard said. "So it would be a miracle if you can do anything with it. But I suppose it can't hurt to try."

"But if we can," Harley said, holding onto this slim hope, "it should tell us where she was prior to her disappearance?"

"Going back about two months, yes—assuming the information is still there. It was supposed to transmit her location in real time, but there are a lot of dead spots out in the desert where she was camping, so a lot of the time—more often than not, I'd say—it couldn't upload. But the information should still be on there if it hasn't been corrupted."

Harley glanced at Callaway. It was worth a shot. They had a lead, even if it was a shaky one.

Callaway's expression grew thoughtful. "I think I know someone who might be able to help us with that."

Harley groaned inwardly. She knew he was thinking of Ray Ranganathan, a young techie who consulted for the Bureau and hit on Harley every chance he got. He drove her up the wall, but she had to admit he was good at what he did.

Aware the governor was watching them, Harley extended her hand to him. "Thank you for your cooperation, governor. Again, I'm truly sorry for your loss."

Ballard shook her hand and nodded with a look of weary resignation. She suspected that, deep down inside, he had known he would probably never see his daughter alive again, but one could never give up hope as long as there was a chance. Harley understood this intimately. It was why she hadn't given up on Kelly.

"So what happens now?" Ballard said.

"We'll need you to come down to the morgue and confirm the identity," Callaway said. "The body should be released to you within a few days. After that, you can begin making funeral arrangements."

Ballard nodded. His face had gone pale, and he seemed to have trouble swallowing.

"Just catch the son of a bitch who did this, will you?" he said.

"We'll get him," Harley answered, nodding sympathetically. "One way or the other."

CHAPTER FIVE

Herb—a moniker that stuck to him like a burr in high school and never fell off—stalked along the beach with his book tucked beneath his arm, smiling to himself as he listened to the screams of the young girls playing in the water.

There really wasn't much difference between a playful scream and a terrified one, he mused. It was all about location. A shriek at a crowded beach would be shrugged off as innocent fun, but the very same sound uttered at an isolated motel in the dead of night—

Well, that would be enough to convince every resident within a country mile to check the locks on their doors and windows.

Herb, of course, had heard enough cries of terror to discern the subtle differences between the two. He enjoyed the sound of genuine, heart-throbbing fear. People would lie to your face just to be polite— "letting you down easy," they called it, like lowering a coffin into a grave—but if you scared them enough, you knew their reaction was genuine. True fear could not be faked.

Pausing in the sand, Herb's shaded eyes scanned the swimmers bobbing and splashing in the water. Children paddled around in plastic floaties designed to look like seahorses, crabs, and dinosaurs. A group of men, their chests as hairy as apes, played a game of water volleyball, alternately lunging for the ball and reaching down to keep their swimming trunks from slipping past their crotches.

Herb smiled to himself, thinking how foolish they all looked without even knowing it. Didn't they understand they were just a blip in the history of time, a scratch of ink on a page? Didn't they know how quickly their lives would be over?

Sometimes Herb lay awake, staring at the ceiling with his hands folded behind his head as he dreamed of the world beyond this one. He saw a black gate that had been creaking open inch by inch ever since he was born, a gate hiding an impenetrable mystery. In those solitary hours, he wanted more than anything to throw himself through the gap and see what was on the other side.

But he knew he couldn't do it, not yet. There was still so much work to be done.

A young boy with a bowl cut brushed past him, the boy's salty skin as sticky as a fish left in the sunlight. Herb shuddered with revulsion, and jolted back into the present, continued his jaunt along the beach, his gaze sharper now as he studied the beachgoers.

Most of the women lay sprawled on beach towels, their eyes closed, as defenseless as daffodils. Their confidence came from their numbers, for as much as Americans liked to preach self-reliance, they were—like all human beings—herd animals that felt safer when together.

As much as Herb hated crowds, this herd mentality was their one saving grace because of the anonymity it afforded. You could be anybody, absolutely anybody, and you could think the most terrible things and look right into a person's eyes while thinking those things, and nobody would notice.

You could stare into a man's face, imagining he was on fire and shrieking in agony as his skin shriveled, and he would smile politely and ask if you knew where the restroom was. People did not observe. They were so wrapped up in their own petty thoughts that they saw but did not notice. They were not *mindful*.

He, however, was mindful because he practiced it every day. He was mindful of the toddler picking his nose with a sandy finger while a man—probably not the child's father, Herb guessed—rubbed lotion on the child's mother, his fingers creeping just beneath the edge of her underwear. He was mindful of the trio of young wives talking about going to the Silver Cat later that evening, just the three of them, and seeing who could be the first to take a man home.

And he was mindful of the screams. Yes, the screams. Not as pleasant to the ear as a shriek of limb-shaking terror, but close enough for Herb to imagine it.

He sat down in the midst of the chaos and opened his book, pretending to read while he kept a furtive eye on a woman sunbathing nearby in a one-piece, a phone dangling in her hand as she talked with someone about the latest celebrity gossip. Herb studied the sensuous curves of her lips, the way the tanned flesh of her throat dipped and bobbed as she laughed.

Suddenly a pair of corgis raced past, splashing through the surf, then doubled back again. Herb glanced up and made eye contact with one of the dogs, who seemed to take this as an invitation. It bounded toward him, fur rippling, and before he could warn it away, the corgi shook itself vigorously.

Herb slapped the book shut and covered it with his body as drops of salty water pelted his skin. He felt his hands go rigid. He wanted to drag the dog back to the surf and hold it under until it stopped struggling, simply for being such a stupid and ignorant creature.

"I am *so* sorry!"

Herb looked up to see a young woman—platinum hair hanging just above her shoulders, dark sunglasses, a bikini the color of fresh-cut grass—trotting toward him, one hand on her bouncing bosom as if afraid of what might spill out. Seeing their mistress's approach, one of the dogs snapped at the other and the two bounded off again, weaving around picnic blankets.

"Is your book alright?" she asked. She had the body of a woman and the awkwardness of a girl. There was something endearing in her clumsiness, an unspoken appeal for the confidence and strength of a man.

Herb felt an inner stirring. He found himself staring at her and looked away, pretending to be distracted by an elderly couple walking past along the sand.

"It's fine," he answered, more curtly than he had intended. Why did he have such a difficult time making himself clear? The more his interest grew, it seemed, the more his eloquence shrank.

All Ka's fault, he thought bitterly. If only she had taken the time to understand him, if only she hadn't made a laughingstock of him in front of the whole—

"Oh," the girl faltered, glancing down at her body as if ashamed of herself. A few beats passed in silence. She seemed to think she needed to say something.

"What were you reading?" she said.

If only they were alone, away from judging eyes. Herb imagined himself taking her by the hand and leading her off toward the tumble of rocks a mile down the beach, then climbing into a hollow space among the stones where only the hush of the water could reach them, quieting and silencing them as they became one.

It was, of course, a pipe dream. This woman would never go anywhere with him. Not willingly.

He realized she was still waiting for an answer. "Old textbook," he said, squinting up at her with one eye. "Not very interesting."

He felt two intense urges at the same time. The first was to scare her off as quickly as possible, but the second was to keep her talking at

35

all costs, hoping—the fool that he was—that maybe this time it would go differently.

"Oh, cool," the girl said, hesitating. What did she want, Herb wondered? Why was she lingering? Was she just trying to be polite, or was she after something more?

For a few strange seconds, the two stared into one another's eyes. Herb began to hope she would stay. Deciding to make the most of this rare opportunity, he lifted his sunglasses.

"Please," he said, "have a seat. I—"

He broke off. An unmistakable shiver of revulsion had gone across her face as the sight of his eyes. She had hidden it quickly, yes, but Herb had seen it, nonetheless. He was quick to recognize it by now.

A black fury rose in Herb. The knuckles on one hand turned white as he squeezed the book in a death grip; the other hand clamped down on a fistful of sand.

The girl took a backward step, as if struck by a physical blow. "Well," she faltered, "I'll let you get back to it. Sorry."

Then, as if fearing that at any moment Herb's hand might snake out and grab her, she turned and hurried across the sand.

Herb watched her go, musing on murderous thoughts.

CHAPTER SIX

"When you told me it was broken," Ray said, "I didn't know you meant totally smashed."

Harley crossed her arms and waited as Ray turned the GPS tracker in his hand, a skeptical look on his face. They were in the bedroom of Ray's house, where he lived with his grandmother and too many cousins to count. The cousins were playing outside, but Nani was out in the kitchen, banging pots and otherwise making sure they knew she was still around. She seemed to think it was her personal duty to make sure her guests were comfortable, regardless of how many times they said they were fine.

Personally, Harley would have preferred to have this meeting in the Santa Fe field office. Since Ray wasn't technically on the clock, however, it seemed unfair to ask him to make the twenty-minute drive, especially since all his equipment was at home.

"I bring you tea," Nani announced, smiling proudly as she brushed aside the beaded curtain and entered with a tray of teacups. She pushed the tray at Callaway, who politely smiled and accepted a cup. It looked tiny in his large hands.

"Just leave it on the desk, Nani," Ray said, still examining the tracker.

"There is no room," Nani replied with a sulky air. Then she turned her attention to Harley. "I tell him and tell him, but does he keep room clean? No!"

Harley, eager to speed Nani on her way, shoved a stack of vintage video game magazines out of the way, which in turn pushed a stack of console games, causing several of the plastic cases to hit the floor.

"There," she said, nodding. "Now you have room."

Ray scooped up one of the fallen games and gave Harley a wounded look. "Do you have any idea how much this game means to me?"

"Maybe now you keep things clean," Nani said, winking at Harley.

Ray's voice was low and resentful. "I think you've helped enough, Nani. You're missing your show."

Nani smiled. "Well, you need anything else, you just call me." She gave a low chuckle and returned to the kitchen, the beads clattering together behind her. Harley felt herself release a pent-up breath she hadn't known she was holding.

Ray rolled his eyes. "Grandmothers, am I right? At least she makes good chai. You want a cup?"

"Actually," Harley said, "I'd like to hear what you make of the tracker. Is it fixable?"

The broken tracker was their only link to Daisy Ballard, the only one of the four victims who had been identified. Without the information on it, there would be little for the agents to do except wait for the ME's findings from the autopsies. Harley had little interest in sitting on her hands, especially since there was no evidence to suggest the killer's work was done.

Ray poured himself a cup of chai, mixed it with a generous amount of cream and sugar, and set it beside his keyboard, using an ancient-looking Walkman as a coaster. A few locks of his curly hair stirred in the breeze from the desk fan as he leaned back, his chair creaking.

"It can be done," he said, interlacing his hands behind his head. "It will take a true wizard of technology, but fortunately you've already found one."

Harley rolled her eyes at Callaway. "I'm glad to know this hasn't been a grand waste of time."

Ray craned his neck toward her and blinked innocently into her eyes. "It is never a waste of time seeing you, Harley."

"Careful, Ray. You're on thin ice."

"Just how long is this going to take?" Callaway said, picking up a magazine with a cartoon cover, then tossing it back on the desk. "We don't have all the time in the world, you know."

His tone sounded more bored than impatient, and Harley suspected he didn't enjoy putting the reins of the investigation in Ray's hands any more than she did. Still, Ray had come through for them in a pinch before. They had no reason to believe he wouldn't do so again.

Ray held up his hands as if to ward off Callaway's words. "Tisk, tisk. Some things can't be rushed."

"How long?" Callaway repeated.

Ray shrugged. "Ten minutes, maybe. Less, if you can keep Nani from interrupting."

Harley glanced at Callaway, thinking of his old-fashioned Southern charm. "You played linebacker in college, right?"

"Yeah."

"How are your blocking skills?"

Callaway groaned. "Why is that my job?"

"Take it as a compliment. You're good with the ladies."

Callaway sighed, resigning himself to this onerous task. "I'll see what I can do."

As Callaway left the room, Ray wove his fingers together and bent his hands forward, cracking the knuckles. Then he opened a drawer and pulled out a kit of mini screwdrivers. He began disassembling the tracker, careful to set the screws aside where he wouldn't lose them.

"So, how do you like your new partner?" he said as he worked.

Harley was studying a music poster. "Callaway? He's great."

"You can be honest with me, you know. If you two are having problems…"

She grunted. "What are you, a marriage counselor now?"

"Just a friend looking out for another friend."

"I'll be sure to remind you of that next time you compliment my looks."

The floor in the next room creaked as Nani bustled about, clattering cookware and occasionally barking a laugh. Callaway's voice was a low rumble, like approaching thunder.

"Is he married?" Ray said after a pause.

"Happily, as far as I know. Not that it's any of my business—or yours."

She thought briefly of Angelina, though she was not sure why. Whatever might have transpired between the CSI and Callaway, it sounded like it had happened years ago. A lot of water had passed under the bridge since then.

Ray shrugged, plugging the tracker into one of the USB ports on his computer. Harley watched as he tried to open the drive. The cursor changed to a waiting circle. Then a window popped up, showing several thumbnails of files.

"Got it!" Ray exclaimed. He clapped his hands together once, hard. "Look out, ladies and gentlemen. The wonderkid has entered the building."

"How'd you do it?"

Ray shrugged. "Just ran a bypass around one of the damaged components—nothing too exciting."

Harley thought he was being too modest. The governor had been unable to crack it, and who knew what hackers he had at his disposal.

The fact that Ray had found a way in so quickly only underscored his value to the Bureau.

Harley studied the image on the screen. "What am I looking at?"

Ray pointed. "These lines are her travels, and these dots are the places she stopped. If you hover over one—" He moved the mouse over one of the dots. "—there's a time signature so you can see how long she stayed there."

From what Harley could tell, it appeared Daisy had moved around the state quite a bit, stopping at wilderness reservations and sometimes just in open areas off the highway, such as the place where her RV was eventually found. One particular dot, however, stood in the middle of many of these lines of travel, like the bullseye at the center of a spiderweb.

"What's that place?" she said, pointing.

"That one's...let's see..." Ray copied the coordinates, then pasted them into a browser. The first result was a link to a website called "CUTLERSPRINGSCAMPING.NET."

"Looks like an RV park," Ray said.

"Pull up the map again? I want to know the exact times and dates of when she stayed at the camp."

"I can do that," Ray answered, returning to the map. "I'll arrange the signatures by order, then print them up for you."

Harley was impressed. "You can do that?"

"For you, *mon cheri*, anything is possible."

She snorted. "Take it easy, pal."

Harley stepped back and pulled out her phone, thinking she would do some reading on the campground's website while she waited for Ray to print the information. She had just entered the internet address when the printer hummed to life.

"Hot off the press," Ray said, pulling out three pages and handing them to Harley. "I won't even charge you for the paper and ink."

"How generous," she remarked dryly.

Taking a quick glance at the time signatures, it appeared Daisy had been roaming the countryside each week and returning to the park each weekend. The park also appeared to be where she had been heading when her GPS got damaged.

"Thanks for the help, Ray," she said, grateful she could trust someone else's expertise in a matter she knew so little about. She almost placed a hand on his shoulder, then thought better of it. No sense encouraging his fantasies.

"Sure thing," he said. Then he paused and leaned close, speaking in a confidential murmur. "Just don't tell Nani this is a part-time thing, okay? She thinks this is a full-time job—it's the only thing that stops her from barging in here every five minutes."

Harley smiled, relieved. "I don't know how you do it, living so close to family. I'd go crazy." As happy as she was to be in the same state as her father and brother again, she was very thankful they didn't share the same house.

Ray shrugged. "They can be annoying, sure. But at the end of the day, if you don't have family to rely on, what's left?"

Harley nodded noncommittally, unsure what to say to this. Her mind was already drifting away, counting the miles to a certain RV park where a certain Daisy Ballard had stayed a number of weekends. What answers awaited them there? Might it have been the very place Daisy crossed paths with her killer?

"Really?" she heard Callaway say for the third time in a row as Nani prattled on, sharing her secrets for making the perfect naan bread.

Harley smiled. "I'd better go save him. Thanks again, Ray."

He grinned back at her. "Anything for you, Harley."

When she entered the kitchen, the glazed expression in Callaway's eyes as he listened to Nani told Harley she had come not a moment too soon.

"Sorry to interrupt," she said, "but I'll need to steal Agent Callaway. Government business, you know."

Nani blinked at her, looking flustered, but Callaway stepped in to smooth things over.

"You know what?" he said. "Why don't you just hand me the recipe?"

Nani's face brightened, and she began rifling through a small wooden box. She came out with an index card covered in scribbles and handed it to Callaway, who smiled.

"Much obliged," he said, holding up the card.

"Stop by any time," Nani said.

Harley waved, keeping her smile fixed in place until they were outside. As they followed the flagstone path to her car, she relaxed her face and let out a sigh of relief.

"Care to tell me where we're headed?" Callaway said as they reached Harley's Jeep.

"There's an RV park Daisy was staying at. Seemed to be spending her weekends there."

"As good a place to start as any."

They climbed into the car. Harley tried not to smile, but she couldn't help it.

"What?" Callaway demanded.

"I'm just picturing you baking naan bread in your kitchen by yourself. Apron around your waist, music playing."

"Screw you. I happen to be a decent chef, believe it or not."

Harley laughed. She did believe it—Callaway was a man of many talents, as she was slowly learning—but the image was funny, nonetheless.

"So what's this place called, anyway?" Callaway said as Harley started the engine.

"Cutler Springs," she said.

A shadow passed over Callaway's face.

"What?" Harley asked. "Do you know it?"

"I know it," he said, nodding gravely. "That campground has been known to attract some shady characters over the years. There was even some human trafficking going on there about a decade ago."

A sense of unease coiled in the pit of Harley's stomach. What shady characters might Daisy have run into during her time at the campground? The kind who liked to wrap their victims in gold?

CHAPTER SEVEN

Harley slipped on a pair of sunglasses as she drove, protecting her eyes against the late morning sun that baked the asphalt and cast shimmering waves of heat across the broken, stunted landscape on either side. She watched the scenery change from scattered junipers to cane cholla. It was a brutal beauty, a land of endurance where only that which could withstand the heat and the sand would survive.

And oh, how Harley had missed it during her years on the East Coast.

Callaway nodded and made murmuring sounds of agreement, his phone pressed to his ear as he spoke with Frank Isidore, the forensic pathologist in charge of conducting autopsies on the four cavern victims. He had tried switching to speaker mode, but Isidore—who, by the sound of it, was old enough to be Harley's grandfather—had struggled to hear them above the noises of the vehicle, so Callaway had switched back.

From the sound of it, Callaway had worked with Isidore before—yet another connection he had that Harley didn't.

How surprised can you really be? she thought. *You were gone for seventeen years. It's perfectly normal to feel like a fish out of water for a little while.*

This was true. As much as Callaway's folksy, slow-as-molasses attitude grated on her sometimes, she was grateful for a partner who knew the lay of the land.

"Thanks, Frank," Callaway said. "Remember to keep us in the loop. As soon as you know something—" He paused, nodding. "That's right."

It took a good deal of patience for Harley to wait for Callaway to hang up. She had been listening along to half the conversation, trying to piece the details together. Now she turned to him and raised her eyebrows expectantly.

"Well?" she said. "Has he started the autopsies yet?"

Callaway slipped his phone into the cupholder by his left arm. "He's about to begin. They just finished transporting the bodies to the morgue, which apparently was quite a process. Just like Angelina said, two of the bodies are in a more advanced state of decay—'soupy', as Frank put it—so they had to be carefully bagged up to preserve the remains."

He grunted and shook his head. "And if it wasn't challenging enough to carry them through that narrow tunnel, one of the interns slipped by the edge of the pool."

Harley covered her mouth with one hand. "No!"

"Almost went into the drink, corpse and all. That would have been fun, fishing it out."

"Talk about a nightmare." A lot of DNA evidence could be disturbed by dropping the body into water, not to mention the challenge of dredging up the corpse again. Harley was grateful she wasn't involved in that process.

Callaway tipped his Stetson back and rubbed the front of his forehead, which was dark with sweat from the heat of the Ranganathan house. "Anyway," he continued, "Frank is doing what he can, but he wasn't prepared for an operation of this size. It's going to take some time."

"Have any more bodies been identified?"

Callaway shook his head. "Thus far, all we've got to go on is Daisy. It may come down to dental records for the other three."

Harley frowned at the road, thinking back to something Callaway had said earlier. "Was Frank able to give you a clearer timeline of the victims' deaths?"

Callaway nodded. "Frank couldn't say much—he didn't want to speculate without further study—but his initial impression is that we have one body two or three years ago, a second body last year, a third body about a month ago, and then a fourth—Daisy—within the past week."

Harley was silent, mulling over Callaway's last words. "Wait," she said. "I thought Governor Ballard reported his daughter missing two months ago. Do you think the killer kept her alive all that time?"

"Not necessarily," Callaway answered. "It would have been difficult for anyone to track Daisy down, given the way she was living. It's possible she just slipped through the cracks until the killer found her."

Harley was not sure she bought this theory. After all, even though the tracker on Daisy's RV had stopped working, it seemed likely she would have talked with someone who knew the police were looking for her, unless she had completely cut herself off from society. But if she had wanted total isolation, why would she have kept returning to an RV park?

She turned her thoughts back to Isidore's tentative timeline. "The killer's accelerating," she said as chilly fingers swept along the back of her neck.

"My thoughts exactly," Callaway answered. "Which means there's a good chance he'll attack again soon, if he hasn't already."

"The question is…what will he do with the next body, now that we've discovered his lair?"

"Your guess is as good as mine." Callaway stretched his arms back and pushed his chest forward, popping his sternum. "I don't know about you, but I'm going to try to catch a few winks. Didn't sleep so well last night."

He turned up the AC and pointed the two nearest fans at himself. Then he leaned his seat back and set his hat over his face.

In her mind's eye, Harley returned to the cavern on the bank of the Rio Grande. She heard the water lapping gently against the stone, smelled the dark odor of decay, and saw the bodies laid out like cocoons in the back chamber.

Four bodies over the course of two or three years. Why had he chosen that cavern? And more importantly, why was he killing in the first place?

"Did Frank say anything about the gold foil?" she asked.

Callaway sighed. "You're not going to let me rest, are you?" he said, his voice muffled by the hat.

"Not a wink. Come on, get your brain in gear. We need to know what we're looking for, which means we need to know what the killer was looking for."

Callaway lifted the hat off his face and sat up, giving Harley a long-suffering glance. "Said it reminded him of an ancient Egyptian burial practice. They considered gold the 'flesh of the gods.' See King Tut for reference."

"So you're saying the killer's clothing them? Dressing them up?"

"He might think of them as trophies, like a hunter mounting the rack of a bull on his wall. It's your enemy in life, but in death…"

"It's a decoration," Harley finished for him. Yes, it made sense. He was demonstrating his prowess. Only…why would he put all that effort into dressing them up if he meant to leave them to rot in the back of a cavern? Why not display them somewhere—smuggle them into a church, for instance, or a public park?

Her mind drifted as the miles of empty scrubland swept past. She pictured the killer dragging one of his victims through that narrow passage, his forehead sweating with the effort, his breathing loud in the confined space. It would be dark too. How would he see? He must have dressed and painted his victims after taking them into the cavern, otherwise there was a good chance the foil would tear along the way.

A giant shadow swept over the hood of the car, blotting out Harley's vision for one terrible second. She felt her heart skip a beat, and she gripped the steering wheel hard in both hands, staring out the window as the turkey vulture landed beside the carcass of a fox at the side of the road. Harley had a momentary impression of the vulture's pink, shriveled head extended as it buried its beak in the fox's gut. Then there was only the yellowing grassland again.

Harley leaned back and let out a deep breath.

"First time driving?" Callaway remarked.

"Screw you."

He chuckled and glanced out his window. Looking at him, Harley decided now was as good a time as any to try to get him to open up.

"So," she said, "you want to tell me about Angelina?"

Callaway let out a surprised grunt. "Not really, no."

"Tell me anyway."

Several moments passed as he went on staring out the window, and Harley began to suspect he really wasn't interested in talking about her. Then he snorted.

"It was stupid," he said. "She was in med school at the time, I was a recruit fresh out of the academy. We met through a mutual friend. Neither of us knew it was a date until he—Kevin Waller, the mutual friend—made an excuse to leave us alone at a cafe. This was years before Sarah came along."

It occurred to Harley that, despite working several cases with Callaway, she couldn't recall him ever mentioning his wife's name before. *He's just a private kind of guy,* she told herself. It seemed a glaring absence, making no mention of one's wife...and yet, Harley had told him almost nothing about her ex-husband, Rob, even though the ink on their divorce papers was still drying.

"Did your friends set you up a lot?" she said, wanting to keep him talking.

He gave her a tired look, as if he sensed a subtle accusation in the question. "Look, it wasn't like I couldn't find a date on my own, okay? I was just busy. It's the way I grew up. Work, sleep, get up, repeat."

"You're worse than I am," Harley answered, not without a faint note of admiration.

"Yeah, well, it took a lot of experience for me to realize work isn't everything."

Harley sensed he might be about to turn the spotlight on her, so she cut him off with a follow-up question.

"What happened with Angelina?" she said.

He shrugged. "It got really awkward, that's what happened."

"You? Awkward?"

"Believe it or not, I wasn't born bursting with masculine charm. I had to work on it."

"Could've fooled me," Harley murmured.

"Anyway," Callaway went on, "I must have said something right because I got her number. We went out a few times after that, realized we weren't looking for the same thing, and went our separate ways. The rest is history."

Harley held up her hand, far from satisfied by this abbreviation version of events. "Hold on. You can't just rush to the finish line and expect me not to be curious about what happened along the way. How serious were you two?"

"I don't know. I looked at rings."

"But you didn't buy one?"

"No."

"How come?"

He shrugged. "It wasn't the right time. We were both focused on our careers, and we both wanted to have kids, but Angelina wasn't sold on getting pregnant. She wanted to adopt—figured, if there are so many kids in the world needing families, why not take care of a few of them instead of making more?"

"And you weren't sure you wanted to sign up for raising someone else's kid?" As soon as she had spoken, she regretted her choice of words. But she let the words stand on their own, trusting Callaway would know she wasn't judging him.

"It sounds heartless when you put it that way," he said. "I just wasn't ready to jump into parenting like that. That's the beauty of having a baby—you start slow, figure it out step by step. You don't have to know everything upfront. I would know—I've been through it three times."

It was yet another reminder of how much Harley didn't know about her partner. She was about to ask a follow-up question when her phone lit up. She pulled it out from the cupholder.

"Shouldn't you be keeping your eyes on the road?" Callaway said.

"I can multitask."

She unlocked the phone and saw a message from a number she didn't recognize.

"Hey, Harley. We need to talk. When's a good time? Greg."

She stared at the message, troubled by those four words.

"Everything alright?" Callaway said.

"Yeah." She turned the phone off and returned it to the cupholder. "Just my brother. Said we need to talk."

Callaway's brow furrowed. "He use those words? 'We need to talk'?"

"Yeah, why?"

"No reason."

"Come on, Callaway. Spit it out."

"When people say 'we need to talk,' it's probably not to inform you you've just won the lottery."

Harley felt uneasy. Was it about Dad? Had he suffered a setback, or had his body simply decided it had nothing left to give? She told herself not to jump to conclusions, but she couldn't help fearing the worst.

While she was still thinking how to respond, a bleached sign came up on the right. "CUTLER SPRINGS CAMPING," it read in bold, colorless letters.

Whatever Greg needed, it would have to wait.

CHAPTER EIGHT

As they pulled into the park, a collection of campers and RVs laid out in irregular lines, Harley tried not to think about Greg's message. It was easier said than done. She assured herself that if something was wrong with Dad, Greg would tell her straight up.

But if it's not about Dad, she wondered, *what else could be wrong?*

Wrong. It was a sad commentary on her family that a spontaneous request from her brother for a sit-down immediately caused her to assume there was a problem. Maybe she was being paranoid. Then again, Callaway was right: People didn't use the words "we need to talk" unless there was an issue that needed addressing.

Which was to say, something had gone wrong.

Callaway, who could have no idea what was going through her mind, gestured at the dry, arid landscape that looked no different from the miles of empty country around it. Water hoses and electric cables snaked from the vehicles like umbilical cords, tethering them to the parched land.

"As you can see," he said, "the name 'Cutler Springs' is a bit optimistic."

"Better than 'Cutler Wasteland,'" Harley said, making an effort to stop thinking about her brother's message.

She pulled up in front of a nineties-looking trailer with the words "MANAGER'S OFFICE" handwritten in large letters on the side of the metal. Judging by the cinder blocks beneath the frame, the flat and cracked tires, and the tendrils of grass fighting for life in the RV's gutters, Harley guessed the vehicle had been there a good while.

As Harley turned off the engine, her stomach gave a low growl, reminding her that she had skipped her breakfast. She would have to grab something to eat as soon as they got back on the road.

An old, sunbaked woman in a camping chair regarded the two agents as they exited their vehicle. Dark sunspots patterned her face, and her puckered mouth seemed to quirk forward and back of its own accord as she popped the tab on a can of beer, her eyes still on the agents. A second can sat in the cupholder on her left, waiting its turn in line.

"Morning, ma'am," Callaway said, tipping his hat. The woman gave no greeting except perhaps the movement of her mouth, a sign in a language Harley could not read.

"Always nice to feel welcome," Harley muttered, turning toward the door of the manager's office. As she climbed the wooden steps, however, the old woman spoke behind her.

"Pokey don't like visitors," she said, the deep and rasping tone of her voice a telltale sign of years of smoking.

"Pokey?" Callaway asked politely. "Is that the manager's name?"

Harley heard the amusement in his voice, though he seemed to be trying to hide it. The name struck Harley as funny as well. Perhaps it was a nickname.

The old woman barked a laugh and crossed her ankles, which were bare except for a blotchy tattoo as illegible as a turd on a windshield. Instead of answering, she merely pointed to the left of the two agents.

Harley turned just in time to see a dog lunge out from the shadows beneath the trailer. There was a hissing sound as the dog's chain rasped along the ground. Then the chain went taut, and the dog—a pitbull with one milky eye—snarled at her from a mere foot away, standing on its hind legs as it strained against the leash. Ropes of saliva dangled and swung from its lips.

"Shit," Harley said, backpedaling in surprise. The dog's one good eye seemed to bulge at her with the intensity of its desire. Purple lips peeled back from yellowing teeth, and its tongue—spotted black, like moldy salami—lolled about in its unbridled agitation.

Suddenly the RV's screen door flew open, banging against the side of the trailer as a man in a baggy t-shirt and denim shorts emerged. "Pokey!" he shouted. "Wait till I learn you some manners!"

There was a hissing sound beside him, and it took Harley a moment to realize the man was holding a cast iron pan in one hand. Several eggs, the whites wet and gray, bubbled and writhed like some high school science experiment.

"Are you the manager here?" Callaway said, seemingly unaffected by the dog.

The man, his eyebrows as dark and spiny as a boar's bristles, nodded. "That's right. Need a lot?" He peered past the Jeep. "Don't see your rig."

"We're with the FBI," Harley said, still keeping a wary eye on the dog, which, though momentarily distracted by the appearance of its owner, had not stopped straining against the leash.

"FBI?" the man repeated. "I'm going to need to see some ID."

Callaway obliged, holding up his wallet to the manager, who plucked it from Callaway's grasp like an eagle snatching a fish from water.

"Say," he exclaimed, grinning, "I ain't never seen one of these up close. It looks official, alright."

"I assure you, it's official," Callaway said with a strained smile.

The manager studied the wallet for several more seconds. Then, as if reluctant, he handed the wallet back to Callaway, who quickly made it disappear inside his pocket.

"What can I do for you fine agents?" the manager said. "Name's Earl Kemper, by the way, owner and manager of this here fine park."

Harley glanced at the dog's bulging eye. "Mind if we come in for a minute? We'd just like to ask a few questions about someone who's been staying here."

"Sure, sure. Come on in." Earl stepped aside, holding the door open with his foot. The pan in his left hand continued to sizzle.

The room Harley stepped into began and ended with a plaid couch, the chewed arms of which were a clear indication that Pokey wasn't always kept outside. To the left of the couch was a closed door marked "OFFICE." To the right lay the kitchen—dirty dishes scattered along the counter, an open bag of flour that had belched a white cloud across the stove, a smoldering cigarette on the edge of the sink bleeding a thin trail of smoke into the air.

"Can I get you agents anything?" Earl said, gesturing with the pan. "I've got eggs, waffles in the box—"

"No thank you," Harley answered with a tight smile, not wishing to stay in the trailer any longer than necessary. The sight of those graying eggs had caused her stomach to pucker like a child tasting a cranberry for the first time.

"Suit yourselves," Earl said with a shrug. "Just let me set this back on the oven, then we can go talk in my office." A shadow passed over his face and he paused. "You *did* say this would only be a few minutes, right?"

Harley smiled again. "That's the plan."

The shadow passed. "Good," Earl said. "Then they might still be hot. If not, I can always nuke 'em, right?"

After returning the pan to the kitchen, Earl led them into his office, a low, dark room crowded with racks of files.

"So," he said, lowering himself into a chair from which the paint was peeling like blisters, "what can I do you for?"

"Do you know a woman named Daisy Ballard?" Harley said.

"Ballard, Ballard," the man muttered to himself, searching through the papers scattered on his desk. "Not one of my long-termers, I can tell you that much."

"She stayed here a few months back," Harley explained, hoping to jog his memory. "Liked to keep her RV here on the weekends."

Frowning, the manager consulted a stack of sticky notes. Then his eyes brightened. "Drove a puller, that right?"

The two agents exchanged an uncertain glance.

"Puller?" Callaway said.

The manager seemed pleased to know something they didn't. He leaned back with a magnanimous smile. "It's a type of RV. Just means the engine's at the front, not the back. Usually lighter than pushers, but don't have the same torque."

"Okay," Harley said slowly, wondering what relevance this had to the conversation.

The manager watched them a moment longer, and Harley had the impression he was hoping they would ask a follow-up question about pullers versus pushers so he could wax eloquent on the subject. When neither agent spoke, however, Earl dropped his gaze and cleared his throat.

"Anyway," he continued, "I've got her down here." He tapped the page in front of him with a hairy knuckle. "Came...oh, let's see...about three months straight, weekends only, just like you say. Is she in some kind of trouble?"

"She was murdered," Callaway said.

Earl blew a long sigh between his lips, shaking his head. "I'm awfully sorry to hear that. Don't know why anyone would want to hurt such a good, innocent kid."

"Any idea what she was doing between visits?" Harley said.

Earl stared at the desk a few minutes longer, as if still absorbing the news. Then he roused himself with an effort and, regaining his former folksy charm, said, "Lot of people round here like to boondock. Closer to the land, less crowded, that kind of thing."

Once again, Harley found herself at a loss. She waited, hoping Earl would explain, but he simply leaned back and folded his hands across his stomach, one thumb brushing up and down his ribs.

Finally, Harley gave in. "Boondock?"

"Camping out in the country. No hook-up, just a generator or solar panels, along with whatever water you've got in the tank. Wilderness living at its finest."

His words reminded Harley of her previous case with Callaway, a series of murders that had taken place around a community of off-gridders. In a society growing increasingly dependent on technology, there was an undercurrent of people moving toward self-reliance. Harley wondered if Daisy had been part of that group.

"Of course," Earl continued, "she might just as easily have been Wallydocking."

Wallydocking?" Harley said, feeling certain he was just pulling her leg now.

"It's a term for camping in one of those big discount store parking lots." He raised his hands in self-defense, perhaps having read her skepticism on her face. "Hey, I didn't make it up. I just report the facts."

"They let people do that?" Callaway said. "Just camp in the parking lot?"

Earl shook his head. "Not if they know you're doing it, no. The trick is to move around, even if it's only from one end of the parking lot to the other. That, and keep the shades drawn. If people see you're living in there, they're likely to treat you as if you're homeless—it's a prejudice a lot of people have against mobile living. So if a policeman comes by and knocks on the window, you just lay low and pretend you're not home."

Harley became aware of a faint scratching sound below her. Probably Pokey tunneling in the soft dirt beneath the trailer.

"Where did Ms. Ballard stay when she was here?" she said, trying to get the conversation back on track.

Earl tapped the paper again. "Lot Seventy-Four, way down at the end. There's a group of long-termers in that section, which is why I put her there. Figured she'd like being with her own kind."

"Her own kind?" Callaway repeated.

"Disaffected youth, kids tired of the nine-to-five grind and wanting out of their cubicles and condos. She was looking for adventure, that girl—you could see it in her eyes. A free spirit in the truest sense of the term."

"Do you always do that?" Harley said. "Play matchmaker with your guests?"

Earl's brow furrowed, as if annoyed by the implication. "My guests appreciate that I notice them, thank you very much. This is a quality campground, and I work hard to keep it that way."

Yeah, it's a real Versailles here, Harley thought. She was feeling edgy. Maybe it was the pressure of dealing with such a high-profile case. It could also have been the heat, the sour reek of cigarettes, or the fact that she hadn't eaten all morning.

Callaway seemed to sense her disquiet. He cleared his throat, drew a card from his breast pocket, and set the card on the edge of the desk. "Be sure to call us if you think of anything else," he said.

Earl nodded, keeping a wary eye on Harley. "Will do. And if the city life gets to be too much for you, I can hook you up with a fiver."

Harley sensed this invitation was directed more toward Callaway than toward her, so she said nothing. Then she realized that, in all the talk about Wallydocking and boondocking, she had forgotten a crucial question.

"When did you see Daisy last?" she asked.

Frowning thoughtfully, Earl consulted his notes. "Weekend before last," he said. "Stayed here Saturday and Sunday, then hit the road early on Monday. Does that help?"

Harley nodded, thinking it over. It fit the timeline.

"Yes, it helps," she said. "We'll let you know if we have any more questions."

Earl followed them out. As they slipped past Pokey, who immediately resumed his barking as soon as he saw them, Earl spoke up from behind them.

"How sure are you that Daisy's dead?" he said.

Harley stared back at him, unsure what to make of the question. "Her body was identified by a police officer. Her father hasn't confirmed the identity yet, but we have no reason to suspect the officer was wrong."

"Is there something we should know?" Callaway said.

Earl squinted one eye as he surveyed the horizon. "First time Daisy came here, she told me that if anyone showed up asking for her, I should tell them I hadn't seen her. Told me she was just trying to get some space from her father."

"*Did* anyone come looking for her?" Harley said.

"A couple of police officers. They said her father had filed a missing persons report. She was fine, though—up until this past weekend, that is, when she didn't show."

"And she never gave you any cause for concern? Never expressed any fear for her personal safety?"

Earl shook his head. "Nope. Just her personal privacy."

Harley thanked Earl, and the two agents continued on their way.

As they climbed back into the Jeep, Harley said, "That explains how she hasn't been dead more than a week. Her father lost touch with her and filed the report, but she probably wasn't attacked until much later."

Callaway nodded, but she could tell he was still thinking it over.

"I can't help wondering about Earl," he said. "He hid Daisy's whereabouts from the police, despite knowing she was the focus of a missing persons case. What else might that man be hiding?"

CHAPTER NINE

Harley and Callaway drove down the deserted lane, scanning the trailers on either side. The old woman had abandoned her post, leaving a single can of beer into which a yellow jacket crawled, its pulsing abdomen pointing skyward for a moment before disappearing.

"It's a ghost town," Callaway said. "Where is everybody?"

Harley rolled her window down a few inches and, as if in answer to Callaway's question, the mutter of several TVs reached them.

"Staying out of the heat," Harley answered. "Not that I can blame them."

She slowed as the lot numbers ticked up into the seventies. Toward the end, where a chain link fence separated the campgrounds from the surrounding desert, stood a cluster of five vehicles drawn up in a circle like a wagon train.

In the midst of all these vehicles was a smoldering fire surrounded by six figures, none of them over thirty. One sat in the red dirt, playing a set of dirty bongos in a rhythm that didn't quite match the tempo of the music. Four others lounged in the shade of the bus, two in camping chairs and two with their backs pressed against the tires. A sixth figure lay stretched on the ground, half in shadow and half in sunlight, lazily puffing on a joint and blowing wisps of smoke that were caught in the updraft of the fire.

And I thought Woodstock was over, Harley thought as she and Callaway got out of the Jeep.

The smiles of several of the campers, who seemed to have been engaged in a lively discussion moments before, fell slack as they eyed the agents with cool suspicion. The bongo player slowed, then stopped altogether. Only the smoker, a long-haired youth wearing only board shorts and a charm bracelet, seemed oblivious to their arrival. He laughed abruptly as if someone had told a clever joke, then dragged a hand down his face.

Harley scanned the faces looking back at her, uncertain which one to focus on. "Any of you fine fellows know a girl named Daisy Ballard?" she said.

The bongo player tossed his head, clearing a lock of thick hair from his eyes. "Yeah, I know her," he said. "Read all about her."

This puzzled Harley. It was awfully early for Daisy's name to be in the news.

"What do you mean, read about her?" she said.

The bongo player leaned back on his hands, a cocky grin on his face. "She's the one who was in that car accident, right? Killed the other girl?"

Several of the other campers grinned.

"You're thinking Daisy Buchanan," Callaway said. "From *The Great Gatsby*."

"Oh, that's right!" the bongo player said, a sly twinkle in his eyes. "Man, it's been forever since I read that book—high school, probably. They should've had us read, like, *On the Road* or something. Something relevant, know what I'm saying?"

Harley felt her cheeks getting hot. "Do you know Daisy Ballard or not?"

"Why?" the bongo player said, seemingly unaffected by the sharpness of Harley's tone. "Is there a reward? Wanted, dead or alive?"

One of the girls giggled at this.

"She's not running from the law, dumbass," Callaway said. "She's dead."

This news seemed to sober the group. Their self-satisfied smiles fell, and they stared at the ground.

"Shit," the bongo player muttered. "We were only joking around."

"Why don't you do us all a favor and cut the crap?" Harley said, tired of their games. "Unless you want to tell her father why you didn't share what you knew, even though it could have helped us find her killer?"

A young man seated against one of the bus's tires cleared his throat. He looked more preppy than the others: blue polo, salmon chino shorts, and thick chestnut hair combed away from his forehead in a wave.

"We knew Daisy," he said in a quiet voice. "Nice girl. Just wanted to live life on her own terms, know what I mean?" He shook his head. "I can't believe she's dead. Who would want to hurt her?"

"That's what we're trying to find out. When was the last time you saw her?"

"Must've been—I don't know—a week ago, maybe two?" He glanced at his companions for confirmation. A few nodded in answer.

"Did she seem scared, like she was running from something?" Callaway said. "Did she ever mention being afraid of anyone?"

The young man's face clouded. "Daisy? No, she didn't have any problems with anybody."

The girl seated beside him in a canvas chair—a brunette in a yellow swimsuit that stood out sharply against her bronzed skin—flinched as he said this. Harley turned her attention to the girl.

"What's your name?" she said.

The girl gave Harley a sullen glance, as if deciding whether to talk or not. "Parker," she finally said.

"Do you know something your friend doesn't, Parker? Something about Daisy?"

Parker glanced at the young man beside her, as if gauging how he would react. Then she dropped her gaze again and began pulling at a loose thread on the seat of the chair.

"You should talk to Cobra," she said.

"Cobra?" Harley repeated, wondering if this would prove to be yet another joke at the agents' expense.

"He's this creep down at the other end of the camp. Likes to walk around, hit on girls. Says he's a reporter working on articles, but for some reason he never seems interested in talking to guys."

"Why do you call him Cobra?" Callaway said.

"Carries this walking stick with a cobra on it. You know, like the terrorist organization?"

"Did he ever give Daisy any trouble?" Harley said.

Parker took a slow, hissing breath between her teeth, as if deciding how much to say.

"Someone murdered her," Harley said. "Do you really want the killer to get away with it?"

Nobody spoke for several moments. A slow breeze, swollen with the day's heat, rolled across the open landscape and billowed through the campground. An eighteen-wheeler rattled by along the road, blatting its horn.

"One night," Parker said in a low voice, "Daisy shows up, says she needs to talk to me about something. I could tell she was real scared, rattled, you know? My mom used to look like that when she'd come back from picking my brother up at my dad's house." She bit her lip, as if sensing she had said too much.

"Anyway," she went on, "I get Daisy a beer—she had a fondness for amber ales—and we sit down on the couch in my unit, just the two

58

of us, and she tells me Cobra came to her RV, banging on the door, claiming he was a reporter. He wanted to go inside and 'interview' her."

She shook her head, disgusted. "Daisy said he had just about forced the door open, but then Earl came strolling by and he backed off. She broke down crying when she told me about it, she was so scared."

The reaction did not surprise Harley. Perhaps the experience had opened Daisy's eyes to how vulnerable she was, moving around on her own with nobody to watch her back. If she had learned anything from the experience, however, the lesson had come too late.

"Is he still staying here?" Harley said.

Parker and the young man in the blue polo exchanged a glance.

"Actually, he walked by about fifteen minutes ago," the young man said. "Looked like he was hiking toward the canyon. There's a trail right behind the bus here—can't miss it."

Harley was moving almost before the man had finished talking. "If he shows back up before we do," she said over her shoulder, "see if you can stall him."

It was a rare opportunity. On foot, this "Cobra" character would have little chance of escape. They needed to act now, before he had a chance to return to his vehicle.

Before she could escape the wagon train of vehicles, however, the bongo player's sardonic voice reached her, "Are you seriously thinking of going after him?"

She turned back, not understanding the question. "Yeah, why?"

The bongo player glanced at the girl in the yellow bikini, the outline of a smirk on his face. "No offense, but the two of you...you're not exactly spring chickens."

There was a low murmur of laughter. Six pairs of eyes gazed at the agents, bright with mocking amusement.

Harley arched an eyebrow. "Excuse me?"

"You're just a little past your prime, is all. It's a tough hike. If the heat's not bad enough, you also have to watch out for rattlesnakes, scorpions..."

"Don't forget mountain lions," the smoker added. "Someone spotted one just the other day, not far from here. You've gotta have eyes in the back of your head."

Harley stared at him, uncertain whether he was being serious or pulling her leg. Either way, she wasn't about to let this kid tell her what she could or couldn't do.

She gave Callaway a measuring glance.

He shrugged. "I'm game if you are."

"Your funeral," the bongo player said. "If you find out he really did do something to Daisy, let us know. I'll be the first to slash his tires."

"I'm going to pretend I didn't hear that," Harley said, not without some appreciation for the sentiment.

With that, the agents left the ring of vehicles and hit the trail.

CHAPTER TEN

As they hiked into the canyon, the sun beating down on them without a cloud in sight or even the faintest stirring of wind, Harley thought back to what she'd had to drink that day: a coffee, a 16.9-ounce bottle of water, and…

And that was it. Nothing else.

We haven't even found this Cobra fellow yet, she thought dismally. *At this rate, there's a good chance we'll be nothing more than a pair of shriveled husks at the side of the road as he comes whistling back. If he tries to run or fight…*

She stopped to take a breather, planting her hands on her hips. Beads of sweat rolled down her ribcage, her legs, and the small of her back. Her head was beginning to feel buoyant, like a balloon slowly filling with helium.

"Doing alright, princess?" Callaway said.

She didn't need to look up to know he was grinning—she could hear it in his voice. He had to be feeling the fatigue too—she could hear that in his voice as well—but she knew he had too much manly pride to let her show him up. What he didn't know, though, was that she was just as motivated to prove herself.

"It's okay if you need to turn back," Callaway added, his tone casual. "We can always wait for him back at the campground."

"Don't quit for my sake," Harley said, refusing to back down. "I just need to get my hair out of the way."

She pulled a ponytail from her pocket. Then, clamping the elastic circle between her teeth, she gathered her hair behind her head, peeling it off her sweaty skin.

"Unless *you'd* rather turn back," she said, slipping the elastic band over her hair and doubling it.

Callaway grunted. "I didn't say that."

"So what's the problem?"

"No problem. I just wanted to make sure—" He broke off abruptly as Harley began to unbutton her blouse, her fingers moving deftly from top to bottom.

"It's too hot to be dressed like this," Harley said. "I should've changed in the car."

Callaway glanced away and cleared his throat. "Suit yourself," he said, a clear strain in his voice. "Just keep something on, would you? I'm still a married man."

"Don't worry," Harley said, adjusting the straps of her white cami. "This is a matter of survival, not seduction."

Cooler now that she had adjusted her clothing, she resumed climbing the trail, Callaway in step beside her. The trail was a mixture of clay and sand, a parchment on which was written the prints of humans and dogs, as well as the crosshatched tracks of bicycles and an occasional round impression that looked like it might have been made by a cane.

Cobra's cane, Harley hoped.

They crested the hill and began descending toward a wooded ravine choked at the bottom by boulders and stunted trees.

"Where are we, the devil's oven?" Callaway said, wiping his brow. His face was beet-red, and he paused to take a large swallow from his water bottle, which was nearly empty.

"You gonna make it?" Harley said with a teasing smile. "No shame in being beaten by a girl, you know. If you need to take a break, just say so."

Callaway laughed. "I could do this in my sleep. Besides, this is the easy part. Just wait till we have to go back up."

"I'm trying not to think about that."

Harley would have paused several times already had she been alone. But the presence of Callaway fueled her to keep going. Though there were plenty of women in the Bureau, they were significantly outnumbered by men, and not all men respected her abilities. It was this lack of belief that so often drove her to prove herself. She wondered if the impetus of that drive had been a desire to impress her father, who had grown so distant after the loss of Mom and Kelly. Maybe she was still trying to prove herself to him, even after all these years.

Callaway came to a sudden halt.

"What is it?" Harley said, catching her breath.

Callaway held a finger to his lips.

As Harley listened, she heard a footstep in the brush to the right of the path. Then one of the creosote bushes rattled, and Harley thought of what the campers had said about mountain lions. How many nine-millimeter rounds would it take to bring down such a large cat, she wondered?

Then a man pushed out through the brush, buckling his belt. Sweaty strips of brown hair clung to the skin beneath his bandana as he leaned on a wooden cane. Harley couldn't see the head of the cane, but she had a pretty good idea what it resembled.

Removing his bandana, the man with the cane mopped his face. His eyes—small, keen, and sparkling with an introspective intelligence—swept across the trail before resting on the pair of agents. He gave a little nod of acknowledgment and turned his face away, but not before Harley glimpsed something between fear and animal alertness.

Just as the man picked up his cane to move forward, his back to the agents, Callaway called to him.

"That's a mighty nice cane you've got there! Where'd you get it?"

The stranger remained perfectly still, like a rabbit that does not know whether it has been spotted or not. After a few seconds, he twisted back toward them, his head lowered so that he had to raise his eyes to see them.

"Do I know you?" he finally said.

Callaway's voice was cheerful and good natured. "Not yet, but that can be amended. I'm Anthony, and this is Harley."

"Your wife?"

Callaway chuckled. "Heavens, no! Just a friend."

Harley would have rolled her eyes if she hadn't been so focused on the stranger. His body was coiled tight as a drawn bowstring, his knuckles showing white on the handle of the cane.

Don't do it, Harley thought. *Don't even try it.*

"What's *your* name?" Callaway said.

The stranger stared back, unsmiling. The silence lengthened. Ordinarily, Harley would have found such a silence in the middle of a conversation awkward. This was no more awkward, however, than a pair of boxers circling one another in the ring. He was measuring them, just as they were measuring him. And whatever he was seeing, he didn't seem to like it.

"Sorry," the stranger said, "I'm not really in the mood for talking right now." It was probably the least sincere "sorry" Harley had ever heard.

"That's too bad," Callaway said. "Because we have a lot to talk about."

The stranger nodded and lowered his eyes, a small smile on his face. It was the smile of someone who has just discovered a silly trick played at one's expense.

Just then there was a burst of laughter from behind Harley and Callaway. Harley glanced back to see a pair of middle-aged couples coming down the path, the man in the lead gesticulating wildly as the others laughed at his story.

When Harley looked forward again, the stranger—Cobra, she was sure of it now—was already sprinting away.

With a burst of adrenaline, Harley forced her exhausted legs forward as she and Callaway gave chase, kicking stones that went bounding off the path and disappeared hundreds of feet below in the ravine. Washouts cut into the trail, creating stony slides that would carry them away if they weren't careful. There wasn't room on the trail for the two agents to run abreast, so Harley was forced to remain behind Callaway, who had been half a step ahead of Harley.

As she ran, she tried to see around Callaway to judge how far they were behind Cobra. All she saw was an empty trail, however.

"Where'd he go?" she said between deep breaths, confused by his sudden disappearance. He couldn't have simply vanished out of thin air, could he?

"Down," was all Callaway managed to answer, pointing to the left.

Harley glanced to the left and saw the trail running along a dozen or so feet below her. The path ahead must have switchbacked as it looped itself down into the canyon. If that was true, it meant Cobra would be running straight back toward them.

Following her instincts, Harley stopped at the edge of the path and paused there, listening for the hiker's approaching footsteps. Several seconds passed in silence as Callaway got farther and farther away.

She began to worry that Cobra might have had a similar idea and dropped down to the next level, bypassing this part of the trail entirely. Then she heard the scuff of his boots and saw him, his head turned over his shoulder as he searched for Callaway, oblivious of the woman perched above him like a gargoyle.

Harley's legs tensed. She had to be careful—if she jumped too far forward, she might tumble right over the edge of the path.

This one's for all the marbles, she thought and jumped.

CHAPTER ELEVEN

Earl took one look at the three figures standing by his front door and whistled. "I'll be damned," he said. "You kill that girl, Mayhew?" He sounded more intrigued than angry, as if he thought it might make a good story.

Rather than driving the half hour back to the Santa Fe field office for the interview, Harley and Callaway had decided to use Earl's trailer instead. The idea had been Callaway's, and despite Harley's distaste for the crowded, sour-smelling building, she had reluctantly agreed it would be better to question their suspect immediately rather than give him time to invent a story. He was off-balance now, and she wanted to keep him that way.

The man Earl had called Mayhew did not answer the question. He stared at the ground, sullen and stony-faced, as he had been doing since they handcuffed him. He seemed to think complete silence might be his best bet at regaining his freedom.

Harley smiled up at Earl, hoping they hadn't made a mistake by involving the campground manager in the process. "Mind if we use your office, Earl?" she said. "We just need a place to ask this man a few questions."

"And some AC wouldn't hurt," Callaway added, knuckling sweat from around his eyes.

Earl's eyebrows pinched together, as if he thought he must have misunderstood. "You want to use *my* office to conduct a federal interrogation of a suspect? Am I hearing that right?"

"Interview," Harley corrected. The Bureau made a conscious effort to avoid the word "interrogation," along with its connotations of coercion and torture.

Earl's face split wide in a grin. "Why the hell not? It's something I can brag about to my kids, if the good Lord ever sees fit to give me any. But I suppose I need a woman first, don't I?" He let out a burst of laughter as he backed into the trailer, holding the door open for them to follow him inside.

They climbed the steps and filed into the office: Harley leading, followed by Mayhew, with Callaway taking up the rear of the group.

Earl crept in behind Callaway and stood there, hands in his pockets, looking like a kid at the theater.

Harley raised her eyebrows at him, as if to ask what he was waiting for.

"Well, don't mind me," he said. "I'm just a fly on the wall."

"I'm afraid this is a bug-free zone," Callaway said. "You'll have to leave."

Earl's face went slack with disappointment. "Come on, I won't interfere. I just want to know what happens."

Callaway put a hand on his arm and escorted him out of the room. Then he returned, closing the door behind him. He glanced at Harley and rolled his eyes.

Harley sighed. It occurred to her that one of the downsides of asking for favors was that, for some people, it implied a quid pro quo.

Satisfied they could now conduct their interview in relative quiet (Pokey's persistent digging beneath the trailer notwithstanding), Harley turned her attention to the hiker who watched her with eyes that were both curious and distrustful, his presence a physical weight on the silence.

She decided to start him off slow, toss a few easy pitches and see how he did.

"Is Mayhew your real name?" she said.

The man shrugged one shoulder. "It's on my birth certificate if that's what you mean. Derek Mayhew. I'm not carrying around a bag full of fake passports like Jason Bourne."

Callaway picked up the cane, which Mayhew had left resting against a filing cabinet, and turned it in his hands, studying the cobra head. He placed both hands on the cane and pulled in opposite directions.

"Do you mind?" Mayhew said in disbelief, glancing at Harley as if to see if she would rein in her partner.

"This isn't one of those sword-in-a-cane deals, is it?" Callaway said. "Because I've gotta tell you, those are really cool."

Mayhew gave Harley a confused look. "Is he always like this?"

"Like a five-year-old? Not always, but he has his moments. I wouldn't concern myself with him, though. You have bigger things to worry about right now."

She caught him staring at the open V of her camisole as she leaned toward him. She straightened, wishing now that she had taken the time to get dressed again.

Yes, she thought, drawing on that woman's intuition she had honed over years of working with and around men. *He's a pig, alright. I can definitely see him getting a little too friendly with Daisy.*

But was he capable of putting his hands around Daisy's throat and choking her to death—and killing an additional three other women, no less? That remained to be seen.

The corners of the man's mouth curved upward in a knowing smirk. His eyes seemed to say, *what do you say you and I go for a little roll in the hay after this?* Harley wanted to slap the smirk right off his face, but she kept her cool. She had dealt with such men too often to let them rattle her.

"What do you do for work, Derek?" she said.

He shrugged. "This and that. Busted up my knee in an oil rig accident, so I collect disability."

Harley glanced at Callaway, who gave her a knowing nod. So much for Mayhew's claim about being a reporter. She decided not to call him out on the lie just yet.

"Do you know a girl named Daisy Ballard?" she said.

Mayhew made a show of trying to remember the name. "Daisy Ballard, Daisy Ballard. Now where have I heard that before…" He drummed his fingers on the edge of the desk. "You know, I'm actually drawing a blank."

Harley stared at him, unimpressed by the act. "That's funny because we spoke with someone who remembers Daisy talking about you. Sounds like Daisy felt you were getting a bit too friendly with her. You told her you were a reporter?"

Mayhew's gaze grew sullen, and his jaw clenched.

"Go easy on him," Callaway said in his slow drawl. "He's friendly with all the girls. Aren't you, Mayhew?" He tapped Mayhew's knee with the head of the cane. "And I get it. A man sees a fine piece like Daisy come strolling in, he's gotta at least try, right? What'd she weigh, a buck-thirty? Man like you could throw her around like a bag of horse feed."

Mayhew's gaze went from Callaway to Harley, as if sensing a trap. "I didn't lay a finger on her," he said tightly.

"But you thought about it, didn't you?" Callaway continued in that same companionable tone. "Lonely girl like her, far from home. Probably thought she needed a strong man in her life—other than her father, I mean. You know who her father is, don't you?"

Mayhew's brow furrowed, but he said nothing.

Callaway looked at Harley and shook his head in a pitying way. "He doesn't know who she is."

"Bet he wouldn't have touched her if he did," Harley said, keeping her gaze on Mayhew.

"What are you talking about?" Mayhew demanded, his leg beginning to bounce rapidly. "Who was she?"

"*Was?*" Harley repeated, leaning forward. "What happened to her, Mayhew?"

"Nothing—I don't know! I only talked with her the one time, so how would I know?"

"Only talked with her once," Callaway agreed mildly. "But that wasn't the only time you saw her, was it? How long did you watch her before you pounced? How many times did you circle her RV, hiding in the shadows, watching her windows? Did she leave the blinds open while she changed? Was that when you knew you had to have her?"

"I didn't touch her, okay?" Mayhew shouted, rising from his chair. "You've got the wrong man!"

Callaway took a quick step forward. "Sit down," he growled, his face inches from Mayhew's. "Before I make you."

Mayhew's anger faltered as he stared into Callaway's hard face. He slumped back into his chair, defeated.

"Now," Callaway said, "we can get you a good deal if you work with us: reduce your prison time, maybe make a way for you to breathe clean air again while you're still kicking. But to do that, you have to cooperate."

Mayhew hung his head miserably. Everything about his posture indicated that he was moments from throwing in the towel and confessing to everything…and yet, it seemed far too easy to Harley. Was the person who murdered four women and painstakingly wrapped and painted them going to crack after just a few questions?

"You want to know who she was?" Callaway said, unrelenting. "She was the governor's daughter. Every woman is someone's daughter, but you really kicked the hornets' nest this time, buddy-boy. Ballard has been looking for answers for the past two months, and when his lawyers get their hands on you—"

Suddenly Mayhew's head snapped back, his eyes bright with a furious hope. "That's it! I can't believe I didn't think of it before!"

Harley glanced at Callaway, but he didn't seem to have any clearer of an idea of what Mayhew meant than she did.

"The GPS!" Mayhew said, a triumphant grin spreading across his face. It was as if he had just figured out the solution to a puzzling math equation.

"What are you talking about?" Callaway said, looking troubled.

In answer, Mayhew leaned back as he dug his phone out of his pocket. He slapped it down hard on the table and grinned at the agents as beads of sweat rolled down his face.

"You said she went missing two months ago, right?" he exclaimed. "This will *prove* I had nothing to do with it!"

Harley stared at Mayhew, unsettled by his confidence. What could he possibly have on his phone that would clear this up? Was he just kidding himself, or did he really have an alibi?

Still skeptical, Harley pulled the phone toward herself. "What am I looking at?" she said.

"That's synced to the built-in GPS on my RV. Just tap the GPS icon."

Harley did and found herself staring at a map of colored lines showing Mayhew's travels. He hadn't been anywhere near the Rio Grande cavern around the time of Daisy's disappearance. He had, in fact, been far to the south, close to the Mexican border. She felt her heart sink down like a stone inside her chest.

"Why were you talking with Daisy, then?" she said, her former certainty slipping away.

Mayhew shrugged. "It's a free country. She wasn't in a chatty mood, so I went on my way. No harm done."

Harley, trying to hide her disappointment, moved toward the door. "Would you excuse us a moment?" she said to Mayhew. "My partner and I need to talk in private."

Mayhew leaned back and stretched his arms, grinning like he'd just been named the heir to a Fortune 500 company. "Take all the time you want, little lady," he said.

Callaway followed Harley out of the room, then closed the door behind them. Harley was pleasantly surprised to see that Earl wasn't in the building—he must have taken Pokey for a walk.

Callaway planted his hands on his hips. "You're thinking he's not the guy," he said. It was more a statement than a question.

Harley ran a hand through her hair, exasperated. "We've got him on harassment, but that's it. There's no evidence he was ever anywhere near that cavern."

"Could have used a different vehicle."

Harley knew this was true. But there was a world of difference between what was possible and what could be proven.

"Other than a witness who claims she saw him talking to Daisy," she said, "we have nothing to tie him to any of the murders. How far do you really want to take this?"

A series of deep ridges formed between Callaway's eyebrows as he frowned at the floor. She sensed he was balanced on the edge of a knife, and all he needed was a little more convincing to fall on her side.

"He's a creep, sure," Harley continued, "but that doesn't make him a murderer. Do you honestly think he would have the patience and the skill to dress those bodies up like that?"

Callaway let out a long, regretful sigh. "Shit," he said. He dragged his hand across his face. "We have to cut him loose."

Harley didn't like it any better than Callaway did. The sooner they moved on from a suspect who didn't fit the bill, however, the sooner they could find one who did.

Callaway opened the door and poked his head back into the office. "Come on out, Mayhew. You're free to go."

Mayhew swaggered through, grinning. "Good seeing you both," he said. "Stay in touch, okay?"

It sickened Harley, watching him get away scot-free like that. Then again, unless someone filed an actual charge against him, they couldn't arrest him for being despicable.

Mayhew bumped Callaway's shoulder in passing. Quick as a striking snake, Callaway grabbed him by the collar and shoved him against the wall.

"Listen to me," Callaway growled. "Stop harassing women and learn to take no for an answer. I'm going to talk with the sheriff, and if he hears you've so much as looked at a woman without her permission, I'll be on your ass like tar on a towel. You understand me?"

Mayhew was still grinning, but there was a queasiness to the expression now, as if his bowels might loose at any moment. He nodded, licking his lips.

Callaway held him a couple seconds longer, just long enough for Mayhew's queasy grin to change to a bitter grimace. Then he released him and jerked his head toward the door. "Piss off."

Mayhew stumbled out, casting a resentful glance over his shoulder before the door slammed shut behind him.

CHAPTER TWELVE

"Come *on*," Jesse whined, dragging his hand down the side of his eight-year-old face. "We've been here *forever*."

For a moment, the way Jesse stretched the skin beneath his eyes looked to June like that of a character from a horror movie, the kind her friend Betsy was always demanding she watch. June was not a big fan of horror movies—she found most of them disgusting. A good thriller, though, with the lights off and her parents out for the night? Yes, please.

"We just got here," she said, tightening her grip on Jesse's slender hand. "You're being dramatic."

She winced as she said it, recalling the many times her grandfather had used that very line in arguments with her mother. In this case, however, it was true. They had been at Shilowa National Monument, a series of pueblo ruins dating back to the eleventh century, for a grand total of five minutes, and already Jesse was pitching a fit.

"Besides," she added hastily, smoothing over her previous words, "we discussed this already. If I'm cleaning your room when we get home, the least you can do is pretend to have fun."

"*And* I get to have the pool to myself the rest of the day," Jesse muttered, as if reciting the terms of a hallowed contract.

June sighed, already feeling she had given up too much in the negotiation. Then again, the story she was going to write was just the sort of thing to help her ace Mr. Mudgeon's literature class. The only reason she was taking summer school in the first place was that she'd been forced to stay home and watch Jesse more times than she could count, all so her mother—who might have been able to afford a babysitter if not for her disgusting nicotine habit—could disappear for long stretches at a time, supposedly on the road for her new trucking job. June had her doubts. The wads of bills she found hidden around the house only confirmed her suspicion that her mother was up to no good.

"You're hurting my hand," Jesse whined. An older couple—anyone past thirty-five was "older" in June's book, given that she wouldn't be old enough to drink until the end of the year—turned in their direction, staring in curious silence as June dragged her brother along.

Feeling their gaze, June let Jesse's hand slip through her fingers. "If you run off, you're dead," she whispered through her teeth as she smiled at the tourists.

"First you have to catch me!" Jesse said.

Before June could grab him, Jesse raced off between a pair of five-foot-high walls and around a corner, his cowlicked head bobbing with every jouncing step.

June started to follow, then realized there was no need. He was eight years old, for goodness' sake. Baby alligators only stayed with their mothers for the first year or two of their lives before they were entirely on their own. Surely, he could survive twenty minutes without supervision.

With a sigh of relief, June moved away from the older couple, who were now focused on navigating the rocky terrain. She turned her thoughts to the story she was writing, a western thriller about a bank robber who mysteriously gives all his money to a struggling mother of three young children. It turns out later that her husband, who went missing in a war (June wasn't sure which war, but she could figure that out later), actually survived but he was so disfigured from combat (again, June wasn't sure what had happened to him, but inspiration would come to her as it always did) that he was ashamed to return to his family, so instead he chose to rob banks to support them.

These ruins June was visiting were the bank robber's hideout. An officer of the law, who had served in the war with the bank robber but left him for dead when the enemy advanced in the middle of a battle, was slowly narrowing down the robber's hideouts and would soon converge on the ruins. He also happened to be sweet on the robber's wife, who didn't return his interest, and toward the end, he would start finding the money the bank robber was leaving and force the wife to marry him for support. Just when the two were about to marry, the bank robber would hear of it from a trusted friend and go riding into town, masked in a dark cloth that he would slowly unwind to reveal his true identity, and then—

Well, June wasn't sure where it would go from there. She was pretty sure, however, that it would involve a shootout between the robber and the officer, and the townspeople (the wife, too, of course) would side with the robber and tip the scales in his favor. He would probably get a slap on the wrist for his crimes, but everyone would think of him as a hero, considering what he had suffered during the war. He would live happily ever after, reunited with his family.

She stopped in her tracks, troubled as she imagined the family rolling off in a wagon while the townsfolk cheered behind them and waved handkerchiefs. Could *she* be happy with a disfigured man, even if she had already fallen in love with him before he was disfigured? Because if she couldn't, then how could she expect her character to love him?

You're getting too far ahead, she told herself. *You're still at the hideout scene, so work on making the hideout as best as you can. The rest will come later.*

Reassured by this advice, she wandered through a doorway and into a small chamber built right up against the giant formation of red stone that occupied the center of the ruins. It was dark in here, protected from prying eyes—in short, the perfect place for a bank robber to hide.

She closed her eyes and pictured the bank robber seated in the corner, stirring a pot of...something. Rice? No, beans. Yes, that was better. She could smell the beans cooking, and along the wall beside him lay several bags of bank notes, heaped in the shadows.

She tried to picture his face as he bent over the pot. He was disfigured, yes, but what did that mean? Were they burn scars or cuts? Exactly what had happened to him on that battlefield? And what war had he been fighting in anyway, the Spanish-American War? Or had the story transpired earlier?

She was focusing as hard as she could when she heard the scuff of a shoe behind her. She took a deep, frustrated breath. "Jesse, I need some space to work on this. If you could just keep yourself out of trouble for five minutes..."

She waited, but no answer came. Troubled, she turned around.

The man standing behind her was not Jesse. The westering sun was at his back, shadowing his face, and his hands hung limp at his side. He clutched something in his right hand. A handkerchief?

He was staring fixedly at her, his eyes glittering from the cavern of his face. The intensity of his gaze caused goosebumps to ripple up June's arms. She crossed them, feeling as if his gaze could cut right through her clothes and even her skin to the wet, pulsing organs cradled in the framework of her bones.

"Who are you?" she said, the words coming out as a frightened squeak. She glanced over his shoulder, but there was no one behind him. Surely, though, someone would hear her if she screamed. She couldn't have wandered *that* far.

"Is this yours?" he said. "I found it on the ground."

She felt an absurd burst of relief in her chest as she recognized Jesse's baseball cap. "Yes, that's my brother's. He must have lost it. Thank you for picking it up."

Yes, he's just returning my brother's hat, she told herself. *That's all this is.* What had she thought might be going on? Why had she been so scared?

Without warning, he tossed the hat to her. She reached for it with both hands, twisting away at the same time to protect her face. The hard brim of the cap bounced off her hand, and the hat sailed over her shoulder.

As she stooped to pick it up, she heard a movement behind her and realized she had made a mistake. Just as she was about to take a breath to scream, she felt a rag clamp over her mouth. She took a sharp breath, and her nostrils were filled with an odor not unlike that of paint thinner. She tried to scream, but no scream came. Feeling light-headed, she leaned backward, supported by the stranger's torso.

"Just let go," a voice whispered, warm against her ear. "Everything will be alright."

She knew something was wrong, but she couldn't pull her thoughts together. They scattered like leaves in the wind. As she took another breath of the sweet-smelling cloth, her vision darkened further, and she felt herself sinking down as her legs gave way.

"We will see one another again soon," the voice whispered. "I promise."

CHAPTER THIRTEEN

Harley sipped the last of her spiced iced tea and stared out the cafe window, watching the sky burn like a wildfire as the sun slipped behind the trees. Across from her, Callaway picked the last few crumbs from a tray of nachos, his Stetson a lonely lookout perched on the corner of the table.

"So," Harley said, keeping her gaze out the window, "you want to tell me what happened back there?"

Callaway plucked a napkin from the dispenser, rubbed his hands, and set the balled napkin on his plate. "You never let things go, do you? You're like a dog with a bone."

"And you're a loose cannon. It's not like you, having an outburst like that. What would have happened if someone had caught it on camera?"

"Nobody did."

"And you're lucky they didn't," she said. "That's the sort of thing that can ruin a career."

He leaned back, draping one arm across the booth cushion. He was silent for a few moments, and when he spoke again, there was no levity in his voice.

"I don't have a lot of patience for creeps like Mayhew," he said. "They're scum. We throw them in prison for a few years, then expect them to behave like decent human beings. It doesn't work out so well."

"What would you rather do, send them to the chair?"

"If it would keep the world safe for everyone else? You bet."

Harley sat back, shaking her head. She didn't think Callaway really meant what he was saying, but it was apparent his hackles were up. She waited for him to say something.

He let out a long sigh, as if realizing she wouldn't leave him alone until he told her. "That childhood friend I mentioned before, when we were working on the Navarro case? The one who went hitchhiking with the wrong people?"

She nodded, remembering.

"She was sixteen at the time," Callaway said in a strange, unsettled voice. "Unstable home, a parade of her mother's boyfriends coming and going. She'd get into shouting matches with her mother, and when they got so bad that she couldn't take it anymore, Darcey would come over to my parents' place."

He paused, blinking thoughtfully down at the table. "One particular night, though, my parents were staying at a bed and breakfast for their anniversary, and I was at my girlfriend's house. Darcey called and called, but nobody answered. Sometimes when I close my eyes, I imagine the sound of the phone ringing in that big, empty house."

The waitress approached, realized they were deep in conversation, and tactfully slipped away.

"Eventually she gave up calling," Callaway said. "She went walking down the road—it was almost one in the morning at the time, mind you—and got picked up by a stranger. That was the last anyone saw of her for two weeks."

Harley watched Callaway, wishing she had asked him about this story sooner.

"You don't have to go on if you don't want to," she said.

Callaway shook his head, dismissing the suggestion. "The worst part wasn't her winding up dead. The worst part was what happened before that. He kept her alive, Harley—imprisoned in a grain silo. Had to be over 120 degrees in there."

"I had no idea," Harley murmured, surprised by this sudden turn.

"That's the hell of it—no one did." Callaway paused, his jaw working back and forth in a way that had nothing to do with eating. "He'd drop a rope down at night, pull her out so he could take her to the house without worrying about anyone seeing. Then, when he'd had his fun, he'd throw her back in there."

Harley could see the pain written plainly across Callaway's face. She felt an instinctive urge to comfort him, but she didn't think that was what he needed at the moment. She sensed he hadn't told this story to many people, and he needed to get it off his chest.

"How'd they find her?" she said in a soft voice.

"Turns out he was a lot better at hiding a prisoner than hiding a body." He barked an unsmiling, cynical laugh. "Tried burying her in a heap of cow manure, but a neighbor's dog found her. Left her hand, purity ring and all, exposed for the world to see."

It was all too easy for Harley to picture. Murder was an evil act, no matter the victim, but there was something about the victimization of the young and vulnerable that had a way of both breaking the heart and inflaming it with indignation. She couldn't imagine what a toll such a crime had taken on Callaway over the years.

Angry tears wavered in the corners of Callaway's eyes. "She lasted ten days. Ten days. That's how long it took for the heat, malnourishment, abuse, and terror to catch up with her. Ten days alone, seeing no other human face except her abuser's, wondering if her family would ever find her."

He shook his head bitterly and glanced out the window.

"So when I see a creep like Mayhew," he continued, "I can't help wondering what kind of monster is lurking behind those eyes. I can't help wondering if he, given the chance, wouldn't do the exact same thing to that girl."

Harley was silent, sobered by Callaway's story. Knowing what she knew now, she didn't blame him for threatening Mayhew. She probably would have done the same in his place.

"That's more detail than I ever told my wife," Callaway said, sounding surprised at the realization.

"How'd you learn about it all, if you were just a teenager at the time?" Harley said. "I can't imagine the police would have shared those details with you."

"Didn't learn until later when I joined the force. Read all the police reports, talked to the homicide detectives. It was like an obsession, needing to know why and how it all happened. I guess I was wondering how guilty I should feel."

She reached across the table and touched his arm. "There was nothing you could have done."

"I know that, sure, but it doesn't change the fact that somebody should have done *something*—a neighbor, a friend, the mailman. I can't accept a world in which an innocent girl like that can be utterly powerless against such unbridled evil, and nobody can do a damn thing about it."

"You're doing something about it now."

He grunted. "Doesn't always feel like it."

"That's because we're not in the business of preventing crimes," Harley said. "I wish we were. But until the Bureau develops the technology to predict crimes before they happen, we'll always be one step behind the criminal. I don't like it any more than you do, but unfortunately that's the way it is."

They both fell silent. Despite the many times Harley had been reminded in training to keep her emotions in check, she appreciated

Callaway's righteous indignation. She wasn't sure she could have worked as his partner if he hadn't been upset by such a heinous crime.

Just then Callaway's phone rang, breaking the moment. He cleared his throat, composing himself, and then answered. "Agent Callaway. Hold on, I'm putting you on speaker. I'm here with my partner, Agent Cole."

Callaway pressed the button, and the familiar voice of Officer Bullock filled their small corner of the cafe.

"I wanted to let you know we've identified the second body," Bullock said. "Her name is Lolita Reyes—local girl, college student, bartended on the side. Apparently, she had a video channel—posted hiking vlogs, that kind of thing."

Callaway's face clouded, and Harley suspected she would have to explain to him what a vlog was after this conversation was over.

"What do you mean by 'second body'?" she said to Bullock.

"The one who was killed before Daisy Ballard," Bullock answered.

Harley thought back to the timeline Angelina had given her of the victims' deaths. Reyes would have been killed about a month ago, or three weeks before Ballard. It was a rough estimate, she knew, but it helped her keep the details straight in her mind.

"How'd you identify her?" she said.

"She had a port-wine stain behind her right ear. It was easy enough to cross-check that birthmark against the missing persons database."

Harley raised her eyebrows at Callaway, impressed. "Good work, Officer Bullock. Have you ever considered switching teams?"

Bullock grunted. "I'm working my way up to homicide detective, like my old man. That's the grand prize."

"Well, you have my recommendation."

"Any boyfriends we need to know about?" Callaway said, cutting into their conversation.

Bullock's voice became formal again. "There's a kid she started seeing a few months before she went missing. We're looking into it. Otherwise, we've got bupkis."

Harley tried to think of more questions to ask, but the only ones that came to mind were questions for the ME, not Officer Bullock.

"Thanks for the update," she said. "And let us know if you learn anything else."

"Roger that."

Callaway hung up the phone, and they both sat back, digesting the new information.

Callaway scrubbed his forehead just above his right eyebrow, a puzzled expression on his face. "What was that word he used? *Vlog?*" He pronounced it as if it were a loanword from a foreign language.

Harley couldn't help smiling. For such an independent, self-reliant man, he could be awfully clueless when it came to technology.

"It's a video blog," she said. "You're blogging about your life—or your career, or your hobbies, or whatever—but you're recording it instead of writing an article."

Callaway nodded slowly. "So where can we find this vlog of hers?"

CHAPTER FOURTEEN

Harley was already unlocking her phone. "I'm pulling it up now."

Callaway rose and slipped to her side of the booth. She held her phone out in front of her so Callaway could see it. He leaned close, his shoulder brushing hers.

"Sometimes I feel lucky to be born when I was," he murmured. "Before all these newfangled gadgets and apps. Kids these days don't know how to entertain themselves without staring at a screen."

Harley searched for Lolita Reyes on social media. No hits.

"I think everyone feels their childhood was 'the good old days,'" Harley said. "The past gets rosier with time, but that doesn't mean we felt that way when we were young."

Callaway only grunted in response.

Harley searched the internet and came across a channel with Reyes's name. She scrolled down to find the most recent video, which was titled "The Great Outdoors: Part 3" and had been posted five weeks earlier, close enough to Isidore's estimate that it could have been filmed the day she was killed. The video had just over 200 views, a scattering of likes, and a number of comments that appeared to be from younger girls aspiring to be as adventurous as Reyes was.

"Hi, guys," Reyes said, flashing a smile as she waved at the camera. She was in her early twenties and slim, with bangs cut just above her eyebrows and pronounced dimples that appeared and disappeared as she spoke—in short, nothing like the gold-painted cadaver Harley had seen in the cavern.

"I started the morning with a protein shake and a few stretches," Reyes continued, now walking along a path crowded by junipers in the background. "Buster wanted to come along, but when I pulled out the harness I got him for Christmas, he ran under the couch. So it's just me today." She flashed another smile. It was so innocent, so young and unsuspecting, that it tugged at Harley's heartstrings.

If only we could go back in time and warn her, she thought.

Harley let the video play, listening to Reyes talk about work and school and her dreams for the future. It lasted only six minutes, ending with a promise that Reyes would post a follow-up video later that night—a promise she never fulfilled.

"Doesn't look like she was anywhere near the cavern," Callaway said. "Or the river."

"Nope," Harley agreed. "Let's check an earlier video."

She scrolled through the videos, which bore titles such as "Road Trip Alaska: Part 7" and "Burning Man: First Impressions," until she came to one philosophically titled "On Growing Up." The cover for the video showed Reyes standing with a backpack and a bandanna beneath the shade of a mesquite as a pair of hikers passed by in the background.

Harley played the video. Then, remembering she kept the volume low so that she wouldn't be startled when videos auto-played, she turned the volume up.

"It's been a hard-fought seven years since losing my Papa," Reyes said. "I know you guys have been supporting me every step of the way, and I appreciate all the love."

Harley scanned the comments below, which popped up in a continuous feed. Most of them were full of emojis such as hearts and hugs, as well as statements such as, "we believe in you gurl" and "what doesnt kill you makes you stronger."

"I won't lie," Reyes continued, turning her face to the side. "It's been rough. He was really the anchor of our family, especially after we lost my brother in Iraq. That's why I'm always recording this stuff for you guys, because I want it to have some meaning. I want it to be about something bigger than myself."

As she moved down the trail, other hikers passed in and out of focus. A mountain range hovered in the distance, just above the angle of the camera, but it was not enough for Harley to identify where Reyes was.

"Without you guys," Reyes said, "I can't imagine how lonely I'd feel right now. It means so much to know you're all out there, watching me and cheering me on, even if most of you have never met me."

She swung the camera around, and there was a knot of people behind her. Most of them broke away, but one in particular—a tall-looking man with a bucket hat, browline glasses, and a Hawaiian shirt—remained where he was, staring at Reyes.

"Wait," Callaway said suddenly. "Go back to the other video."

"What is it?" Harley said, navigating to the previous video.

"Just let it play. You'll see."

Harley did so. About halfway through, she noticed a figure in the background studying Reyes from the corners of his eyes.

"It's the same man," Harley murmured with growing conviction. "No question about it."

Callaway shifted, the booth cushion squeaking as he turned toward her. "What are the chances they bump into each other twice like that?" he said.

"Not very likely." She let the video play to the end, searching for a better picture, but that one shot was the man's only appearance. Following her curiosity, she scrolled below the video to the comment section.

"What are you doing?" Callaway said.

"Searching the comments. It's possible someone else noticed him. It's also possible he might identify himself if he has his own account— not very likely, but stranger things have happened."

"Let's just hope he likes the attention."

Before Harley could get far through the comments, however, a notification came up. Newbury was calling her.

"Agent Cole," she said as she answered.

"Is Callaway with you?"

"Sitting right beside me."

"Whatever you're doing, drop it. Someone just called in a body over at Shilowa National Monument."

Harley's heart sank. Newbury wouldn't call her to talk about another body if he didn't think it was related to their case.

The station chief seemed to take her silence as a lack of understanding. "It's a bunch of Indian ruins," he explained, "real touristy spot. The place is a maze."

"Are you sure it's related to our case?" she said.

"How many killers you know who wrap their victims in gold foil?"

She cursed. "Fair point. We'll get there as soon as we can." She hung up and shook her head ruefully. Just when she felt they might be putting the pieces together, the killer left another victim.

"Another body?" Callaway said, scooting out of the booth. He stepped aside so that Harley could get out.

"Same MO," she said, rising. She pulled a few bills from her wallet and tossed them on the table.

"You called it," Callaway said.

She turned back. "What are you talking about?"

"Two bodies in as many months? He's accelerating the timeline. He's getting more confident, less afraid of getting caught."

"Well, then, we'll just have to put the fear of God in him, won't we?"

CHAPTER FIFTEEN

Harley was still thinking about Callaway's story as they passed the sign reading, "SHILOWA NATIONAL MONUMENT," which was situated across the road from a crumbling maze of stone walls built around a giant sandstone outcropping.

Despite the differences between herself and Callaway (and there were many), they had one significant thing in common: Both had joined the Bureau due to the loss of a loved one early in life. Callaway had alluded to this shortly after she and Harley met, but without the details of the story, she couldn't possibly have known how much of an effect the girl's death had had on him.

Now that she did know, she thought she understood Callaway a little better. It was something they shared, that sense of childhood bereavement—except that for her, there was still the hope that Kelly might be alive, though the hope was as thin as a strand of spider silk by now.

Callaway was studying the ruins, a thoughtful frown on his face. "Isolated, set back from the highway," he said. "Not as remote as the cavern, but remote enough."

Harley offered no comment. She was watching Callaway from the corner of her eyes, drawn to his pain like a magnet. It comforted her somehow, and it reminded her of something a psychology professor had once told her in college: that friendship comes from the moment one person says to another, "You, too?" That sense of loss was something they both shared, and it caused Harley to look at Callaway with a renewed sense of respect.

Callaway turned toward her, and Harley glanced away, hoping he hadn't felt her gaze.

"Should we do this," he said, "or do you want to sit here all evening?"

Harley nodded, still distracted, and climbed from the vehicle.

They followed a raised platform along the length of the ruins, pale sagebrush on one hand and crumbling adobe walls on the other. The entire structure looked to Harley like an excavated termite hive. Dark rectangles peered into collapsed rooms, though whether they were doors or windows, Harley could not tell.

Off to the side was a playground: colored slides, the plastic cracked by the sun, a heavy roundabout, and a pair of swings with weeds growing beneath them.

As they neared the entrance to the ruins, they spotted Bullock standing just outside the ribbon of caution tape, his radio held close to his mouth. He noticed the two agents and lowered the radio.

"Long time no see," he said. "Crazy day, huh?"

"And it ain't over yet," Callaway answered.

Harley was staring past Officer Bullock, into the ruins. "Where is she?" she said.

Bullock's face became grave, and he jerked his head to indicate that they should follow him. "Right this way," he said.

They followed Bullock beneath the caution tape and through a series of deteriorated rooms, some of the walls of which rose no higher than Harley's hip after years and years of exposure to the desert winds.

"Natives built it around a standing formation," Bullock explained, gesturing toward the wall of unshaped sandstone to their right. "That way they could have part of the structure on top and part below."

Shelves had been chiseled from the stone, as well as small alcoves whose purpose Harley could not guess. She noticed a number of faint drawings on the wall—petroglyphs, she guessed.

After crossing several rooms in a straight line, they took a right and passed through a rectangular doorway in a manmade wall. The doorway was about five-and-a-half feet tall, forcing Callaway to duck as he entered and even Harley had to stoop.

The back of the room pressed up against a dark, vertical slab of stone, and though the roof was missing, the walls remained intact up to about eight feet. On the ground to the left, tucked at the edge of the shadow cast by the stone wall, lay the shape of a woman wrapped in gold foil, her face a painted golden mask. Several drops of dried paint lay in the dust, leaving no doubt where the killer had done his work.

Harley's guts twisted at the sight. There was something grotesque about what the killer was doing to the bodies, something…violating.

"Ah, shit," Callaway muttered, taking off his hat.

"Name's June Collington," Bullock said. "She was a freshman at New Mexico State University."

"Who found her?" Harley said.

"Her eight-year-old brother," Bullock answered. "Says she was writing a story for a summer school class."

"How long was he away from her?" Callaway said.

"Twenty minutes, half an hour?" Bullock shrugged. "He's not sure. Keeps saying it's his fault because he ran off. Should've stayed with her. His parents are on their way—they made it clear they don't want us talking to him anymore, so you can forget about questioning him."

"Nobody saw anything?" Harley said, glancing back out through the doorway and seeing an older couple seated on a bench nearby, watched by another police officer. "Have you interviewed those two yet?"

"Best I could, yeah. They must have been up top when it happened. Didn't realize anything was wrong until they heard the boy screaming."

Harley glanced at the boy seated a short distance from the older couple, his arms wrapped around his knees as he stared at the ground with a vacant expression.

His little mind will be trying to process this trauma for a long time, she thought. *All his life, maybe.*

"You search the area?" Callaway said.

Bullock nodded. "Top to bottom. Trust me, if the killer was still here, we'd have found him."

"What about the boyfriend angle you were working for the second victim, Lolita Reyes?"

Bullock let out a disappointed sigh. "Didn't pan out. He's disabled, can hardly stand without a wheelchair. No way he carried those bodies into the cavern."

Bullock waited, as if to hear whether they had any more questions for him. When neither agent spoke, he said, "You need anything else, you just give me a call."

"Thanks, Bullock," Harley said.

"You got it."

As the crunch of Bullock's boots on the stony ground faded, the evening grew quiet. The only sound was the whispering of the wind as it wore down the edges of stone, undoing the work of human hands grain by grain. A thousand more years, and there would be no sign this place had ever existed.

"She was trapped," Callaway said, studying the walls surrounding the small chamber. "Soon as she came in, he had her. No way out."

"He's careful," Harley added. "She might not have even had time to scream."

Callaway's face grew curious. He stepped into the middle of the room, turned back toward the doorway, cupped his hands over his mouth and shouted, "Bullock!"

They waited for a response. None came except the steady, papery whisper of the wind.

"Or she did scream," he said, "and nobody heard her."

This thought only made the crime seem more tragic.

Harley turned her attention to the body. From the neck down, June was no more than a golden cocoon. Her cheeks, eyes, and forehead were painted gold as well, just like the other victims, but her chin and mouth remained exposed.

"It looks like he got interrupted," Harley murmured, her eyes traveling to the girl's ragged hair. It looked out-of-place somehow, unkempt. "Look how red the skin is around her mouth."

"Could just be her natural skin color."

Harley shook her head. "The skin around her chin and throat is much paler."

Callaway leaned closer. "What do you think it is, a burn of some kind? Something she drank?"

"Or the killer held something over her mouth, maybe to asphyxiate her."

Whatever it was, it must have worked fast. Harley saw no indication that June had put up much of a fight, though she wouldn't know this for certain until Isidore had a chance to unwrap the body and examine it thoroughly.

Callaway made a small, clucking sound as if something had caught his interest. "Check this out," he said.

Harley followed Callaway's gaze to the corner of the chamber, where a number of small stones lay stacked in the shadows. At first, the stones looked entirely unremarkable to Harley. Then, as Callaway began to set them aside one by one, she noticed a scrap of cloth buried in the debris.

"What is it?" she said, curious now.

Callaway went on moving the stones one by one until he had exhumed a tight bundle of clothing. It appeared to be a purple tank top wrapped up with a pair of jean shorts, both of them ruddy with dust.

"Must have hidden it when he got spooked," Harley said, giving Callaway a congratulatory pat on the shoulder for his discovery. "That's why he left the body where he did—so he could come back, take the clothes, and finish painting her. Probably would have come back tonight if the kid hadn't found her first."

"Why not take the clothes?" Callaway said. "He must have been carrying a backpack, a satchel—something to transport the foil and paint. He could have tucked the clothing in there."

"Unless he was afraid of getting caught with it." The realization sent a thrill of satisfaction through Harley. *And if he's not afraid yet,* she thought, *we'll give him reason to be soon enough.*

Callaway ran his knuckles against the bristle along his chin, a sound like sandpaper on wood. "If he was smart," he said, "he'd lay low for a while, wait for the heat to die down before killing again. Either that or stop making his killings so distinctive."

"I don't think it's just a homicidal urge," Harley said. "That's part of it, sure…but there's more to what's going on here. He's an artist, and his canvas just happens to be the bodies of young women."

Callaway said nothing. He was gazing thoughtfully at June's face, his eyes introspective.

Harley glanced at the darkening sky. Night was coming on, and she wanted to conduct interviews while there was still light enough to see faces.

"We should talk to the couple," she said. "They might have seen something, even if they didn't realize it was significant."

Callaway nodded, but he continued to stare at June's body, as if in a trance.

"Callaway," Harley repeated.

Finally, he shook himself and faced her.

"You alright?" she said.

"It's not so different from what happened to Darcey," he said. "She was thrown out like trash, while this girl has been preserved like a piece of art…but in the end, neither had a choice. In the end, they both became the objects of someone's sick fantasy."

Harley nodded soberly, watching him.

Then he roused himself, taking a quick breath and brushing at his forehead. "Look at me, getting all sentimental. That's what you get for talking about your feelings—stirs things up." He laughed, but it was a hollow sound meant only to cover the sorrow beneath it.

He began to move past her, but she caught his arm. "Hey," she said softly. "Are you alright? It's fine if you need a minute."

Callaway stared over her shoulder for a few seconds, his face hardening, though Harley did not think it had anything to do with her.

"It's justice I need, not time," he said. "I've done enough grieving. Finding this girl's killer won't bring Darcey back…but it will sure help me sleep better at night."

"I hear you on that one, partner," Harley said.

She knew they couldn't do anything to protect the dead. They could, however, protect the killer's next victims—and that was a goal worth every drop of sweat, blood, and tears.

CHAPTER SIXTEEN

Harley and Callaway found the couple sitting in silence as a curtain of darkness fell around them. The man had a mane of silver hair and a distant, detached look in his eyes. The woman rocked gently back and forth, her lower lip twitching as if it had a mind of its own.

Harley cleared her throat, mentally switching gears as she prepared herself for the coming conversation. Before she could break the ice, however, the man glanced up at them, frowning.

"We already gave our statement to the officer," he said. "We really need to be getting home now—my wife needs her medication." As he said this, he reached over and squeezed his wife's wrist.

Harley had dealt with plenty of reluctant or avoidant witnesses before, so she was more than ready to deal with the man's brusque tone. "We understand," she said patiently, "and we'll do our best to get you out of here soon. But it's very important we don't miss anything."

The man leaned away from his wife, gesturing toward her as if she were an exhibit at a museum. "Do you see how upset she is? You really want to put her through this again, even though we just talked with the other officer? Why don't you ask him what we saw?"

Already playing the sympathy card, Harley thought. *He's good at this.*

She smiled, trying to show a mixture of firmness and understanding. "Officer Bullock is a fine officer," she said, "and I'm sure he was thorough. But there are facts about this case that only Agent Callaway and I are privy to, so it's possible you may know things Officer Bullock didn't think to ask you about."

The man stared off into the distance for several moments. There was a dune buggy zipping around in all that darkness, the sound of the engine rising to a fever pitch and then falling again, rising and falling.

The man sighed and ran a hand through his silver hair, which seemed both shaggy and stylish at the same time. Harley could not help noticing the large ruby ring on his right ring finger—a class ring, by the look of it.

"Looks like I don't have much of a choice, do I?" he said. "What do you want to know?"

"For starters," Callaway said, "what are your names?"

"Chet Wheeler." Chet pointed his thumb at the woman seated beside him. "This is my wife, Sherry."

"What time did you get here, Chet?" Harley said.

"Five, five-thirty? We grabbed an early dinner at Marston's, then asked the waiter if there were any places in the area for taking a stroll. We're staying at the Best Western on Gulver Drive, flying back to Baton Rouge in the morning."

Harley couldn't help noticing the precise way Chet included the very information they needed. *He sounds like a lawyer,* she thought.

"What's your line of work, Mr. Wheeler?" she said.

"Contract negotiator for Sigma Dental Group," he answered without pause. "Been in the biz for almost twenty years now." He had a confident, take-charge manner that was in striking contrast to the body language of his wife, who continued to rock back and forth, her eyes drifting toward the horizon as she murmured wordlessly.

"What brings a contract negotiator from Baton Rouge to New Mexico?" Harley said, though she suspected she knew the answer.

"Business trip. We're opening a new branch in Santa Fe."

"Was anyone else here when you arrived?" Callaway said.

Chet scratched the silvery stubble on his chin. "In addition to the victim's car?" he said, gesturing to a red sedan in the parking lot. "Just one other vehicle, as I recall. A van." He turned to his wife, apparently looking for her input, then turned back just as quickly, as if realizing it was foolish to look for help from that quarter.

"White," he added, "with tinted passenger windows. Maybe a 2000?"

"How do you know the Fiesta belonged to the victim?" Harley said as she pulled up her phone to take notes. It was too dark for a notepad.

He shrugged. "Process of elimination. It was the only vehicle here besides ours when the kid found his sister, so it's only logical."

"Did you get a look at the van's plates?" Callaway said.

Chet shook his head. "No, sir."

And no security cameras to help us out, Harley thought.

"Did you see anyone else in the ruins?" she said.

Chet leaned back and rested his elbows on the back of the bench. "Like I told the officer, there was a group of kids up there on the shelf." He gestured with his chin toward the top of the rock formation. "They had a little fire going, but God knows what they were cooking. Almost turned around when we heard them laughing."

"I'm sorry," Harley interrupted. "Kids?"

"Teenagers, or maybe early twenties. Bending the elbow, if you catch my drift. I'm not judging—I was a hell-raiser in my day, you can be sure."

This bit of information—about the kids, not Chet's hell-raising youth—caught Harley's attention. "How many of them would you say there were?"

Chet squinted, as if peering through the mists of time. "Six or seven, I'd guess."

"You said they were drinking?"

Chet nodded. "That's right. Smoking something too, and I'm guessing it wasn't tobacco."

"Was June Collington with them?"

Chet frowned and glanced at Callaway for an explanation.

"The victim," Callaway said.

"Ah. No, she wasn't with them."

"You're sure?" Harley said, still trying to decide how much stock she could put in Chet's memory.

Chet, however, had no lack of confidence in himself. "Positive," he answered with a decisive nod. "She came later, along with her kid brother."

"But the other group was still here?" Harley said. "When June and Jesse arrived, I mean?"

Chet considered, then shook his head. "No, they left a little sooner. Ten, fifteen minutes—something like that."

Ah, Harley thought, disappointed. *So, they weren't here at the same time.*

"And you're sure they all left?" she said, wondering if perhaps the killer might have come out with the group, then stayed behind when he chose his target.

"I didn't count heads if that's what you mean. They were there one moment, the next they were gone. I tuned them out just about as soon as I got here, so I didn't notice."

Another dead end. If everything Chet was saying was accurate, that meant the killer must have arrived after the van had left, killed June (and taken the time to undress her, wrap her body in gold foil, and paint most of her face), and escaped all without being noticed by anyone. It seemed like a magic act. Then again, a man so skilled at getting close to his victims surely knew how to move about undetected.

"And what were you doing during all this?" Callaway said.

Chet shrugged. "Walking around, mostly. Sherry had hip surgery couple years back, so we take our time. Our son called, and we were still talking with him when the woman—I'm sorry, I don't remember her name."

"June," Harley said tightly, trying not to let Chet's blasé attitude get to her.

"Anyway, when June and her brother arrived. So everything that happened after that—well, we were a bit distracted."

"Was anyone else around?"

"Not that I recall."

Harley stared at her notes, searching for a lead, anything to go on. Thus far, about the only thing they knew for certain was that the killer had taken a fifth victim, been spooked in the act, and managed to escape. They were no closer to understanding why he used the foil and paint or how he was choosing his victims.

The silence lengthened. Harley tried to think of what to say next, but she had asked them everything she could think of. No, that was not quite right. She had asked *Chet* everything she could think of. Sherry, on the other hand…

She turned her attention to the white-haired woman, whose frail hands lay folded in her lap, the skin as thin and papery as parchment.

"What about you, Mrs. Wheeler?" Harley said. "Did you notice anything?"

"She was with me the whole time," Chet answered immediately, as if it were impossible his wife could have anything to add. "She already told me she didn't see anything."

"I understand," Harley said. "But I'd still like to hear what she has to say."

Sherry took a breath, her lips still quivering, and then let it out again.

Chet placed a hand on her knee. "My wife is very upset by what happened. I really don't think it's a good idea—"

"The cameraman," Sherry murmured.

Chet stared at her sternly. "What are you talking about? There was no cameraman." He smiled apologetically at the agents. "She's thinking of the media, probably. The cameras, the microphones—she's always been a little uncomfortable with the attention, so she wants to get out of here before the news crews arrive."

He leaned forward and lowered his voice, as if doing so would keep his wife from hearing, even though they were so close their knees were touching.

"She gets confused a lot," he explained. "Misplacing the house keys, leaving the oven on overnight. Doctors think it's early-onset dementia."

"He was watching," Sherry said, her rocking growing more agitated now. "Filming everything, everyone."

"That's enough, sweetheart," Chet said, his hand tightening on her knee. "Why don't you go back to the car while I—"

"Mr. Wheeler," Harley interrupted, losing her patience. "You can either let your wife share what she has to say, or Agent Callaway can escort you out of sight. The choice is yours."

Chet stared at her, looking shocked that anyone would speak to him that way. Perhaps no one had ever spoken to him like that before. If not, it was about time someone put him in his place.

"I can't believe this," he muttered. Then, perhaps realizing the weakness of his position, he threw up his hands and leaned back, as if he wanted no part of what was about to happen.

"Go ahead, Mrs. Wheeler," Harley said.

Sherry licked her dry lips. Her blinking came as rapidly as the twitching of a little bird.

"The man was standing there with a camera," she said in a reedy voice, "just standing there and recording everyone." She glanced up, her gaze worried. "Recording us, too. Chet was helping me walk, so he didn't see the man."

"Can you describe this man?" Harley said, eager now.

Sherry was silent for several moments. "He was a big man. I want to say as tall as..." Her eyes flicked to Callaway. "As you. But bigger, barrel-chested."

"Do you recall what he was wearing?"

She paused again. "A loose shirt. One of those touristy ones with flowers on it."

Harley felt a flutter of excitement inside her chest. "Hawaiian?" she said.

Sherry considered the idea for several, agonizing seconds. Then she nodded. "Yes, I think so. And sneakers—no, hiking boots. With shorts. His legs were very hairy."

"What about his face?" Harley said, hoping for just a few more details to compare against the man from Reyes's vlog.

Sherry squinted, then shook her head. "I'm not sure. His camera was in the way."

"That's okay," Harley said, undeterred. "How long would you say he was filming?"

Sherry shrugged one shoulder. "I couldn't tell you. I just saw him that once, and then he was hidden behind a wall. I forgot about him."

She fell silent. As if sensing this was his opportunity to reassert himself, Chet patted her hand and smiled at the two agents. "I'm afraid that's all we can tell you. You can see my wife is very tired, and it's high time I get her home."

He took his wife's hand, and she let him help her to her feet.

"Best of luck, agents," Chet said, as he led his wife toward the parking lot. "We'll be watching the news."

Harley stared at Chet's back and shook her head. "If I ever marry a man like that," she said to Callaway, "shoot me."

"If you ever marry a man like that," Callaway answered, "you'll shoot him first."

Harley grunted, knowing he was probably right.

They both fell silent.

"Hawaiian shirt," Harley said. "Tell me that doesn't sound like our creeper friend from Reyes's vlog."

"It does indeed," Callaway murmured. "But there's only one way to find out."

Harley nodded, already one step ahead of him. "What do you say we find somewhere to sit down and look through that comment section?"

CHAPTER SEVENTEEN

Harley felt almost like a kid again as she sat down on the edge of the roundabout, which was divided into four quadrants of different colors. Despite how little use the playground had seen (Harley wondered who had thought the ruins would garner enough attention to merit its own playground), the slides, swings, and roundabout were clean and usable, at least once one wiped away the patina of sand.

"Used to love sitting on these," Harley said. "Kelly and I would hold on as hard as we could, and Greg would try to get us 'seasick' as he called it."

"Who won?" Callaway said.

"Kelly, usually. She'd grip one of the bars like she was a koala, get this tight little frown on her face. She might turn green, but she wouldn't let go." She smiled at the memory. It was strange how many memories the mind could hold onto without actively thinking of them.

Callaway sat down next to her, his knees comically high on the low seat. A second dune buggy had joined the first, and the pair of them zipped across the hills together, sounding like June bugs buzzing around a streetlight.

Talking about Kelly made Harley think of the papers strewn across her office floor back home, and she felt a stab of guilt that she wasn't back there now, scouring them for clues. She knew it was silly to blame herself—she couldn't be in two places at once, after all—but she felt as if she were letting her sister down somehow.

Patience, she reminded herself. She had to prioritize the case at hand—not just because it was her job, but because their killer was taking new victims, and Kelly—well, how much reason did she really have to believe Kelly was out there now, waiting for Harley to find her? Unless she had been kidnapped and brainwashed, or held prisoner for all these years, the obvious conclusion was—

She's not dead, she told herself stubbornly. *Not until you see her body with your own eyes, touch her bones with the fingertips of your own hands. Until then, she's as alive as ever.*

"It's never easy, is it?" Callaway said, interrupting her thoughts.

She glanced at him and gave a noncommittal nod, though she wasn't really sure what he was talking about.

"They say it gets easier," he continued. "And I suppose there's nothing as shocking as seeing that first body, especially when you're dealing with homicide victims. But it never really becomes normal, does it? We just grow numb to it."

Harley nodded again, realizing now that Callaway had assumed her somber mood was directly connected to the sight of June Collington's body. Harley supposed it was, in a way—every time she approached a new body, she couldn't help wondering if she would find herself gazing at her sister's face. When she imagined this happening, she saw Kelly as the teenager she had been, perhaps because she didn't want to imagine how different Kelly would look now. Such a difference would only underscore how much of Kelly's life Harley had missed.

Not trusting herself to speak, Harley dug her toes hard in the dirt as a wave of grief washed over her.

Callaway's hand rested gently on her shoulder. "All I'm trying to say is, it's okay to be a little shaken up. It just means you're still human."

Pulling herself together, Harley sniffed hard and cleared her throat. "We should take another look at Lolita Reyes's vlog, see if we can't identify that man we saw in the background."

Callaway gave her a long look. She could feel his eyes on her, though she didn't look back.

Finally, he said, "Okay," in a quiet voice, as if he had accepted that Harley would not share more than she wanted to share. "You still have the link?"

Harley unlocked her phone and pulled up her browser, which was still on the victim's vlog. Her eyes drifted to Reyes's profile picture, which showed her leaping in the air beneath the Arc de Triomphe.

Well-traveled girl, Harley thought, still trying to detach herself from her emotions. She couldn't help wondering how big a family Reyes had, and where they had been when they learned of her death.

Harley returned to the video titled "On Growing Up," then fast-forwarded to the image of the hiker with the Hawaiian shirt. She paused the video and scrolled down to the comment section again.

"We're not the only ones who noticed him," she said.

"What'd they say?" Callaway said, leaning closer.

Harley scrolled slowly, letting Callaway read the comments for himself:

Goalicious414: total creeper
Alejandro K: lol I know right
HottieBoddie: wtf is he doing? Defiantly stalking her
ClinicalSalad: holy shit I knew I recognized him!!!

Below this last comment was a link, which led Harley to a channel called "The Big D." The description read, "Calling out all fakers, frauds, and phonies, got nothing but luv for my homies. Keep it real yall, like and subscribe."

Harley scanned through the videos. Several showed Big D's attempts at rapping—Harley listened to a few seconds of one, then quickly stopped it, not seeing any need to torture herself further—but most involved him hiking a number of popular trails across the state, sometimes rhapsodizing about the "fakeness" of society and sometimes provoking arguments with other hikers.

Harley paused on an image of Big D staring at the camera. He wasn't wearing the Hawaiian shirt, but he did have the browline glasses and bucket hat.

"That's our guy," Callaway said. "Now let's see if he's serial killer material."

The most popular video, which had garnered a whopping 120 views, showed him recording a couple's argument. When the man noticed he was being recorded, he turned angrily toward the camera.

"Do you mind, buddy?" he said, his eyebrows making an angry V.

"Not at all," the vlogger answered. "This is great material. Why don't you get back to the part where she suspects you were getting a little handsy with her sister?"

"Get the hell out of here, you prick!" the man said, trying to shove the camera away. Big D ducked away and backpedaled, laughing. It was the laughter of someone who has just played a hilarious prank on someone else, except that there was no prank here, no cleverness. This was straight up being a jackass.

"I'm not the one with the problematic prick," Big D said, a smile in his voice.

The man pursued him for another twenty or thirty yards. Then, with a look of haggard defeat, he shook his head and turned back. Big D followed, laughing to himself.

"Dooon't this guy have anything better to do?" Callaway said. "What a loser."

"Apparently not," Harley answered. She was studying Big D, trying to decide if he was capable of murdering five women and displaying them like mummies. Was his behavior simply a symptom of immaturity, or did it go deeper than that? If nothing else, his proximity to Reyes—not to mention the intentional way he had been staring at her—deserved further investigation.

"We need to find this guy," she said.

Callaway nodded, a sober look in his eyes. "Damn straight, we do. Is he there now?"

Harley was puzzled by the question. "There?"

"Active. You know what I mean."

"No, his stream is down, probably for the night. By the look of it, though, he's on here a lot." She scrolled through his channel, searching for any clues as to where he might live and what he might do when he wasn't harassing hikers.

After a few moments, Callaway cleared her throat. "Harley?" he said.

She didn't look up. "Yeah?"

"Harley," he said again.

She glanced at him, slightly annoyed now by the interruption. "What?"

"What are you doing?"

"I'm studying our suspect. What does it look like I'm doing?"

He sighed. "You might not believe this, but you're a human being like everyone else, and that means you need sleep just like everyone else."

She blinked at him, not registering his words. "I'm fine, Callaway. I'll sleep when we catch this guy."

She turned her attention back to the phone. Callaway, however, put his hand on her wrist, gently pushing the phone down.

"This isn't a hundred-meter dash," he said. "It could take weeks to find him, months. Hell, before I met you, the last case I worked took five years to wrap up."

"That's because you didn't have me." She gave him a wry smile, despite herself.

He grunted. "I'm not sure you would have done any better extraditing a Colombian national, but maybe I'm wrong. Knowing you, you'd probably have flown down there, stuffed him in a suitcase, and brought him back."

She raised her eyebrows, impressed by his creativity. "That's not a bad idea."

"Look. Tomorrow we can get up bright and early and check his channel. If he's on, we'll try to use background clues to track him down. If he isn't, we'll see if we can't identify him another way." He paused. "But tonight, we need to sleep."

She studied him. "That canyon hike is really hitting you, isn't it?"

He stared at her patiently, refusing to take the bait.

"I don't love the idea of making the long drive home," she finally said. "Now that I think about it, though, I know a place nearby. Ever been to the Welcome Wagon?"

A look of distaste came over Callaway's face, and he sucked a breath between his teeth. "I don't know, Cole. The Welcome Wagon isn't quite what it used to be."

"I know it's never been the Ritz, but it can't be that bad, can it? Is Ned still there?"

Callaway shook his head. "It's his son now. Austin, I think his name is."

Harley remembered Austin as a freckled, heavyset boy with scabs on his legs, a sheepish smile, and a propensity for wearing shorts that were not much longer than underwear. She had gone out of her way to befriend him in school, and in response he had given Harley the spare key to the pool area. She smiled fondly at the memory.

"So how about it?" she said. "We'll catch a few hours of sleep, then get back at it first thing in the morning."

Callaway looked like he wanted to protest, but the expression on Harley's face seemed to convince him to let it go. He raised both hands. "Don't say I didn't warn you."

CHAPTER EIGHTEEN

Harley flopped down on the bed, exhausted.

As Callaway had warned her, the hotel was far more rundown than she remembered. Despite the outdated wallpaper and peeling exterior, however, it was bug-free and clean, even if there was a faint odor of tobacco lingering in the air. It wasn't perfect, but it would do.

Her mind, which had been hyper-focused on the case all day, now began to wander like a boat cut free from its moorings. She found herself thinking of the message Greg had left her.

We need to talk.

The words sounded ominous, a harbinger of bad tidings. Tired as she was, she didn't intend to go all night wondering what Greg wanted to talk with her about. Better to bite the bullet and hash it out now.

She dialed his number and waited, chewing her lip while the phone rang. The call went to voicemail, and she hung up, unsure what to say.

"At least I tried," she mumbled, tossing the phone onto the comforter and lying back again.

She tried to relax. She planned to hit the ground running in the morning, which meant she needed all the rest she could get. Try as she might to get comfortable, however, she couldn't stop thinking about the case. All the details—the gold foil, the paint, the timeline of the murders—kept running circles in her brain.

Knowing she wouldn't be able to sleep until she wrote her thoughts down, she turned on the lamp and threw back the sheet. Next, she retrieved the guest book and pen from the drawer and wrote the following:

"MOTIVE?"

Given the age and gender of the victims, the most obvious answer was a sexual motive. Though she couldn't rule such a possibility out, not until the ME had carefully examined all the victims, nothing about the way the bodies had been left—the foil, the face paint—suggested a sexual motive.

What kind of motive *did* those details suggest, then? Was he just a hunter mounting his trophies, as Callaway had suggested? Or did he bear some particular hate toward his victims, some old grievance?

Whatever else he is, Harley thought, *he's dedicated, motivated. Probably someone on the fringes of society, whether or not others see him that way. A zealot.*

Harley wrote the word "RELIGIOUS" and underlined it twice.

She sat back. Did the man who styled himself Big D seem like the zealot type? No, not at first glance…but Harley had the impression there was a lot going on beneath the surface with him. He was definitely on the fringes of society, that was for sure. And his camera might be a way for him to get close to his victims without alerting them to his true intentions.

I need a sounding board, she thought, blowing out a slow breath between her lips. She considered waking Callaway, but remembering how tired he had looked, she decided to let him rest. Instead, she picked up her phone and dialed the number of Josiah Emerson, an old friend from the Bureau's Massachusetts field office. He had helped her talk through the Felix Navarro case. Maybe he could help her again.

She listened to the phone ring several times. *He's probably asleep,* she thought. *It's past midnight, after all.*

Then, to her surprise, there was a faint click and she heard Emerson's familiar voice. "Hello?"

"Hi, Emerson. Sorry to bother you so late at night. This is—"

"Harley!" Emerson's voice was bright with happy surprise. "Burning the midnight oil, as always. Just wait till they put you on Microzide and you have to get up every couple of hours to take a piss—then you'll wish you'd appreciated your sleep more when you could get it."

She smiled, pleased to hear his voice again. "I'll make a note of that."

"So what's going on with you? Still chasing that billionaire? I'm out of the loop here, so I might be behind the times."

He was referring to the Felix Navarro case, the first one Harley had worked since returning to New Mexico.

"Actually, we found the killer," she answered, pleased to be able to deliver this piece of good news. "It wasn't the billionaire, though he did get convicted on other charges. I can't say enough about what a difference talking with you made."

"A pleasure, Harley, a pleasure. Any time you need to brainstorm, you know where to find me."

Harley gave a little laugh. "Well, how much time do you have now?"

She could hear the smile in his voice. "Still all business, huh? It wouldn't be so bad if you reached out one of these days just to catch up, you know, but I won't hold it against you. What are we dealing with here?"

Harley wasted no time sharing the details. "Five bodies, two different locations. All young women."

"Cause of death?"

"Asphyxiation, it appears. Burns around the fifth victim's mouth suggest a chemical agent." She paused. "But here's where it gets interesting. He's wrapping his victims in gold foil and painting their faces gold as well."

The line was silent for several heartbeats.

"I swear they get weirder every year," Emerson muttered. "I'll give him props for originality, though. What's it all about?"

"That's the million-dollar question. It seems…ritualistic somehow, which suggests a religious background to me, that, and the parallels to ancient Egyptian burial practices."

Emerson made a murmur of agreement. She could hear him descending a flight of stairs.

"What's your profile so far?" he said.

"Sketchy, to be honest," she said. "I haven't had much time to work on it."

"Stop pulling my chain, Cole. I know how you work. You must have at least some idea who you're dealing with."

She grunted. It was a double-edged sword, talking with someone who knew her well. He could see right through her, whether she wanted him to or not.

"My best guess," she said, "is that we're looking for a young man, probably in his twenties or thirties. Someone who knows how to fit into the college scene. Possibly a college student himself."

"A ladies' man?" Emerson said.

"Not necessarily. There's a good chance he's socially awkward, emotionally stunted. Might have even been bullied." Even as she spoke the words, she thought of Big D. He was not what she would ordinarily describe as "awkward," but socially backward, to the point of deviancy? Absolutely yes.

"How'd you draw that conclusion?" Emerson asked.

"He's interested in the dead, not the living—otherwise he'd discard them just as soon as he's finished with them. Instead, he wraps them in gold and paints them. Why?"

"He's creating art."

"Then why hide it in the back of a cavern? Why not leave his victims in churches, public parks, outside national monuments?"

Emerson said nothing. Harley heard the soft whimper of a dog, followed by Emerson's soothing murmur, "I know, girl, I know. You'll be chasing those hares in just a few minutes."

Then Emerson's voice grew firmer as he addressed her. "How do you think he's choosing his victims?"

Harley closed her eyes, considering. "There's a good chance he's frustrated with women," she said. "Might even be a virgin. He's been rejected numerous times, and now he takes out his frustration by killing them. It's hate, but it's also self-hate."

She paused, thinking Emerson would comment. After several seconds passed in silence, however, she decided to continue.

"He probably has a domineering, controlling mother. He feels impotent with women, unable to get a woman's attention—which becomes a self-fulfilling prophecy, because women know better than to put their confidence in a man who doesn't put any confidence in himself."

"So he kills them," Emerson said. "It's his way of getting back at the people who hurt him."

"That's my theory, anyway."

"Not a bad one, for what it's worth." There was a metallic rattle. It sounded like Emerson was letting his dog out of her crate.

A new thought occurred to Harley. "If he did know his victims," she said, "he could have a list of women who've rejected him over the years."

"A kill list."

"Exactly."

The thought sent a shiver up Harley's spine. How many names might be on that list? Ten? Twenty? Dozens?

The dog whined again, and Harley heard the sound of nails scratching on linoleum. "I'd love to stay and chat," Emerson said, "but Maggie really needs to go out. I can leave the phone on and come back after I've tied her outside if you want."

As good as it was to hear Emerson's voice, Harley was finally feeling the day catch up with her. It was time to get some sleep.

"That's alright," she said. "I'll let you go. You've been a great help, as always."

"I'm not sure I did much more than listen, but you're welcome."

104

Harley ended the call and let out a deep sigh. Then she lay back, thinking of Emerson's words as she pictured the bodies laid out in a row in their golden skins.

CHAPTER NINETEEN

Harley dreamed she was swimming to the bottom of a dark pool. Something glinted down there in the soft shadows. As she approached, she discovered the legs of a woman with golden skin. She pulled herself along the body until she reached the face, which was stretched wide in an expression of horror, the eyes rolled back to reveal the milky whites.

At first, she thought it was Daisy Ballard, but no—the face was wrong. Then, with dawning dread, she realized that she was staring into Kelly's face. Kelly had not aged a day. She had been dead all this time, just waiting for Harley to find her.

What took you so long? Kelly's aggrieved, accusing face seemed to say. *Why did you leave me here for so, so long?*

Harley stirred in her motel bed, her sweaty legs dragging across the sheets as her eyes fluttered. Just as she was realizing it had been a nightmare (*Just a nightmare,* she reassured herself, *no truth to it at all*), she heard a sound that was clearly not from her imagination: the distinct click of the door latch pulling free.

Still unsettled from the dream, Harley curled the sheet back and slipped her feet to the floor. With the light coming through the gap in the curtains, she could just make out the outline of the door as it swung slowly toward her, then caught on the latch fixed to the door frame.

A cold prickle of fear ran along her spine. *He doesn't know it's locked,* she reminded herself. She did not know who "he" was, but she had a feeling she would find out before the night was over.

But who would want to harm her? Who even knew where she was?

The door retracted, separating the bolt from the latch, and then a card appeared through the gap between door and frame. The card pushed the latch back so that it wouldn't come into contact with the bolt again.

Then there was a pause. Breaking free of her paralysis, Harley hurried to her nightstand and drew her Glock from the holster. She turned on the lamp just as the door opened.

"Well, you're up early," Callaway said, slipping the credit card back into his pocket. He was dressed in yesterday's clothes: button-up shirt, faded jeans, undyed Stetson.

Harley relaxed, sighing in disbelief as she returned the Glock to its holster. "Ever hear of knocking?"

"Didn't want to wake the neighbors," he answered. "They kept me up half the night."

"So you decided to break into my room?"

"Neat little trick, huh? Learned it from this Italian kid who would sneak into people's rooms and steal their things. That was back when I was still with the police department."

"As much as I'd love to hear all about your life, the only thing I'm curious about right now is why you found it necessary to wake me in the dead of night." She glanced at the clock, whose red letters glowed like taillights on a desolate midnight highway. "It's five in the morning, Callaway."

Callaway nodded. "I know. Our friend is an early bird."

This caught Harley's interest. "Big D?"

"That's right. He's already up and live streaming. You'll never guess where he is."

Harley frowned, thinking. Then it came to her in a flash, and her eyes widened. "No way."

Callaway nodded, looking pleased by her surprise. "Scene of the crime. Couldn't resist the urge to go back."

Harley cursed under her breath. She couldn't believe it.

"Still wish I hadn't woken you?" Callaway said.

*

A single, solitary vehicle was parked in the Shilowa National Monument's dirt lot, a gold SUV with a "BABY ON BOARD" warning decal in the rear window. The car did not appear to have been washed in at least a decade.

"Decent amount of trunk space," Harley murmured, peering through the dusty glass. Whoever the killer was, he had to have a way to transport the bodies of his victims, unless he had somehow lured all four of those women into the back of that cavern, something Harley did not find particularly likely.

"Come on," Callaway said, touching her arm. "Let's go get him while his guard is down."

The sun was still hidden over the horizon, but the eastern sky blazed in a maelstrom of red. *Red in the morning, sailor's warning,* Harley thought, wondering how often the old adage was actually true.

The low shushing sound of traffic on the highway filled the background as they entered the ruins. The caution tape remained where it had been left the previous night, the only sign that a crime had been committed there.

As they neared the walled room in which June Collington's body had been found, Callaway stopped suddenly and pressed a finger to his lips. Harley listened. At first, she heard nothing. Then, as an eighteen-wheeler on the highway faded from hearing, Big D's muffled voice came through the stillness.

"Like I always say, I bring you guys the real shit. Most of you princesses are probably still getting your beauty sleep, but I had to come out here early, before the pigs came back." He laughed. "Let me get a selfie real quick."

As Harley came around the wall, she saw Big D sprawled out on the ground in the exact spot where June's body had been found, one hand cocked behind his head like a model sunbathing as he pointed a compact camera at himself. He was wearing a Hawaiian shirt—not the same as the one in the video; this one had crimson daylilies in place of palm trees—and a pair of baggy cargo shorts that had ridden up his hairy legs, exposing the fine down of his newborn-pale thighs.

He started to say, "How do I look?" but his words faltered at the end as he saw the two agents. For a moment his eyes were filled with a blank, uncomprehending expression, as if he had gone over a math equation a hundred times only to be told the answer was in fact not the number he had written down. Then, with a frantic sort of nervousness, like an overturned beetle desperate to right itself, he scrambled to his feet and blinked at the agents in confusion.

"What do you want?" he said, casting a quick glance to the side as if to plan his retreat. He was cornered, however—just like June had been, Harley realized with a grim satisfaction.

Callaway gave Harley a look of tired disbelief. "You believe this guy? He has the stones to come back here, and he asks us what *we* want?"

Harley could see a series of calculations firing quickly behind Big D's eyes. Then a new idea seemed to occur to him, and he pointed one long, accusing finger.

"You're not supposed to be here!" he said. "This is a crime scene!"

"Then what are you doing here?" Callaway said. "Besides shooting your cover image for a fashion magazine, that is."

"I'm documenting the crime scene." Big D looked from one agent to the other, as if unsure which of them he should try to convince. "The public needs to know what happened here."

"Come on, Big D," Harley said, unimpressed. "You're going to have to do better than that."

To her right, Callaway moved in the shadows, flanking Big D like a wolf with a cornered lamb.

The man swallowed hard. He glanced down at the camera, and the sight of it seemed to fill him with fresh vigor. He spun the camera around so that it faced the agents. Harley doubted many people were watching at this early hour (not that many people watched Big D's videos at *any* hour, to be fair), but she still disliked being filmed without her consent. There was no telling what little slip-up might be used later to undermine the investigation.

"When I file harassment charges," he said, a bead of sweat rolling past his eye, "I want the whole world to know your faces."

"Harassment?" Harley repeated, amused. "You're trespassing on a crime scene. We're federal agents."

Big D gave Callaway a wary glance and edged away, moving toward the corner. "You can't touch me," he said, backing up as he recorded them. "First Amendment. Right to free speech. Maybe you've heard of it."

"We don't want to touch you," Callaway answered, his voice low and threatening. "We want to talk to you."

"We're talking now."

"Without a camera in our faces."

"Go ahead, knock it out of my hand. Show the world how tough you are."

Harley stepped forward, worried Callaway might take the bait. "Listen," she said, speaking calmly. "All we want is for you to tell your side of the story."

"My story?" Big D laughed. It was a heartless, chilling sound, the laugh of a man who is used to laughing alone. "Go to my vlog—*that's* my story."

"Interesting you'd bring that up," Callaway said. "You were here just last night, weren't you? Two visits to a crime scene in under twenty-four hours—does that seem a little odd to you, Agent Cole?"

"It does indeed," she answered.

Big D's tone became more conversational as he addressed his online audience. "Buckle in, guys," he said. "You're about to witness some A-level police brutality. But rest assured, no matter what kind of shit they pull, I'm taking this all the way." He raised his voice for the agents' benefit. "You hear me? I'm not just going for your jobs—I'm going for your bosses' jobs too. Take the whole damn corrupt patriarchy down on your heads. I'm Sampson, and you're the two pillars I'm about to bring down, so by all means, start swinging."

Callaway gave Harley a befuddled look, as if to say, *You believe this guy?*

"You're not under arrest," Harley explained patiently. "We just need to talk with you."

"Yeah, right. You want to get me to the station so you can fingerprint me, probably lift my DNA off a can of soda."

Callaway shook his head in disbelief. "You've been watching too much TV."

"Then you'll keep badgering me till I say something that sounds remotely incriminating," Big D continued, "and you'll start threatening me with jail time if I don't cooperate."

"You've already incriminated yourself," Harley said. "You unlawfully entered a crime scene."

Big D shrugged. "A misdemeanor. I'll get off easy."

"Yeah, but homicide?" Callaway said. "That's a felony."

Big D stared at him and said nothing. Harley could see the thoughts firing off behind his eyes again, calculating.

"If you want to get ahead of this thing," she said, "your best bet is to tell us your side. The more you stonewall us, the more reason we have to dig into your past." They were going to dig into his past one way or the other, but he didn't need to know that.

Harley could see the uncertainty on Big D's face. He knew he'd been caught with his hand in the cookie jar, but he was still trying to find a way to weasel out of the situation.

"And what's to keep me from lawyering up?" he said.

The two agents exchanged a glance. "Nothing," Harley said. "But if you do, keep in mind you'll only make yourself appear guilty."

"I didn't kill anyone."

Harley shrugged. "Maybe, maybe not. Either way, people are wrongfully convicted all the time. You really want to take that risk?"

Big D gave her a resentful stare. Harley had the sense he was thinking several moves ahead, planning his escape.

After a long pause, Big D turned the camera off and lowered it. "Let's make this quick," he said.

CHAPTER TWENTY

Harley stared at the man seated across the table from her in the gray, nondescript interview room of the Santa Fe field office. She had the sense there were two sides to the vlogger who called himself Big D: the internet persona, a troll who alienated everyone around him with his mockery and insensitivity, and then the man who hid behind that persona, protected from scrutiny by a shield of tasteless jokes, pointless arguments with strangers, and claims of authenticity that rang as hollow as pumpkins on Halloween.

She didn't like the look of him: the greasy, taunting smile, the eyes that buzzed about like a fly, never landing on anything. It was like he had a big secret, and he was just waiting for the opportunity to show everyone else how stupid they were.

Who was the man behind the mask? Harley wondered. A hurt, misunderstood child who had never grown up, or something much more sophisticated, something…monstrous?

The door opened and Callaway entered with a trio of water bottles. He set one in front of Harley, then skidded the second one across the table toward Big D, who caught it just before it could crash to its side. The third he kept for himself, running his thumb along the ridges of the cap as he leaned against the wall.

"Why don't we start with your name," Harley said.

Big D's eyes flickered with amusement. "What, you don't like the name on my channel? Too racy for you?"

Harley had no interest in playing his games. She stared back at him, unimpressed.

Big D gave up the attempt at humor and snorted. "Dale McCann, celebrity vlogger." He glanced up at the corner of the room. "This is being recorded, right? I want it on record I was coerced into this interrogation."

"Interview," Harley said. "It's an interview, and there was no coercion involved. Now, if you'll please refrain from interrupting—"

Dale sank back into his chair and crossed his arms. "You'll just edit it out, anyway."

Harley sighed and looked down, already feeling she was on the edge of losing her patience. *Be careful,* she told herself. *That's exactly what he wants: for you to blow up and say or do something you'll regret. Don't let him get under your skin.*

To her relief, Callaway stepped in. "That's not how this works," he said. "We don't tamper with the evidence until we like how it looks."

"I think that's exactly what you do."

Callaway passed a weary hand over his forehead and murmured, "Lord, help us."

Harley decided to take another turn. "Mr. McCann," she said, "can you tell us where you were yesterday evening around seven o'clock?"

"At the Shilowa ruins."

The willingness with which he admitted this surprised Harley. She said, "The same ruins where a woman's body was found, is that correct?"

He nodded nonchalantly, as if it were merely a coincidence.

"Can you tell us what you were doing there?" Harley asked.

He shrugged. "What does anyone do there? I was seeing the sights, learning the history."

"What were you videotaping?" Callaway said. "From what I hear, it sounds like you were more focused on the people than any history."

Dale snorted. "Videotaping?" He gestured at Harley's phone, which rested on the edge of the table. "What does that look like to you, a VHS camcorder?"

"Just answer the question," Harley said.

Dale's eyes pivoted to hers. "I'm an artist, okay? I take in everything—the scenery, the people, all of it. It's all connected."

At the word "artist," an image of gold-painted faces popped into Harley's head. She stared at Dale, imagining him on one knee beside Daisy's body, his lips pressed together in an expression of concentration as he stroked the cleft beneath her nostrils with a fine brush.

"What kind of art do you create?" she said.

"Human art. Life. I capture the world as it is, not as people want it to be. I cut through all the bullshit and show people how things are under the surface."

Harley frowned. She was having a hard time tracking with him. First, he was talking about art, then he was talking about truth. She couldn't tell whether he was being deliberately vague to throw her off the scent, or if he was genuinely sharing his perspective.

113

Before she could formulate a response, Callaway spoke up.

"You know what the bullshit is?" he said. "Your story. You're not interested in the scenery, the ruins, the history. You're not an 'artist.'" He made air quotes as he said this. "You're just a lonely jerk who gets attention by annoying people."

This got Dale's attention. His face darkened, and his hands moved beneath the table. Based on the way his forearms were flexing, Harley guessed he was squeezing his hands into fists.

"Is that right, pig?" Dale said softly. "The world's just black-and-white to you, isn't it?"

The two stared at one another. Had the two met in an alley, Harley was not sure she would have been able to recognize Dale's face afterward.

She decided to play her next card. "Lolita Reyes," she said.

A shadow passed over Dale's face. Was it guilt, or the fear of being discovered? Whatever it was, it disappeared quickly.

"Never heard of her," he said.

"Maybe not," Harley agreed. "But you've seen her. You were watching her, in fact."

She pulled up the video from Reyes's vlog, showing Dale a still image with him in the background.

Dale stared at it for a few seconds before sinking back into his chair with a shrug. "Looks like me, sure. Doesn't mean it is me."

"You got a twin brother we don't know about?" Callaway said.

"What if I do? You gonna arrest him because he was looking at some broad?"

"That 'broad' was murdered," Harley said, her voice brimming with anger. "She and three other women—four, counting the one at the ruins."

Dale's face went pale as if the blood had suddenly been siphoned out of him. He began to blink rapidly, glancing around the room, and his breathing became quick and shallow.

"Oh, man," he said, leaning forward and cradling his head in his hands. "Oh, man."

"You didn't think we'd make the connection, did you?" Callaway said, stepping closer to him. "You had no idea that while you were watching her, the world was watching you."

Dale's chest rose in deep, hitching breaths. His hands turned to claws, digging into his scalp.

114

Callaway went on, each word a dagger. "You really are an artist, Dale—just not the kind you pretend to be. The one thing I can't figure out is all the gold. Is it a religious thing? A way of showing off?"

Dale began muttering to himself under his breath, perhaps trying to drown out Callaway's words.

Callaway leaned close to Dale's ear. "You slipped up, Dale. You left something in that cavern. You want to know what it was?"

Dale went still and silent, waiting.

"Three letters," Callaway said in a hushed voice just above a whisper. "D-N-A."

Dale sprang to his feet, his chair clattering to the floor behind him. Callaway took a quick backward step, his hands coming up, but Dale didn't come toward him. Instead, he backed toward the far corner of the room, his eyes hollow and mad as he shook his head repeatedly.

"I didn't kill them, I didn't kill them!" he insisted, now on the verge of tears.

Callaway crossed his arms. "The evidence says otherwise."

"Then the evidence is lying!" Dale pointed his finger at Callaway. "You planted that DNA! You don't know who the real killer is, so you decided to frame me!"

"Nobody's being framed here," Harley said, trying to regain control of the situation. "Please sit down, Mr. McCann."

"Yeah, right," Dale muttered. "So you can trick me into saying something damning. That's been your plan all along because you can't prove shit."

He began to smile, regaining some of his former confidence. "There *is* no DNA evidence because I never touched that Rita girl, or whatever her name was."

"Reyes," Harley corrected.

"Whatever. I saw her, sure, but I didn't get within ten feet of her, and you can't prove what didn't happen."

Harley sensed they were losing their opportunity. She leaned forward, speaking in a low, confidential tone.

"I'm going to be honest with you," she said. "Right now, you're in the crosshairs of this investigation. If you want to change that, you need to be truthful with us—one hundred percent."

He snorted. "Yeah, because the truth can never do any damage."

"Not as much as lies," she countered. "You don't need to trust us, but unless you give us a reason to trust you—"

He raised a hand to stop her. "Okay, okay. I get it. You don't need to keep going with your pitch." He sighed, rubbing his temples with one hand.

"Let's start over," Harley said. "What were you doing at those ruins, Dale?"

He ran a hand through his wiry hair. "I was just trolling, okay? That's what my whole channel is about."

Harley saw Callaway's confused expression.

"It's a way to annoy people, get attention," Dale continued. "There were some chicks up there smoking weed at the Monument, so I went and mingled. You gotta get those hotties in the thumbnails, man. Sex sells."

Callaway made a disgusted face. "So do snuff films," he said. "Were you planning to record it, maybe post it somewhere anonymously?"

"Hell, no! I didn't kill that girl!"

"You expect us to believe it's a coincidence you were at the ruins last night?" Callaway said.

Dale sighed and shook his head. "I told you already, I was filming."

Callaway's voice was firm, not budging an inch. "Bullshit. You knew she was going to get killed there, which means you either killed her yourself or know something about the person who did. Which is it, Dale?"

"Neither. You want proof? Go back to my vlog. I live-streamed for *hours*."

"Didn't step away from the camera for a minute? Not even to go to the bathroom?"

"Thirty seconds, tops. You think I can murder a woman and wrap her up in foil in the time it takes to piss?"

Harley looked up sharply from her notes. "How do you know about the gold foil if you didn't see the body?"

There was a beat of silence as both agents stared at Dale. He blinked back at Harley, thinking.

"I heard that old couple mention it, okay?" he finally said. "Something about, 'the girl with the golden face'."

"Why didn't you stick around?" Callaway said. "If you knew there was a story, why didn't you get in the middle of it?"

Dale shrugged. "I guess I'm not a big fan of brushing shoulders with cops. I knew the place would be swarming, so I dipped. End of story."

Harley studied him, unsure what to believe. She compared his version of events to the timeline Chet Wheeler had given her. Even if Chet had remembered everything with complete accuracy, he could not have had his eye on the parking lot the entire time, not if he was wandering the ruins with his wife. Besides, he hadn't even seen Dale there. What other details might Chet have missed?

"The video you mentioned," she said, trying to get back on track. "We checked your channel, but I never saw that one."

"That's because I took it down," Dale said. "I was afraid some shit like this would happen. I wanted to look it over, make sure there was nothing that would make people think I might have been involved."

"We need to see that video," Harley said.

Dale pulled his phone from his pocket and set it on the table. Then he hesitated. "And you'll let me walk?"

"You know we can't guarantee that. But if it shows us what you say it will…" She paused, not wanting to draw any conclusions without talking with Callaway first. "Let's just say having an alibi never hurts."

Dale didn't seem to be entirely appeased by this answer. He bit his lip, staring at the locked screen of his phone.

"The other option," Callaway said, "is we get a warrant for your phone. It'll take longer, sure, but then there won't be anything off-limits. I'll be waist-deep in your IMs, DMs, and whatever other kinds of electronic messaging people use these days."

"All we want is the video," Harley said. "But if you make us get a warrant, your entire digital history will be at our disposal. You sure you want us digging through that?"

With a steadying breath, Dale's fingers danced across the surface of the phone, unlocking it. Harley moved around the table so she could see what he was doing. It occurred to her that he might just delete the video if it contained anything incriminating. Such an action would only convince them of his guilt, however, and besides that she was pretty sure there were ways to recover deleted videos, anyway.

"Here it is," he said, passing the phone to her. "Knock yourselves out."

CHAPTER TWENTY ONE

Herb paused in the lobby of the Shady Oaks Museum of Natural Science, scratching his chin indecisively as if deciding which of the many fossil displays to approach first. In truth, he was searching for a certain dark-haired girl he had seen enter the museum only a few minutes earlier.

The question was, where had she gone?

Herb knew that Ka had been coming to the museum quite often lately. She was working on applying for an internship at the Fletcher Museum of Natural Science and History, which, if she was accepted, would allow her both to advance her career in her desired field while also living close to her extended family.

The problem for Ka was that Herb had different plans for her—plans he had been mulling over for a long time, ever since her callous rejection of him back in middle school when she had laughed at him in front of all their peers for offering her a flower.

Of course, Ka had no knowledge of Herb's plans, and she almost certainly wouldn't have liked them if she had known about them. But that was okay. Herb would convince her.

He could be very convincing when he wanted to be.

All he had to do was find her first.

The man at the desk—fifties, wearing a tan blazer over a salmon-colored dress shirt—was looking in his direction, and Herb suspected that at any moment the man would ask if Herb was looking for anything in particular. He was looking for some*one*, in fact, but Herb couldn't tell him that.

Ducking his head, Herb moved toward the nearest display at hand. According to the plaque, the "ERYOPS" was a kind of extinct amphibian, though to Herb it looked more like a flat-headed dog with stubby legs.

Herb ran his hand along the pebbled snout of the fossil, dipping his fingers into the quarter-sized holes of the nostrils. As he did so, he turned his body slightly away from the display so he could survey the room, searching for Ka. Flocks of people came and went. A large man in shorts and flip-flops waddled past, perspiring heavily despite the museum's seventy-degree temperature.

Then Herb spotted her. She was several displays to his left, biting her lower lip as she tapped the end of her pencil against a notebook. She was no more than a pencil shadow in his peripheral vision as she studied a series of fish fossils…but nevertheless, Herb would have recognized her anywhere.

"Hello, beautiful," he murmured, barely moving his lips. He felt a flush of relief at the sight of her, even though less than fifteen minutes earlier he had been tailing her, doing his best to stay with her while keeping one or two vehicles between them. The truth was he needed her. He couldn't finish his plans without her.

The man with the flip-flops doubled back, pausing by a collection of rocks. Ka disappeared behind his bulk.

Cursing under his breath, Herb left the display and strolled across the middle of the room, searching for Ka. He tried to keep his breathing level, but he was so excited to be near the end of his quest, so ready to finish, that he could barely contain himself. He wanted to shout his good news to the world, like an explorer who has discovered the fountain of youth.

Except…why would he want to share it with anyone else? Why would he want to let anyone else follow in his footsteps?

He spotted her again. He watched the swing of her hips as she drifted toward the tunnel—an unconscious gesture, he was sure. She wasn't the type of girl to draw attention that way. If she had been, Herb would've had no interest in her.

No, she was a good girl: smart, well educated, with good genes and a high IQ. Exactly the type of girl he wanted but could not have, not if he played by the rules. He had never been one to play by others' rules, however. He preferred doing things his own way.

Herb followed a large family—two parents, two strollers, and three additional children who swarmed about like wasps searching for something to sting—into the tunnel. It was cool inside, and he felt as safe as if he were back in his mother's womb. He had always been safe in the darkness—safe from prying eyes, safe from the attention of those who could never understand the way he thought.

He stood in the darkness and stared at Ka. He loved the length of her straight, charcoal hair and how it fell down her back, a waterfall of ink reaching down to her hips. He loved the proud arch of her eyebrows, the softness with which her jawline dissolved toward her throat, and the flat and unfeeling glance of her dark eyes.

She was strong, oh yes. Like a wild mare tossing her mane as she gallops the plains.

And, like a wild mare, she needed to be broken. And Herb was just the person to do it. He would break her gently, because he didn't want to extinguish the fire in her eyes, didn't want to frighten her spirit into retreating far inside herself.

After all, he would need her again soon.

He hung back as the group moved on. Ka was taking notes as she stood in front of a display showing a pair of dinosaurs battling one another, claws extended. Herb moved closer, drawn as much by the notebook as by her scent. He had always been blessed with a tremendous sense of smell. He was not drawn by the manufactured scents she wore—her perfume, shampoo, and deodorant—but the underlying odors of her flesh, the smells she tried so hard to hide.

You can't hide them from me.

She shifted, and her elbow brushed against his arm. She did not seem to notice. An electric thrill coursed through his body, and a rush of blood began pounding in his head. All the details around him seemed to sharpen into focus, as if magnified.

He was so close he could touch her hair without her noticing.

This, he realized, was what it meant to be alive. Everything else, all the inane details of maintaining his body and keeping up societal expectations, was just sleepwalking compared to this.

He leaned close and took a slow, deep breath, closing his eyes as her scent curled up his nostrils, billowed into his chest, and spread into every cell of his body. The rush was so heady that he almost thought he might pass out.

Then she shifted her weight, bumping his hip.

"I'm sorry," she said, moving away. "I didn't see you there."

"No harm done," he answered, his eyes half-lidded.

She smiled, her teeth strikingly white in the darkness, and continued down the tunnel.

Herb felt a twist in his guts as he watched her walk away. He wanted to catch up with her, cut her off. But this wasn't the place. There were too many people about, too many chances he'd be seen. He couldn't afford being discovered, not before he'd finished his mission.

Leaning against the glass window to steady his trembling arms, he watched Ka move back out into the light.

It won't be long now, he thought. *Not long at all.*

This time, he would not try to win her heart with a flower. He would take it by force.

CHAPTER TWENTY TWO

Harley stared blankly at the whiteboard menu hanging from the side of the taco truck. She tried to focus on the ingredients, but somehow counting calories seemed a bit less interesting than trying to decide how to pursue a murder investigation now that Dale McCann was no longer their chief suspect.

A voice interrupted her thoughts. "Ma'am? What kind of cheese, ma'am?"

Harley stirred herself from her reverie with a sheepish smile. "Pepper jack is good, thank you."

The owner, a Hispanic man with eyes as dark as the soul patch on his chin, gave her a long look before turning to bark orders to the pair of teenage boys mopping their sweating brows with their forearms as they rolled fresh tortillas.

"You okay?" Callaway said, touching her arm. He peered at her closely, as if wondering if he had missed something.

She shrugged it off. "I'm fine. Didn't sleep well last night, that's all."

She avoided his eyes, hoping he would take the hint that she didn't want to talk about it. He did not, however, drop it.

"I'm disappointed, too," he said. "First Mayhew, then McCann. Can't help feeling like that's two strikes. I don't want there to be a third."

"It doesn't work like that."

"Not for us, no. We have the luxury of time. But for his victims?" Callaway shook his head.

The man with the soul patch slapped down a pair of tightly wrapped burritos on paper plates, then rang up the bill.

"I got it," Callaway said, pushing forward before Harley could protest. He pulled a few bills from his wallet and slid them toward the man, leaving a generous tip.

Hot burrito in hand, Harley nodded toward a nearby bench. "What do you say we go have a seat?"

Callaway nodded as he slipped his wallet back into his pocket. There was a thoughtful, determined look in his eyes that had been there ever since leaving the field office. Even though he had been reluctant to release McCann (a sentiment Harley shared herself), he appeared more than ready to move forward with the investigation and pursue new leads.

They sat down at a picnic table in the shade of a white mulberry tree. They were in downtown Santa Fe, not far from the Georgia O'Keeffe Museum. It was almost noon, and the streets were thick with tourists dressed in bright colors, the faces of many hidden beneath broad-brimmed sun hats. Harley could not smell much more than the savory cocktail of scents wafting over from the taco truck, but she knew from past experience that the smell would change to the fragrant odor of pinon in the fall, the tree of choice for wood-burning.

They sat down, leaning over their burritos as they watched the passing tourists.

"I keep wondering," Harley said between mouthfuls of seasoned beef, "if there isn't more to the locations than we've realized."

Callaway was silent for a few seconds as he swallowed. Then he said, "What do you mean?"

Harley gestured at Callaway's face. He plucked a napkin from the pile that had come with the burritos and wiped at the runaway grease spilling down his chin.

"The cavern, for example," she said. "Why did he choose it?"

"It's remote, secluded. We went over this already." He sounded more puzzled than annoyed.

Harley held her burrito carefully over her plate as a stream of beef grease filtered out. "Half of the state is remote and secluded," she said. "He could have just driven out and left the bodies in the middle of the desert. Why go through all the work of hauling them into that back chamber?"

Callaway took another bite and chewed thoughtfully.

"Or look at the other site," she continued. "If your goal was to find somewhere secluded, would you really choose a national monument? He must have known someone would discover Collington's body before long."

Callaway leaned back, using his tongue to work bits of food free from his teeth. "So why did he pick those locations, then? It can't be about opportunity—Collington may have been at the ruins of her own will, but the other four didn't have any reason to be in that cavern, as far as we know."

123

Harley said nothing. She had the feeling she was missing one little detail—a detail that, for all she knew, might prove to be the linchpin to the whole investigation.

"Maybe his methods are changing," Callaway suggested. "He could have been planning to take Collington back to the cavern, but then we discovered his hiding spot. So he gave up on hiding the bodies."

Harley, however, was not listening. She was thinking of Officer Bullock's retelling of events when the agents had first reached the cavern.

Suddenly it hit her, and her body straightened as if she'd been struck by lightning. "Petroglyphs!" she exclaimed. "Bullock mentioned there were petroglyphs in that cavern!"

She studied Callaway's face, waiting for him to make the connection. His expression remained blank for several seconds. Then his eyebrows rose, and his mouth made a small, surprised circle.

"Just like the ones at the ruins," he said.

Harley nodded, her body thrumming with excitement now. "The foil and face paint have clear religious overtones. It's only logical the locations would have religious significance as well. Whatever ritual he's performing with his victims, I think the location is just as important as the way he prepares their bodies."

Callaway nodded, but his face grew serious again, his tone measured. "You might be right," he said, "but how does that help us stop him? How does that help us discover his identity?"

Harley pushed her half-eaten burrito aside, unable to focus on food at such a moment. "If he's planning to kill again, as I assume he is," she said, "that means he needs a new place to leave the next body."

"You don't think he already has a list of places picked out?"

"I don't think he was planning on anyone going into that cavern," she said with growing conviction. "He's been scrambling since then, which means there's a good chance he's making mistakes—mistakes someone might have noticed."

She pulled out her phone. "We need to start calling up park districts, preserves—any type of place that might fit the bill—and ask if they've seen anything suspicious."

Callaway was not convinced. "And what do we say? Could you please take a quick look around, just to make sure you haven't overlooked any corpses on the property?"

"There's no harm in asking, is there?" she said.

Callaway stared off into the distance. She knew she had him cornered. The case had ground to a standstill, so he could hardly argue they were wasting their time if he didn't have anything better for them to do.

Clearing his throat, he set his jaw and nodded. "Alright," he said. "Let's just hope we can find a pattern or some kind of lead, because if we don't, Newbury's going to be calling us about another body."

*

Forty-five minutes later, Harley set her phone aside and dropped her face into her hands, exhausted. Many of her calls had gone unanswered, forcing her to leave cryptic messages that revealed little more than that she was a federal agent conducting an investigation about things she couldn't disclose. Among those who had answered, none had seen anything remotely suspicious.

"I can tell you've had about as much success as I have," Callaway said, his elbows perched on the table as he leaned his mouth on his clasped hands. He sounded discouraged rather than defeated. Harley knew the feeling.

She watched as a shirtless boy in swimming trunks clung to the leash of a beagle. The beagle, frenetic with excitement over all the smells surrounding it, raced down the street, nearly pulling the boy off his feet until an adult stepped in and caught the dog's leash.

Harley rubbed distractedly at the corner of her mouth. If they could not make any connections between the locations, then they were back to waiting for results from the lab, crossing their fingers that Isidore would discover something to give life to the investigation again. That process, however, could take weeks or even months, and there was no guarantee it would lead them to the killer.

Mired in these thoughts, Harley was startled by the harsh buzzing of her phone as it worked its way across the bench. She held it up but did not recognize the number.

"Hello?" she said.

"Is this Agent Cole?"

"Speaking."

"This is Patrick Donovan, outreach director here at Shady Oaks Museum of Natural Science. You called earlier about some kind of investigation you're undertaking?"

Having had so many unsuccessful conversations already, Harley held little hope this one would turn out any differently.

"Yes," she said. "I can't provide more details than that, given it's an ongoing investigation."

"I understand. What is it you want to know?"

Harley rattled off the same questions she had already repeated a few dozen times. "Have you noticed any suspicious persons at the museum? Has anyone reported being stalked or assaulted?"

There was a thoughtful pause. "No, I don't think so," Donovan said. "We have a group chat with the staff here, so if any of our visitors came forward with a complaint like that, it would be shared with the whole group—not the person's identity, you understand, but the nature of the problem."

"Sure," Harley said, her heart sinking. "Thank you for calling back anyway, Mr. Donovan. I won't take any more of your time."

She was getting ready to hang up the phone when he said something that surprised her.

"What about stolen artifacts?"

She sat up, curious. "What kind of artifacts?"

"Dinosaur bones, Native American items. That kind of thing."

Harley snapped her fingers to get Callaway's attention. "When did these go missing?" she said.

"I can't tell for certain," Donovan answered cautiously. "A number of the items were taken from large displays, so their absence wasn't noticed right away. One particular item, however, was taken this past week."

"What was this item?" Harley said.

"A large effigy pipe. Priceless."

Harley was silent for a moment, unsure what to make of this. On the surface, she didn't see an immediate connection with their case. Then again, there was so much they didn't know about the killer that it seemed unwise to overlook any lead, no matter how far afield it might take them.

"Do you have any idea who might have stolen these items?" she said.

A note of exasperation entered Donovan's voice. "I'm afraid not. We contacted the police, but no matter how many times I call them, the answer is always the same: They're pursuing all leads and will let me know as soon as they have new information to share."

126

Harley did not hesitate. "Mr. Donovan, would it be possible for us to come by and talk this over with you in-person? Say, in the next hour or so?"

There was another pause. "Well," he said cautiously, "we have some events going on today, so I can't leave the property, but I can probably step away from my work for fifteen minutes or so. Will that be enough?"

"It'll have to be," Harley answered optimistically. "Thank you, Mr. Donovan. We'll be there in fifteen."

She felt Callaway's gaze on her as she hung up the phone. "Not another body, is it?" he said.

She shook her head. "Not a body. A break-in."

CHAPTER TWENTY THREE

Harley remembered the Shady Oaks Museum of Natural Science from a school trip she had taken there many years earlier, though it had changed a great deal since then. The planetarium was new, and the old, cartoonish illustrations of dinosaurs had been replaced by lifelike banners showing the creatures at their true height. It was a positive change, though Harley had to admit she had preferred the mom-and-pop feel back when the museum was privately owned.

They spotted the outreach director, an erect willow of a man in a tan blazer, surrounded by a semicircle of middle schoolers. He looked like a Roman senator giving a speech to the assembly.

He must have spotted them earlier because he waved them forward without glancing in their direction. An older woman with a nest of gray curls—the students' teacher, Harley supposed—watched the agents approach, one of her doughy hands spinning the pearl bracelet on her wrist.

"And do you know why they're eating peacefully together?" Donovan asked, gesturing toward the display. The attentive tone of his voice made it clear that he was addressing the middle schoolers.

A freckled boy with a face as round as a tomato scrunched his eyebrows in an expression of intense focus. "Because they're friendly with each other?"

"And why are they friendly with each other?"

A girl with pigtails raised her hand.

"Yes, Marie," Donovan said, pointing toward the girl.

"Because they're herbivores!" She pronounced the *h* rather than keeping it silent. Harley could not help smiling, despite the gravity of their visit.

Donovan nodded. "Herbivores, yes. Which means…?"

"They eat plants!" another child said.

The excitement among the children was palpable. They stole glances at one another, wondering who would be next to answer correctly. Harley tried to remember how it had felt to be that age, but it seemed like a lifetime ago.

128

"And because they only eat plants," Donovan continued, "they *don't* eat…what?"

"Each other!" the boy with the tomato face exclaimed.

Donovan smiled, pleased. "They don't eat each other. That's right. Because they both eat plants, and have no interest in eating one another, they can stay side by side without worrying what the other might do, just like rabbits and squirrels are safe around one another."

Several hands shot up immediately. Rather than call on them, however, Donovan rose. "That's all we can go over now. Mrs. Platt will tell you what's next on your schedule."

This was met by a chorus of groans and several downcast faces. Before they could offer further complaint, however, Mrs. Platt—she of the pearl bracelet—stepped forward and began herding the children away.

"Come on, kids," she said. "Who wants to see some fossilized poop?"

"And don't forget to stay curious!" Donovan called after them. Harley watched the children turn a corner and disappear, their curious murmurs fading into the background.

"Magical age," Donovan said, shaking his head in wonder. "You can learn anything. If I could go back, I'd study about four different languages at the same time."

"Heck," Callaway said, "I'd settle for paying attention to how my mom cooked. I didn't learn a damn thing."

Harley, knowing their time was limited, offered Donovan her hand as she introduced herself. "Agent Harley Cole," she said. "This is Agent Anthony Callaway. Thank you for agreeing to speak with us."

"Of course. This is about the Mummy Killer, isn't it?"

Harley had not heard the term before. She glanced at Callaway, who looked just as confused as she was.

"That's what the media's calling him," Donovan explained. "I guess it has something to do with how he dresses his victims?"

How would the media know those details? Harley thought. Then, as she considered the idea, she realized there were several potential leaks. Anyone from that tour boat could have given the information to the media, not to mention Dale. Whatever the case, the cat was out of the bag.

Harley decided to level with him. "We can't discuss the details, since it's an ongoing investigation—"

"Of course," Donovan said.

"—but I can tell you the killer has been using sites that appear to have religious or cultural significance. The first site was a cavern along the Rio Grande, the second was—"

"Shilowa National Monument," Donovan finished. "Yeah, I've been following the news. What was special about the cavern? Is it on Indian land?"

"No," Harley said, "but there were some petroglyphs in there, just like at Shilowa."

Donovan nodded. "Very common in the area. Contrary to what some think, petroglyphs are not designed to be art. They're symbols meant to communicate messages—teachings, warnings, that kind of thing." He frowned, as if struggling to make a connection. "And you think your killer might be the person responsible for the thefts I mentioned?"

"That's what we're here to find out," Harley said, trying to remain open-minded. "The more details you can share about what happened, the more easily we can decide if the two are related."

Harley knew there was a good chance that, fifteen minutes from now, they would find no reason at all to believe their killer had anything to do with the thefts, and then they would have to go back to the drawing board. Considering how few leads they had to go on, however, they didn't have much to lose by looking into it.

Donovan watched them silently for a few moments, as if deciding how open he wanted to be with them if they couldn't be entirely open with him. Finally, he took a deep breath, crossed his arms, and leaned back against the edge of the display behind him, which showcased the skeleton of a once-mighty mammoth, its fierce tusks curling back like bullwhips.

"A few months back," he began, "I'm working late, planning an event with a local special needs organization. There's nobody here but me and Mike."

"Mike?" Harley said.

"He's the security guard. Been here almost as long as this building has been standing."

Harley nodded. "Go on."

"Anyway, I'm about to lock my office when the alarm goes off. I track down Mike, and he tells me the alarm was triggered by one of the emergency exits."

Donovan's face lit up with a polite, professional smile as the gang of middle schoolers trooped past again. "Enjoy the rest of your day," he said, waving.

After the group had gone, Donovan returned to his story.

"Here's where it gets interesting," he said. "A few days before the break-in, we had the safety inspector here for a routine inspection. He says everything's up to code except for one little detail: One of the emergency exit alarms is disabled. Not broken, but manually disabled."

It only took Harley a few moments to make the connection. "Let me guess," she said. "It was the same door your thief used."

Donovan nodded. "Must have jumped out of his skin when he heard it go off."

Interesting as this was, Harley was not yet certain if it had anything to do with their killer. "Did you get a look at the thief?" she said.

Donovan hesitated. "Yes and no. Come on, I'll show you."

Intrigued, Harley and Callaway followed Donovan out of the main room and through a door marked "EMPLOYEES ONLY." Next, they proceeded down a dim hallway to an unmarked door at the end, where Donovan wrapped several times with his knuckles.

"It's unlocked!" a muffled voice called from the other side.

They entered the security room. A man with a horseshoe of graying stubble on his head glanced at them. Heavy bags hung beneath his eyes, reminding Harley of a bloodhound.

"Hey, Mike," Donovan said. "I've brought a few federal agents to look at the security footage from the break-in. Think you can bring it up?"

Mike's pale eyes studied the agents for a few seconds without acknowledgment. "You got it, boss," he said.

Harley, Callaway, and Donovan leaned over Mike's shoulders as he pulled up the video feed. Harley stared at a grainy video showing the museum's parking lot, framed by a steel fence on one side and the road on two other sides. Mike had apparently created shortcuts to the appropriate time signatures, because he had no difficulty navigating to the night of the break-in.

"We've been meaning to update the security cameras for years," Donovan said apologetically. "Every time I bring it up in board meetings, though, there are a thousand areas of greater need."

"Here he comes," Mike said, pointing at the corner of the screen as a gray minivan rolled into the lot. The van crawled forward, turned, and began backing beneath the camera.

"No brake lights," Callaway said. "He came prepared."

At the bottom of the screen, the driver's side door opened and a large man clambered out, his face hidden by a hood. He kept his head down as he walked beneath the camera.

"Now he's walking to the emergency door," Mike said. "Little does he know the alarm has been fixed."

There was a blur of movement as the man suddenly reentered the field of view. He jumped into the vehicle and—true to Donovan's description—peeled out of the lot. As he did, Harley noticed something peculiar through the van's back window.

"Wait!" she said. "Go back to when he's just starting to pull away."

Mike did so.

"Can you zoom in on the window?" Harley said.

Again, Mike obliged. Despite the graininess of the video and the narrowness of the window, Harley could nevertheless make out a rectangular, shimmering material laid out across the van's carpeted floor.

Her breath caught in her throat.

"Callaway," she said in a low, spellbound voice, "what does that look like to you?"

"It looks like some kind of metallic foil," Callaway said, sounding every bit as taken by the discovery as Harley was.

"Big enough to wrap around a body?" she said.

"Maybe so."

"A body?" Mike said, frowning up at Donovan with his bloodhound eyes. "What are they talking about?"

Callaway, however, interrupted before Donovan could answer. "The plate," he said. "Can you zoom in on it?"

Mike let out a beleaguered sigh, as if he really would have preferred for someone else to take a turn at the keyboard, but he offered no protest as he enlarged the vehicle's license plate. Harley, surprised that a thief who had taken the time to disable his brake lights had forgotten to hide his license plate, wondered if this might just be the breakthrough they needed.

Then something else occurred to her. "If you already spoke with the police," she said, "haven't they been through this already? It doesn't take long to run a set of plates."

"I spoke with the police," Donovan said, "but they haven't reviewed the footage yet. There have been a number of similar break-ins in the area, and it appears they simply haven't gotten to us yet."

132

Harley thought this might prove to be a blessing in disguise. She didn't want anyone else interfering with her suspect.

"Is that a one or a *t*?" Callaway said, gesturing at one of the symbols.

"We'll run them both," Harley answered, scribbling the plate number down. "You want to handle it, Callaway?"

Callaway gave her a teasing smile. "Sure you don't want to make the call?"

"I'm sure."

Chuckling quietly, Callaway pulled out his phone and dialed Ray's number. While the two of them talked, Harley asked Mike to replay the van's arrival and departure. She was searching for distinguishing marks, anything that might help them identify the vehicle later.

"What year is that?" she said to Mike.

"Early 2000s, I'd say," he said.

"Lots of space back there," Harley murmured.

"Thanks, Ray," Callaway said. "I owe you." He hung up the phone and turned to Donovan. "Does the name Boris Poletov mean anything to you?"

"Boris?" the archaeologist repeated, looking puzzled. "Are you saying that's *his* van?"

"You know him?" Harley said.

"Of course. He's a colleague of mine—former colleague, I should say."

"Former?" Callaway said.

"Yes. He was fired…" He paused, a look of understanding dawning on his face. "I can't believe it."

"What?"

"He was fired for stealing items from a dig site."

Harley could not believe her ears. "And you didn't think to mention him before?" she said, annoyed by the outreach director's oversight.

Donovan held up both hands, like a police officer stopping traffic at a construction zone. "Let's not jump to conclusions here. Boris is a thief, sure—he proved that already, so I guess the fact that he came back to rob us again shouldn't be a surprise. He'd known his way around the museum, after all." A touch of color crept into his cheeks, as if he was embarrassed he hadn't done more to prevent Poletov's thefts.

"But theft and murder are two very different things," he continued. "I worked with this man for almost ten years, and I can tell you he's not a murderer. A bit rough around the edges? Sure. Likes to keep to himself? Absolutely. But that doesn't make him a murderer."

Harley watched Donovan, unsure whether he was defending Poletov on principal because he was a former coworker, or because he genuinely didn't believe Poletov to be capable of murder. Either way, Harley and Callaway would have to form their own conclusions.

Rather than arguing about what Poletov might or might not be capable of, Harley decided to cut to the chase. "Does this guy have an address?" she said.

Donovan sighed wearily, as if it were a long story. "He's moved since we let him go. I only know because we tried sending him his last paycheck, but it got returned. He had to come by and pick it up. I'm not sure where he's living now."

Harley thought it was more than generous to settle accounts with someone who was helping himself to the organization's property. She was getting the impression, however, that Donovan was loyal to a fault when it came to his staff. If others in the organization behaved the same way, she could understand how Poletov might have hidden his crimes.

"You mentioned he was stealing from a dig site," Callaway said.

Donovan blinked thoughtfully. "Yeah. It's just off Highway Twenty-Five, near Santa Ana. It's believed to be the location of a skirmish between Coronado's troops and the Zuni. Why? You think he'd go back there?"

Harley decided to be honest with Donovan. "I know you don't think he's our killer," she said, "but if he is, he might be looking for a new location to hide his victims. A dig site at the side of the highway? From what we know so far, it fits the bill."

Donovan nodded, looking sobered by this possibility. He said, "If you do recover any of the artifacts—particularly the effigy pipe—try to return them in one piece? They're highly valuable."

"We'll do our best," Harley assured him.

"And if you run into Boris," he said as the agents prepared to leave, "be careful. He can have a bit of a temper sometimes."

As the agents left the building, Harley couldn't help thinking about Donovan's final words. *What kind of temper does he have?* she thought. *The kind that leads to an occasional angry outburst, or the kind that leads to killing five women?*

CHAPTER TWENTY FOUR

Harley parked on the edge of the bluff overlooking the dig site in the valley below. They were surrounded by mesquites, which she hoped would keep the afternoon sunlight from gleaming off their vehicle and giving them away. She didn't want to drive into the dig site and spook Poletov, not until they knew where he was.

She would have liked to study the history of the location more—the lives of the pre-colonial Native Americans had been one of Kelly's favorite subjects, which made it of greater interest to Harley—but given the lack of cell service and the need to keep a close eye on the area, it appeared now was not the time.

"Must get tiring, spending all that time digging in the dirt," she observed, staring down at the cratered site. Heaps of earth loomed beside broad trenches, several of which were covered by white canvas tents. A pair of portable toilets stood at a discrete distance on the far side of the site. As far as Harley could tell, nobody was working at the site today.

Callaway shrugged. "Until you find something, I guess. Not unlike investigating murders. The fun starts when you get a lead."

Harley supposed he was right. Most of an investigation involved paperwork and background research that usually didn't lead to anything. It was a general rule that investigators spent a lot more time figuring out what hadn't happened—who hadn't killed the victim, how the murder hadn't been perpetrated—than what had. Only by following the process of elimination could they narrow down the list of possibilities.

"So what's the game plan?" Callaway said, stifling a yawn. "If we go down there now, he might see us and get spooked. Unless we hide the vehicle, that is."

Harley's gaze panned across the site. "I was thinking we wait for him to show."

Callaway glanced at the dashboard. "It's only three o'clock. You really think he's going to do this in the middle of the day?"

Harley considered. "He attacked our last victim in broad daylight, didn't he?"

"That's true," Callaway agreed. "But we don't even know if there *is* another victim. Maybe he got it out of his system, and he won't get the itch again for another few weeks. How long do you plan to sit here? We don't even know if he's coming to this location at all."

Harley knew he had a point. The investigation was mired in uncertainty. For all they knew, this whole effort could be a waste of time that would bring them no closer to finding the killer, but that didn't mean they shouldn't give it their best.

"If you come up with a better plan for finding Poletov," she said, "I'm all ears. But until then…" She pressed her lips together and shrugged.

"Well," Callaway drawled, "since you're looking all bright-eyed and bushy-tailed, why don't you take the first shift?" He tipped his chair back, then rested his hat over his face. "Wake me when Poletov comes back," he said, his voice muffled.

Harley stared at the dig site as Callaway's breathing grew deep and measured. As much as she hated the waiting, it did give her time to slow down and think more carefully over the details of the case, presenting an opportunity to pick up on things she might have missed.

She had a feeling the man they were looking for was a fanatic— another reason Dale didn't fit the mold. Neither he nor Mayhew possessed the dedication necessary to prepare the bodies the way the killer had.

But a man like Boris Poletov, who might have spent years excavating remains? He couldn't have done his job if he wasn't meticulous and detail-oriented. Brushing dust from a skull wasn't so different from painting gold on a face, was it?

And then there was the matter of that object in the back of Poletov's van. As much as Harley cautioned herself not to make assumptions, she felt certain it had been the same kind of material as the kind that the killer had used to wrap his victims. That would be a difficult coincidence to swallow.

The minutes rolled on, and Harley felt her lack of sleep taking a toll on her. She slapped her cheek, tapped her fingers on the wheel, bounced her leg—anything to keep herself alert. She would have turned on the radio if Callaway hadn't been sleeping.

Despite her best efforts, however, her eyelids began to grow heavy. Her head dipped forward, and her blinking slowed. A dull ache began in her neck, but she barely felt it. Then, just as she was about to close her eyes entirely, something flashed at the edge of her vision. She sat up, sucking in saliva from the corner of her mouth.

A gray minivan was heading toward the dig site across the open ground.

"Callaway," she said urgently, shaking his arm. "Wake up. We've got company."

"What's going on?" Callaway grumbled, sitting up and rubbing his face. He raised his eyebrows comically high as he blinked, struggling to focus. Then he noticed the vehicle.

"Shit," he said. "If it isn't Comrade Boris. Well, what are you waiting for?"

Harley started the vehicle and backed away from the bluff. As they followed a winding path down into the valley, Harley couldn't help thinking of the hike she and Callaway had taken the previous day in pursuit of Mayhew, a hike her calves and thighs still remembered. She was grateful to have a vehicle this time.

They lost sight of the van as they came level with the dig site. The site had appeared small from the height of the bluff, but at ground level it seemed huge, a labyrinthine world of tents and pits.

"Where is he?" Harley muttered, leaning over the wheel as she searched for the van. "He's gotta be here somewhere."

Suddenly Callaway pointed. "There! He's on foot."

Harley followed Callaway's pointing finger and caught a glimpse of movement between two tents. Then the figure was gone.

Parking the Jeep behind an outcropping of stone, the two agents drew their sidearms and moved at a crouch toward the place Callaway had seen the suspect. The wind rustled the edges of the tarps, creating a disorienting din of noise. It was like being in the middle of a flock of birds.

"He was right here," Callaway whispered, looking around. "I don't know where he went."

Harley motioned toward a low, crumbling wall. She and Callaway hunkered down against it. The adobe was hot against Harley's back. A bead of sweat ran down the bridge of her nose, stinging her eye. She knuckled it away.

Rising on aching legs, she peered over the wall. At first, she didn't see anything. Then she caught movement as a large man with shoulder-length curly hair lifted a canvas flap, peered quickly around, and then ducked beneath it.

"Time to roll," Callaway said, rising.

Harley felt her adrenaline kick in as she and Callaway trotted toward the tent. As they neared the entrance, Callaway made a circular motion in the air with his finger, indicating he'd go around toward the back in case Poletov tried to run. Harley nodded.

She waited, counting the seconds as Callaway moved around the side of the tent and out of sight. Her hands were slick on the Glock, and she kept shifting her grip, glancing sharply around as the wind played tricks on her mind: snapping the canvas, hissing against low adobe walls, teasing her with the possibility that Poletov was beside her, ready to wrap her tight in a cocoon of gold foil.

Then the wind fell, and everything went deathly still. Realizing she had probably given Callaway far more time than necessary, Harley stepped forward and, bracing herself for the possibility that she might soon find herself face-to-face with the killer, swept the flap of the tent aside in one quick motion.

Poletov, however, was not there. The inside of the tent was dim. Long, foldable tables ran in rows, covered with boxes of dirt to be sifted. A wall of plastic buckets, each stack sorted by color, sectioned off the area to Harley's left, while to the right lay a pair of coolers next to a garbage bag brimming with empty soda cans. Toward the back of the tent lay a shallow, grave-like trough beside which a pair of shovels were crossed.

She did not see any sign of Poletov.

Where are you? she thought, panning the room a second time. She glanced toward the back of the tent, searching for Callaway, but she did not see him. He was probably waiting for her to flush Poletov out.

"Boris Poletov?" she called, moving into the room. "We were just talking with your former colleague, Patrick Donovan. Remember him? He told us an interesting story about artifacts being stolen from the museum. From what we heard—"

Harley saw movement out of the corner of her eye and ducked just in time to avoid the terracotta figurine that was careening toward her head. As she straightened again and turned, she barely had time to register the large, bear-like shape beside her before he extended both arms, shoving her off her feet.

She fell against one of the tables, the sharp edge of a sifting box punching into her ribs. A hot flame of pain ran up her side. It was almost enough to distract her from the sight of the bearded, broad-shouldered man bearing down on her, his eyes burning so fiercely they could have evaporated water.

One of the man's large hands reached for Harley's pistol. Knowing she would be no match in a contest of brute strength, Harley tried to roll away. Before she could do so, however, the man's hand clamped down on the barrel of the gun and, in one savage twist, wrenched it from her hand.

She cried out as a searing pain shot up her arm. To her surprise, the man did not turn the gun on her but tossed it aside as if it were merely a toy.

His face contorted into a grotesque smile as he looked down on her. "You're just like the others, aren't you?" he said, his voice thick with a Russian accent. "So weak, so pathetic. Helpless as a newborn babe."

Staring up at the giant, it occurred to Harley that all of those women put together would have been helpless against this brute. She thought she understood now why he had used that cavern—a man of such strength would have little trouble carrying those women all that distance.

There was a rustle of fabric behind Poletov. A flicker of uncertainty entered his eyes, and he half-turned away to investigate the sound, just in time to see Callaway's fist as it pistoned toward his face. The blow rocked Poletov's head back, but the Russian was smiling a moment later, licking blood from his lips.

"So this is how you Americans fight, is it?" he said. "Two against one?"

Harley rose to her feet on the table, then sprang at Poletov like a wildcat, slipping one arm around his throat. As Poletov, still grinning, worked to pry her arms free, Callaway began to steadily pummel the Russian's stomach. A look of grim determination came over Callaway's face.

Then, just when Harley thought Poletov had had enough, he caught hold of her hair and wrenched her forward. She screamed, her hold on his throat loosening, and he threw her forward into Callaway. They tumbled to the ground in a heap.

"It's been fun," Poletov said, panting, "but I'm afraid I must go now."

He made to dash past them. Before he could get away, however, Harley hooked both her feet around the Russian's ankle. He jerked his leg away, stumbled, and fell right into the open pit.

Harley and Callaway rose, brushing dirt off themselves. As Harley retrieved her gun, Callaway drew his and stood over Poletov.

139

"Boris Poletov," he said, "we're going to need to take a drive together. We have a few questions to ask you."

CHAPTER TWENTY FIVE

The first thing Harley saw as they neared the FBI field office was the swarm of media gathered on the steps leading up to the door. At the center of this swarm stood none other than Governor Ballard, a look of stern aggrievement on his face as he spoke into the thicket of microphones.

"Shit," Harley said, slowing. There was no telling what might happen if Ballard saw them drag Poletov into the office in handcuffs. Would he trust them to run the interview their own way, or would he try to take matters into his own hands, perhaps by reminding them of their failure to prevent his daughter's murder? As governor, he could apply a tremendous amount of pressure on Newbury but trying to force results—extracting a confession from Poletov at all costs, for example—could backfire.

It was not a risk Harley was willing to take.

Poletov chuckled from the backseat. "What, afraid of some cameras? You see the lights, so you scurry back to shadows like little rats." His accent had thickened since his arrest, though whether this was a strategic move or simply a case of his native tongue creeping out, Harley could not tell.

Callaway stared rigidly at the crowd of media for several moments. Then, as if on impulse, he said, "Turn right here."

"Why?" Harley said.

"Just trust me, okay? There's a safe house nearby, hasn't been used in years."

Harley had no interest in arguing. She turned right, steering them away from the field office and the crowd of media. She thought the governor's eyes shifted in their direction, but she could not be sure.

As the field office disappeared behind them, she breathed a sigh of relief and sank back into her seat, watching the buildings of downtown Santa Fe roll by. College students flocked the sidewalks, carrying hot dogs and ice cream cones, a striking reminder that summer break had begun.

Callaway directed her through a few more turns until they reached the safe house, a rundown two-story building with caution tape across the door. The yard had grown riotous with weeds, and several of the windows were covered with sheets of plywood.

"Home sweet home," Harley remarked dryly. "We should really talk to Newbury about turning this into an Airbnb. Throw up a few cobwebs and skeletons, and you'd have a perfect Halloween getaway."

Despite the joke, she was just happy not to have the governor breathing down their necks. She put enough pressure on herself already, and she didn't need any politicians adding to it.

Callaway got out of the vehicle and opened Poletov's door. "Going to be a good boy?" he said.

"Screw you, American," Poletov said. He didn't sound particularly worked up, however. It sounded more like he was just playing the role he was most comfortable with.

Is that his disguise? Harley wondered. *The clueless foreigner, unfamiliar with American ways?*

Callaway put one hand on Poletov's arm and guided the burly man out of the vehicle.

"What is this place?" Poletov demanded. "You torture me, yes? Make me talk?"

"This might be the West, but it's not the Wild West," Callaway answered, slapping the door shut. "No iron maiden today, I'm afraid."

The two agents flanked Poletov as they led him down the path of cracked flagstones. As they reached the porch, a snake uncurled itself and slithered through a knothole in one of the boards.

"You sure know how to pick them," Harley said.

While Harley kept an eye on Poletov, Callaway stood on an empty planter and stretched one arm up over the edge of the gutter, feeling inside with his fingers. He frowned as his fingers scratched at the aluminum. Then his hand came down, grasping a key covered in a wad of rotted leaves.

"There we are," he pronounced, unlocking the door. "Make yourselves at home."

Given the dilapidated state of the exterior, the interior was in better shape than Harley had expected. Other than a leak that had bubbled the plaster in the kitchen ceiling, all it really needed was some TLC.

"It'll do," Harley said, satisfied.

Callaway led them into the living room, where he pulled out a chair at the end of the table and gestured for Poletov to sit down. The Russian paused inches from Callaway's face and stared at him. Then he snorted and dropped heavily into the seat, holding out his cuffed hands for Callaway to unlock them.

"You sure that's a good idea?" Harley said, worried what Poletov might do if they lowered their guard.

Callaway shrugged. "I can handle him. Besides, he's going to be good for us. Isn't that right, Boris?"

Poletov said nothing. Callaway unlocked the cuffs and removed them, leaving the Russian to rub his chafed wrists.

Despite Callaway's confidence, Harley couldn't help feeling this was a dangerous gamble. Poletov was a bear of a man, as he had demonstrated at the dig site. She would have preferred to see him in a straitjacket. Still, sometimes she had no choice but to trust Callaway, for better or worse.

The floor creaked as Callaway retreated toward the wall. He pulled out his phone and began typing away.

What's he doing now? Harley thought, growing increasingly worried. *Checking the weather?*

Poletov leaned back and stared at Harley with a haughty expression. "In my country," he said, "women don't do this. Women cook, clean, wash clothes. But this?" He grunted and shook his head. "It is man's work. For strong." He clapped his left bicep with his right hand. Harley had to admit it was a beefy bicep. There was a tattoo on it too, but his shirt covered part of it and she couldn't make out the rest.

"There's more than one kind of strength," she answered, unfazed. She was keenly aware that Poletov could lunge forward and reach her long before she drew her weapon, but she was trusting Callaway to back her up if that happened. He was the one who had uncuffed Poletov, after all.

Poletov smiled, revealing teeth stained brown. "Look at you. Little American woman, so much power. You think you play with dogs, but you are cat. Cat is for running, for hiding. Dog is not running."

Callaway, looking bored, set his phone on a bookshelf to his left that was decorated with the shriveled, bone-gray remains of an assortment of potted plants along with a piece of wood shaped like a tennis racket and engraved with the words "BOARD OF EDUCATION." He rubbed his forehead with his thumb and first two fingers.

"Can you please state your name?" Harley said to Poletov, ignoring his little speech.

Poletov only smirked at her. It was the expression of a poker player who knows he has a winning hand—or wants others to believe he does, anyway.

Harley tried a different tactic. "What were you doing at the dig site?"

Again, Poletov remained silent. Now he looked like he was enjoying this, as if he wanted them to get all worked up just so he could disappoint them. If this kept up, they might as well call in his lawyer and be done with it.

Harley drummed her fingers on the edge of the table, thinking. They had to get him to start talking, but how? She had a feeling scare tactics wouldn't work with this guy. They hadn't brought him all this way, though, just so he could amuse himself at their expense.

She was still considering their predicament when Callaway's phone rang. Callaway had to twist to reach it, partly turning his back on Poletov. At the same time, the Russian's eyes flicked to the phone and his hands gripped the edge of the table.

Sensing what was about to happen, Harley started to rise. Before she could do so, however, Poletov kicked her chair, shoving her away from the table. She only skidded back a foot or two, but it was enough to separate her from what happened next.

Poletov launched himself from his chair. He was surprisingly limber for such a large man. He had almost reached Callaway just as Callaway's arm came back with the phone...except that he wasn't holding the phone. He was holding the "BOARD OF EDUCATION" racket. He swung it like a club, smacking the side of Poletov's head.

The Russian staggered, blinking and shaking his head. Before he could recover, Callaway barreled into him and they landed across the table, which screeched as its feet clawed grooves into the hardwood floor.

Callaway held his forearm across the Russian's throat, pinning him. "Quit playing games," he said. "We know who you are, we know you were working at Shady Oaks, and we know you were fired for theft. What were you doing with the artifacts, huh? Why did you want them?"

Poletov grunted and tried to throw Callaway off. Callaway held on like a bull rider. He might have been slimmer than Poletov, but he had his weight to help hold Poletov down.

"*Suka*," Boris whispered, barely able to get the word out as Callaway increased the pressure.

Sensing an opportunity, Harley stepped forward. "We have agents searching your van as we speak. What are they going to find, Boris? What mementos did you keep?"

"You have wrong person, policeman," Poletov said, his voice scratchy. "But maybe you do not care, eh? Maybe you just want person in prison."

Callaway grabbed Poletov's shirt with both hands, lifted him off the table, and slammed him down again. "You're lying to us!" he shouted, pinning the Russian's throat with his forearm again. "We saw the gold foil in your van! What were you doing, wrapping presents for your grandmother?"

Poletov wheezed, each breath labored and slow. His face was turning an angry shade of red.

"That's enough, Callaway!" Harley said, alarmed.

Callaway went on applying the pressure. He lowered his head and stared directly into Poletov's eyes. "Tell us what you know!"

"Callaway!" Harley shouted, ready to grab him and pull him off the Russian. Before she could do so, however, Callaway sat up, relieving the pressure on Poletov's throat. Poletov twisted to the side and coughed, misting the table with spit.

When he straightened again, he was smiling. "You want to kill me, agent, yes?"

"I'll kill you myself if you don't start talking," Harley said. It was an obvious bluff—they were already getting too close to FBI brutality for her liking—but she was losing her patience.

"Tell us about the gold foil," she said.

Poletov's smile faded. His eyes looked genuinely puzzled. "Foil? What is this foil?"

Harley, hoping he wasn't just playing dumb, pulled up a picture on her phone. She showed it to Poletov.

"Ah, blanket!" he said. "Yes, for keep warm."

Harley glanced at Callaway, who was staring intently at the Russian.

"Keeping warm?" she said. "Like in an emergency?"

"Well, not emergency. I live in van now."

Harley felt a flicker of doubt. Was it possible that was all she had seen, a space blanket Poletov was using to stay warm?

She decided to change the subject.

"Where were you last night around seven o'clock?" she said.

The Russian's eyebrows pulled together in concentration. "Last night? I sleep in van, like always."

"Where were you parked?"

"Gas station. Murphy Express."

"Can anyone confirm that?" Harley pressed.

Poletov shrugged. "How do I know? Ask people at gas station!"

Not much of an alibi, Harley thought.

Callaway appeared to be growing impatient with this line of questioning. "What were you doing with the artifacts, Boris? A little home decorating?"

"I kill no one," Poletov said. "You have wrong man, policeman. You let me go, and I do not make fuss for choking."

Callaway grunted, unsympathetic. "You attacked me, pal. I've even got a witness to back up my story. You're the one who didn't want to play nice."

Poletov let out a low laugh. "You say America so good, so fair. I say America bad apple. On the outside, so shiny and tasty, but inside? Soft, like sauce."

"Listen, man, as much as I enjoy listening to your insights on our hopelessly corrupt country, I'm not buying your story. You really expect us to believe this is all one big coincidence?"

Poletov shrugged. "I not care what policeman believe. And now I want lawyer. You get me lawyer, yes?"

Harley glanced at Callaway. It was amazing what power those simple words contained. She understood why the system had checks and balances to protect citizens against government corruption, but sometimes she wished it weren't quite so easy for criminals to throw a wrench in the works.

"Alright," Callaway murmured. "We'll get you your lawyer. In the meantime, stay put."

They stepped out into the hallway, leaving the door open so they could keep an eye on Poletov.

"He fits the bill," Callaway said. "His job explains the religious sites."

"What about motive?" Harley said, not wishing to rush to judgment.

"We'll run a background check, see if he has any priors. But I'm telling you, Cole, this is our guy. He's got the foil, the right experience—and if you have any doubt that he's capable of murder, don't forget he's attacked us twice now. He'd put us both in a shallow grave in a heartbeat, believe me."

Callaway's eyes glowed with excitement. Harley wanted to share that excitement, but still she hesitated.

"What is it?" Callaway said, frowning now. "You think it's all a coincidence?"

"I'm thinking about the profile. He's just...a bit rougher of a character than what I was expecting."

Callaway rubbed his face, as if barely able to contain his impatience. "I get that it's what you do, profiling people, and I'm sure you're great at it. But I've been doing this for a long time. I don't need to psychoanalyze that man in there to know he's good for it. He checks the boxes, Cole. Don't overthink it."

Harley grew thoughtful for a moment. "You remember how the bodies looked in the cavern?" she said.

An expression of cautious uncertainty came over Callaway's face. "How they looked?" he said, not understanding.

"The way they were cradled in beds of stone," Harley said. "And their hair—it must have been brushed, don't you think? I'd bet their nails were cleaned, too."

"I don't know what you're getting at."

"The killer didn't just 'dump' the bodies in that cavern. He took his time deciding where to place them. And think of the painstaking work of painting their faces, combing their hair, wrapping their bodies."

She gestured at the large, bearish man slumped in his chair, singing softly to himself. "Does he really strike you as the kind of person who would do that?" she said. "We're looking for an artist—someone sensitive, inward-looking, probably socially awkward and a bit eclectic. Does Poletov check any of those boxes?"

Callaway was silent, thinking. "Those are theories," he said after a few moments, not unkindly. "But now we're dealing with the real thing. Isn't it possible you got the profile wrong? Isn't it possible you missed something?"

Harley knew this was a very real possibility. Maybe Poletov was more complicated than she thought, and she was oversimplifying him by focusing too much on his brute strength. Still, she had a hard time imagining him taking such care with the bodies. If he was murdering women, she'd expect the bodies to be brutalized beyond recognition.

"The first thing we need to do," Callaway said, "is book this guy. We look into his background and see what red flags we find. We can also compare that material in the back of his van to the foil used on the victims and see if we get a match."

It was a sensible plan, Harley knew. She wasn't in the mood to wait for results to come to her, however. There was too much at stake for her to sit around.

"While you're doing that," she said, "I'm going to head to the morgue. With any luck, Isidore will be able to tell me more about how the victims died."

Callaway was silent for a few moments. "You really want to rule Poletov out, don't you?"

"No," she answered softly, shaking her head. "I'd love for him to be our guy. But if he isn't? I want to know about it as soon as possible so we can stop wasting our time with him."

CHAPTER TWENTY SIX

Frank Isidore, a forensic pathologist with a shock of white hair that stood up straight from his head, was lifting a heart from the chest cavity of a corpse when Harley entered the morgue. Plastic gloves covered the pathologist's arms to his elbows—which was a good thing, since that was about how far he had buried his arms inside the cadaver's chest cavity.

An oldies station played from an FM radio perched atop a vintage lunch box next to the sink. Isidore hummed to the music, his back turned to Harley.

"Dr. Isidore?" Harley said, not wishing to startle him. He had to be at least seventy years old, so she wasn't entirely surprised he hadn't heard the door close behind her.

She waited several moments. A trio of bodies lay on steel platforms, each covered by a white sheet except for the one Isidore was operating on. A rolling tray stood beside Isidore, covered with an assortment of sharp instruments and stainless-steel containers. There was even a small hand saw, undoubtedly for cutting bone.

"Frank?" she said, taking a tentative step forward. "I wanted to ask—"

Before she could finish her sentence, the heart pulled free and Isidore held it up admiringly.

"There she is!" he said. "Ain't she a beaut?" He half-turned toward her, just enough to let her know he was talking to her and not himself.

Harley stared at the gleaming muscle, thinking there was a good reason it was hidden beneath so much skin and bone. The pale, pork-like organ bore no resemblance to the symbolic image that had become synonymous with love. It looked more like a dubious cut of meat well past its expiration date.

"Is this the girl from the ruins?" Harley said.

Isidore placed the heart in a stainless-steel bowl. "The very same," he said. "Five bodies in one week—your killer is keeping me quite busy." He chuckled.

He struck Harley as an eccentric man, yet she also had the impression he was comfortable in his eccentricity, even if it alienated him from others. Maybe that was why he was so good at his job: He could be alone in a room full of corpses and not feel lonely.

"Have you finished the autopsies on the four from the cavern?" she said, hoping to divert him from plucking any other organs out. She wasn't squeamish around corpses—she wouldn't have been able to do her job if she was—but she had a pretty good idea Isidore could gross her out if he really tried.

He sighed and began pulling on the fingertips of his gloves. Then, once all his fingers were free, he peeled the gloves off and lay them on the edge of the tray.

"Yes and no," he said. "I haven't had time to do a thorough autopsy on all of them, but I did sate my curiosity."

She raised an eyebrow, waiting for him to explain.

"I cut back the foil and unwrapped the bodies," he went on. "I considered scraping back the paint from the faces, but there's really no need, not unless there's something specific to look for. There were no indications of any blows to the face, so I didn't consider it necessary."

Harley nodded, following along. "Were you able to establish time of death for the first four?"

Isidore waggled his head side to side. "Yes and no. If I were a forensic entomologist, I could take samples of the mature flies, pupil casings, maggots, and so on found in the cavern, then create a timeline off their life cycles to establish time of death. Unfortunately for you, I'm not an entomologist, and the nearest one I know is out in Phoenix."

Isidore held a hand up to his throat, as if to indicate a water level. "He's in it up to here, so even if you got a hold of him, he couldn't come out for weeks, and by that time it might not be worth the effort."

"So what you're saying is," Harley said, "you can't give me a clearer time of death?" She wasn't particularly disappointed by this possibility. Even if Isidore were to tell her the exact hour of each victim's death, that alone wouldn't be enough for her to connect the dots and find the killer.

"Dissecting isn't a fifteen-minute process, not if you're dealing with something bigger than a squirrel," Isidore said, clucking his tongue. "Maybe with a trained staff around me, but as you can see..." He gestured around, indicating the emptiness of the room.

Undeterred, Harley pressed on to her next question. "What about cause of death?"

The doctor's eyes lit up. "That's where it gets interesting. The two that are in the oldest state of decomposition..." He glanced at a chart on the wall. "Gianna Whyte and Kimberly Shao. They bear signs of blunt force cranial trauma."

"Wait," Harley said, bewildered. "They've been identified? When did that happen?"

"Your boss sent a few agents down here earlier," the doctor explained. "They found both victims in the missing persons database."

Newbury probably has the governor breathing down his throat, demanding answers, Harley mused. Still, it would have been nice for Newbury to reach out and let her know. She would have to call him when she was finished talking with Isidore.

"Anyway," the doctor continued, "Whyte and Shao were both killed with a heavy, blunt object—maybe the same one, maybe two different objects. It's too early to say. The other three victims, however, bear no such wounds."

Harley was silent a few moments. "He refined his methods," she said.

The ME pointed the scalpel at her. "Precisely."

"And the burns around the mouth?" she said. "What are those about?"

"I was just getting to that. I won't know for sure until the test results come back, but the burns are consistent with a high dose of chloroform. That appears to have been the cause of death for—" He glanced at the chart again. "—Reyes and Collington. I think he tried to do the same with Ballard, but he misjudged her. Hence the strangulation marks."

"How long does it take?" Harley said. "To kill someone with chloroform, I mean."

"It's not like the movies, Agent Cole, where you simply press a chloroform-soaked cloth over a person's mouth, and they instantly swoon. That's no more realistic than knocking someone unconscious with a hammer, only to see them wake up hours later with no repercussions."

The doctor chuckled and shook his head. "No, chloroform takes longer—probably several minutes or so." He held up a warning finger. "But bear in mind, they would pass out long before then."

Harley grew thoughtful. Blunt trauma to the head sounded like the way Poletov might kill, but chloroform? She just didn't see it. The Russian struck her as impatient and impulsive, while the killer appeared to be careful and calculating, cool enough to hold a chloroform rag over a young woman's mouth until she stopped struggling. The more she learned, the less she liked Poletov for the murders.

"Any sign of sexual activity?" she said.

Frank shook his head. "The first two victims are too old for me to say, but I can guarantee the other three were not sexually assaulted. As far as whether there might have been consensual sexual activity, I haven't found any evidence for it, but I can't rule it out just yet."

Another dead end. As far as Harley could tell, the murders were neither sexually motivated nor acts of passion, but rather cold-blooded, premeditated attacks. Why? What was the killer getting out of it? Why was he targeting these women?

"What does he have against women?" she murmured. "Did his mother do something to him as a child, and now he's taking out his hate on innocent women?"

She was just thinking aloud, not really expecting Isidore to answer. The doctor, however, seemed to think the question was directed at him.

"Hate?" he repeated, cocking his head like a bird studying a peculiar insect. "How do you know he hates his victims?"

Harley was puzzled by the question. "Why else would he kill them? This type of killer is usually someone on the outside looking in, someone who has been rejected and humiliated—and so, in response, he kills those he considers unattainable."

"That hardly means he hates them," Isidore replied.

"Murder isn't an act of love," she answered. Then, as the words lingered in the air, she grew thoughtful. Could she be wrong? Could this somehow be the murderer's way of connecting with his victims?

"There is nothing loving about strangulation or chloroform," Isidore said, "but everything he did afterward? Brushing the hair, cleaning the fingernails? Wrapping them and painting their faces? If that's not an act of love, my dear, then what is?"

Harley was silent, absorbing this. Suddenly she was aware of two things: first, that Poletov couldn't be their killer—he was simply too brutal of a man. And second, that the real killer wasn't killing women at random.

He was killing the women he wanted. The women he—in his sick, twisted way—*loved*. And that meant that if she and Callaway put together what they knew so far of the five victims, they might be able to figure out the killer's type—and just possibly guess who was next.

"I need to get back," she said suddenly, turning away. She needed to share this news with Callaway.

Isidore watched her as she hurried to the door, a look of amusement on his face. "Always happy to help," he said. "Give my best to Tony!"

CHAPTER TWENTY SEVEN

Callaway was sitting with a tray of nachos, watching Poletov through the one-way glass. His brow was furrowed in a look of concentration, as if he were studying a puzzle he couldn't quite figure out.

"Learn anything new?" Harley said as she entered the room. She grabbed a cheese-covered chip from the corner of his tray and popped it into her mouth.

Callaway shook his head. "I told him he needs to get ahead of this thing, tell us his side of the story, but his lawyer shut that down pretty quick."

"Who's his lawyer?"

"Some big shot out of California. Apparently Poletov isn't quite as down-on-his-luck as he appears. He's sitting on a small fortune. He just doesn't like to spend it."

It was always disappointing to have to communicate through a lawyer instead of directly with a suspect, but Harley took the news in stride. She felt certain Poletov wasn't the man they were after, and she was much less concerned about getting him convicted for trespassing, theft, and assault of a federal officer than she was about catching a serial killer.

Callaway picked up another chip and dipped it in a plastic cup of sour cream. "What about you?" he said. "Has Frank identified any more of the bodies?"

"Both of them, actually," Harley said, an undercurrent of excitement thrumming through her words. "Newbury sent a few agents down to the morgue earlier."

Callaway frowned at her, looking equal parts offended and wounded. "He didn't think to let us know?" he said.

"Don't worry, I cleared it up with him on the way over. Someone was supposed to reach out, coordinate with us. They dropped the ball." She shrugged, trying to convey that it was water under the bridge by this point.

"He was able to tell me a few things about the oldest victims, though," she said. "Apparently the first one, Kimberly Shao, went missing a few years ago at a college party. Nobody ever saw her leave."

"And the second victim?"

"Gianna Whyte. She went on a blind date."

"Let me guess," Callaway said. "Her date forgot to have her home by midnight."

"Something like that," Harley said. "She was never seen again—until Spencer Newman discovered that chamber at the back of the cavern, that is."

Callaway sat back, taking this all in. He held up his left fist and opened his fingers one by one as he recited the names. "Kimberly Shao, Gianna Whyte, Lolita Reyes, Daisy Ballard..." Then his thumb came out. "June Collington."

He dropped his hand to the desk, where his fingers began to tap in a restless, thoughtful rhythm. "He takes Shao at a college party," he said, "and Whyte on a blind date. He attacks Ballard in her trailer."

"Presumably," Harley said, not wanting to introduce any assumptions.

"Presumably," Callaway agreed. "And he attacks Collington at Shilowa—that much we know for certain." He frowned. "What do these women have in common?"

Harley was ready for this question. "They're all in their early twenties, slim, intelligent, and well-educated. The killer has a type, Callaway. They may not all have the same hair color or belong to the same race, but there's a type nonetheless."

Callaway's eyes wandered to the one-way mirror, watching as Poletov and his lawyer—a balding man in a crisp, tight suit—leaned together, murmuring. "And you think that's how he's choosing his victims?" he said.

She nodded. "I think he admires them because they're unattainable for him. Somehow, his pursuit of them is an act of love. It's twisted, I know, but from his perspective, it makes sense."

Harley could see Callaway was considering this. The fact that he didn't shoot the idea down right away was a good sign in and of itself.

"It makes sense he'd have at least a passing familiarity with them," Callaway said after a few moments. "It might cause them to lower their guard."

Harley fell silent, considering this. Then a new thought struck her, and she straightened.

"We're so stupid," she said, digging into her pocket for her phone.

"Speak for yourself, Einstein."

"I'm serious. What kind of person would have the opportunity to get close to a bunch of college girls?"

"A professor?" Callaway ventured.

She unlocked her phone and began searching for the video McCann had recorded during his visit to Shilowa the previous night. "Or a student," she said, feeling the conviction grow inside her. "Like that group at the ruins, the ones Chet Wheeler said were doing drugs."

She played the video, then fast-forwarded until she could see the teenagers gathered around the campfire…only, not all of them were teenagers. One looked a bit older, and he sat a short distance from the others, his baseball cap pulled low over his face and his hands hidden in his pockets. A backpack rested on the ground beside his chair.

"He's not with the group," Harley said. "He's just blending in, using them for cover so he can isolate his target."

Callaway scratched his chin. "You might be on to something, Cole. It's not much of a description to go on, though, not with that baseball cap hiding his face. We can't exactly put an APB out if we don't—"

"Hold up." Harley pointed, this time indicating the man's backpack. "Do you see that?"

Callaway shrugged. "It's a backpack."

"Not just any backpack." She zoomed in until they could see the logo. It was grainy, but she could still make out the symbol stitched on the back: *ETERNO*.

"That's a designer company," Callaway said, looking intrigued now. "They make quality products, but you have to pay out the nose."

Harley nodded. "Our friend has expensive tastes. How many of those do you think they sell a year, a few hundred?"

"*If* that." Callaway was already looking up the company number. "It's not a chain, so I'll be surprised if they have more than one or two locations. If we can get his name—" He stopped abruptly, his expression changing as he listened to the person on the other end of the line.

"Hello, yes," he said. "Can I speak with your manager?"

"Put it on speaker," Harley whispered.

Callaway held the phone out and stared at it for a few seconds while he located the speaker button. A nasally voice filled the room.

"This is Horton. May I ask who I'm speaking with?" There was a tired civility to his tone, as if he would have preferred to tell them to piss off if it wouldn't hurt his company.

"Mr. Horton, my name is Agent Callaway. I'm with the FBI. My partner, Agent Cole, is here as well."

"Okay," Horton answered in a cautious tone, drawing out the second syllable.

"We're conducting a criminal investigation," Callaway continued, "and we're trying to identify a suspect seen carrying one of your bags."

"Plenty of people use our bags, Agent Callaway," Horton said. "Just because someone suspected of a crime used one of our bags doesn't mean we were involved in the crime."

Callaway shot Harley a confused glance.

"Of course not," Harley said. "We're not accusing you of any wrongdoing. We just need to find out—"

"I'm sorry, who is this?" Horton interrupted petulantly.

"Agent Cole. My partner already introduced me."

"Agent Cole, if I go buy a set of kitchen knives and murder my wife, are you going to go after the store that sold the knives?"

The analogy, which seemed to come out of left field, struck Harley as a complete non sequitur. "That would be ridiculous," she said. "And that's not what—"

"You can understand my disbelief, then," Horton continued, raising his voice to drown hers out, "at the FBI calling me, insinuating that I might have something to do with one of my customers—"

"We don't mean to insinuate anything," Callaway said. "All we're trying to do is—"

"And to be frank," Horton went on, as if he hadn't heard, "it causes me to question what kind of call this is. How am I supposed to know that you're actually with the FBI? This could be a prank call, a joke at my expense."

Harley felt her jaw drop, like a door swinging open in the wind.

"Mr. Horton," Callaway said patiently, "I need you to listen to me very carefully. Are you listening?"

"Of course, I'm listening. What do you think I'm doing, playing Solitaire?"

"Neither you nor your company is under any suspicion. You selling a product to a customer does not make you responsible for what your customer does with that product."

"Thank you," Horton said emphatically, as if Callaway were surrendering to a hard-fought point. "That's exactly what I've been trying to say this whole time."

"And what we've been trying to say," Callaway explained with admirable patience, "is that we are trying to track down the name of a particular customer of yours so we can continue investigating a crime that otherwise has nothing to do with either you or your company. Is that something you could help us with?"

Silence. Harley waited, not sure what to expect.

"You want me to give you the personal information of one of our customers?" Horton said.

"That's right," Callaway said. "This is a man suspected of five homicides, so you would be doing a great service not only to us but to the entire country. There is a very good chance you would be saving lives."

Again, Horton remained silent. Harley imagined him mulling it over. She couldn't imagine he would refuse such a simple request now, not after Callaway's hero pitch.

Horton, however, continued to surprise her.

"I wish I could help," he said. "I really do. But our company has a policy about protecting the information of our customers. If it were up to me, I'd give you the name. But when it comes to the rules dictating how this business is run—"

This rationale was more than Harley could take. "You care more about company policy than helping us catch a serial killer?" she shot back, furious now. "*That's* not worth making an exception for?"

Callaway groaned and sank back, covering his eyes as if he knew there was no chance of convincing Horton now. Harley waited, breathing heavily and wishing she could reach through the phone and throttle this man.

"Like I said," Horton said unctuously, as if he was above such emotions as anger, "we take the privacy of our customers very seriously. If you can prove one of our customers is guilty of the crimes you speak of, we might be able to make an exception. But as long as it remains speculation—"

"Hard to prove guilt when you're hiding his identity," Harley said.

"Well, the rules are the rules, sweetheart. Tough titty, said the kitty."

Harley took a deep breath, ready to give Horton a piece of her mind, but Callaway quickly pressed the speaker button again and turned away, shielding the phone with his back.

"Thank you for your help, Mr. Horton," he said into the phone. "We'll be in touch."

Harley stared at him in disbelief as he hung up the phone. "How can you talk with him like that?" she said. "What a self-righteous, small-minded, idiotic ass."

He raised an eyebrow. "Are you finished?"

"I could go on, but I'll stop there for now."

"Good." Callaway leaned against the wall and sighed. "I'm not going to defend the guy. He's a class-A stooge in my book."

"Thank you."

"But that doesn't mean it will do us any good to burn bridges."

"There wasn't a bridge to burn. He was hostile and paranoid from the start." She ran a hand restlessly through her hair. "We need that information, Callaway. It's our only shot at identifying that man."

"I know it is. But before you suggest breaking in there in the dead of night to steal information that won't be admissible in court, let me see if I can call in a favor."

Harley had a hunch she knew what kind of favor he was talking about. "Your judge friend?" she said, remembering how Callaway's friendship with a local judge had helped in a previous investigation.

He made a circle with thumb and forefinger. "Bingo," he said.

"Must be nice, having friends in high places."

"That's what happens when you're polite."

They were silent for a few moments.

"You really think I'd break into that building to get that information?" Harley said.

"I think you'd do whatever it takes to put the killer behind bars. And as much as your determination drives me up the wall, I also respect the hell out of it."

Harley nodded. She appreciated the compliment, but she was still concerned their plan might not work.

"I just hope you get that warrant," she said. "Because if you don't, those people at Eterno might not let us through the front door—and it just might cost another young girl her life."

CHAPTER TWENTY EIGHT

The sporting goods store was sandwiched between a women's fashion store on one side and a custom footwear shop on the other. The smells of grilled steak and French fries drifted across the outlet mall from a nearby restaurant.

Harley, who had driven separately from Callaway, got out of her Jeep and waited for him at the entrance to the store. He climbed out of his truck a few moments later, absently flipping through a printed document as he approached her.

"Everything in order?" she said.

Callaway got to the last page, then looked up. "All good. Nothing like having the full weight of the law on your side. So long as the sales records haven't been deleted, we should be able to get what we need."

"Considering how Horton was on the phone," Harley said dryly, "I wouldn't put it past him to delete those just to spite us."

As they entered the store, a saleswoman rearranging men's shirts on a rack glanced up and smiled at them. Her smile froze, however, when she saw the badges on their hips. It probably wasn't very often they got federal agents in their store.

"Can I help you?" the woman began tentatively, as if unsure whether to offer.

Harley, however, had no time to waste on pleasantries. She strode straight toward the front desk—and the clerk standing on the other side of it. He had slicked-back hair, a pencil mustache, and tortoiseshell spectacles. His eyebrows rose in a patrician arch as he gazed at the agents.

"Can I help you with something?" he said.

As soon as Harley heard his voice, she knew she was looking at Horton. She smiled and, without turning away from Horton's narrow-eyed gaze, held her hand out to Callaway. He passed her the warrant, and she slapped it hard on the desk.

"It's all there," she said.

"*What's* all there?" he said, a note of doubt entering his voice. He stared at Harley for several long moments before his curiosity overpowered him. His eyebrows pulled together in a disdainful frown as he scanned the cover page.

"We asked nicely on the phone," Harley said, enjoying Horton's sudden discomfort. "But you made us do this the hard way."

Horton cleared his throat and looked up, adjusting his spectacles. "Don't take this the wrong way, but I'll have to read the fine print— one can never be too careful about these things, you understand. It might be a while."

"I think you misunderstand," Harley said. "We don't need you here. In fact, I think I'd prefer not having you looking over our shoulders. Don't you agree, Callaway?"

"One hundred percent." Callaway moved around the desk and took the clerk by the arm.

"Get off me!" Horton cried. He tried to shake his arm free from Callaway's grasp, but Callaway held on.

"You bullies!" Horton shouted as Callaway pulled him away. "This is police brutality! Whatever happened to personal privacy?"

Harley smiled politely. "Company policy, I'm afraid."

She watched as Callaway hauled Horton through the front door. Then, as the door closed shut again, she slid behind the desk and moved the mouse, waking the computer. She moved the cursor across the icons, not sure what to look for.

"There have to be records in here somewhere," she murmured.

But what would they look like?

She noticed QuickBooks was open. She maximized the window, then navigated to "CUSTOMERS," where she discovered a massive list of names. She searched "backpack" but didn't come up with any results.

She drummed her fingers on the desk, thinking. Then she noticed another employee—the woman who had watched the two agents enter the store—lingering nearby, making a show of organizing a stack of cans of airsoft pellets.

"Ma'am?" Harley said.

The woman went on working, as if she hadn't heard.

"Excuse me, ma'am?" Harley said, more loudly this time.

Finally, the woman turned, raising her eyebrows in an exaggerated expression of surprise. "Hmm?"

"How many kinds of Eterno backpacks do you sell?"

"A few. What are you looking for?"

Harley pulled up the image on her phone and held it toward the employee. "What's this one?" she said.

The woman lifted her glasses, which hung from a chain around her neck, and studied the image. "Ah, the Cosmopolitan. Popular choice. One hundred percent calfskin leather."

"And what do you call it in your database?"

The woman glanced out the window to see Horton standing just beside the front door, remonstrating with Callaway. Horton's hands flew comically in the air.

For a moment, Harley thought the woman would decide not to help her. Then she surprised Harley.

"Look for 'Eterno underscore Cos'," she said.

Harley did and came up with ten sales. Of the ten, only three had been bought by walk-ins—the other seven had been ordered out-of-state.

Harley pulled out her phone and took a deep breath, preparing herself for the conversation she was about to have. Then she called Ray.

"How's it hanging, Harley?" he said before the first ring had even finished. Harley could hear children screaming with laughter in the background, accompanied by splashing and the sound of running water.

"What is it, bath time at the Ranganathan household?" she said.

"Just the kids enjoying the slip-n-slide. Wanna come over?"

"Afraid I'll have to pass. I need you to run a few names for me."

Harley heard Ray cover the phone and yell. It sounded like he was telling his grandmother she needed to come out and watch the kids. This was followed by the sound of a sliding door, which closed and shut out the children's laughter. A few moments later, Ray's chair creaked as he sat down.

"Okay," he said. "I'm all ears."

Harley began reading the three names. "Todd Balaskas, Tyler Ferrill—"

"How do you spell those last names?"

Harley spelled them out for Ray, then waited.

"Got 'em," he said. "Had to write them down with a pencil. Surprised they even make these things anymore—pencils, that is."

"You're not *that* young," Harley remarked dryly.

"What was the last name?"

"Reggie Hughes."

The pencil scratched out the name. "Got it," Ray said. "What do you need to know about them?"

"Everything. I'm looking at them for five homicides in the area."

Ray whistled. "When did these murders take place?"

"The past few years. The last one happened within the week."

She listened to the sounds of his fingers on the keyboard.

"Alright," Ray finally said. "Todd's out—he's over in Spain for the summer. Posted a selfie outside the Alhambra Palace half an hour ago, so I'm pretty sure he's not your guy."

"And the other two?"

The keys clattered again.

"They're both here in New Mexico, both in their...let's see...early twenties, I'd say. I'm sending you a few pictures. What's your Instagram handle?"

Harley knew better than to fall for this. "Nice try," she said. "Text message or email is fine."

He sighed. "You miss all the shots you don't take, right?"

Harley's phone buzzed with a notification. She opened her text messages and saw a pair of profile pictures. Hughes was an African American man with a high-top haircut, a broad nose, and a goatee so thin it might have been drawn with a Sharpie. Ferrill was clean-shaven, with a pile of dark curls that hung boyishly over his forehead as he stared unsmilingly into the camera, his eyes bright in their curiosity.

"Thanks, Ray," Harley said, still studying the two pictures. "I'll let you know if we need anything else."

"You'll mention me if you get the guy, right? Say I helped?"

"Helped? You could practically put the cuffs on him yourself."

Ray snorted, but Harley could tell by his voice he was pleased. "Good luck, Harley."

"Thanks, Ray."

As she hung up the phone, she was surprised to see Callaway standing beside her. He must have convinced Horton not to reenter the building until they were finished.

"What'd you get?" he said, leaning close.

Harley showed him the two pictures. Then, minimizing the window, he pulled up Dale's video for comparison. Even without the baseball cap, it was clear the white man with the dark curls was the one from the video.

"Tyler Ferrill," Harley said, staring into Ferrill's bright, dreamy eyes, unable to get over how young he looked. "That's our guy."

"He have an address?" Callaway said.

Harley showed him the address Ray had sent.

Callaway cursed. "That's…what? Less than twenty miles from the cavern?"

"Even closer to the ruins," Harley answered, feeling as if the pieces of the jigsaw puzzle were finally clicking into place. "He's right in the middle between the two."

They had been wrong before, and Harley knew she had to be careful not to become so focused on one particular suspect that she lost all perspective, but she had a good feeling about this one.

"What do you say we drop by and see if he's home?" she said.

CHAPTER TWENTY NINE

As they drove to Ferrill's apartment, light flashed in the gathering clouds—a sight Harley's mother used to say meant God was taking pictures of her. The air smelled of ozone and the coming rain.

"Looks like the place," Harley said as they drove up to a large metal gate, behind which the road continued between two lanes of stately-looking pines, the lower branches cut close short enough to leave yellowing stumps.

"He's got money, alright," Callaway said, his voice distracted as he glanced back down at his phone. He was reading up on everything he could about the five victims to see if there were any connections they hadn't made.

"Either that or his parents do."

Harley rolled down her window. A voice came over the intercom: "Can I help you?"

"I'm Agent Harley Cole with the FBI," she said, holding up her badge toward the camera mounted high on the fence. "We're here to investigate a fraud charge."

The voice sounded cautious, uncertain. "A fraud charge?"

"A government website was recently hacked. Fortunately for us, the protection software didn't fail entirely—it managed to snag the hacker's IP address."

Callaway looked up from his phone and raised his eyebrows at her, impressed. "Not bad," he murmured.

"And you think this hacker lives here?" the voice said, the doubt clear now in the speaker's tone.

Harley shook her head. "I don't know what to think. These hackers bounce their IP addresses around, and we have to chase them down. For all we know, the hacker could be on the other side of the world. We just have to clear this number—as a formality, you know."

There was silence.

"How long does it take to do that?" the voice finally said.

Harley felt a flutter of hope. "Just a few minutes," she said. "We'll find out whose computer it is, then run the owner's name against our database. More than likely, we won't come up with anything." She sighed. "This isn't exactly the dream job I had in mind when I joined the Bureau, but it pays the bills. Know what I mean?"

Again, the man was silent for several heartbeats. Harley sensed him debating his options.

Finally, there was a buzzing sound, and the gate swung inward.

"Be quick about it," the man said. "I don't want our tenants thinking something's wrong."

"No," Harley muttered to herself. "Wouldn't want that."

"Nice work," Callaway said as they drove through the gate. "Although I have to admit it's a little scary knowing how easy that looked for you."

She shrugged. "Don't tell me you don't have a few stories on the back burner, just in case you need to use them."

Harley slowed as they neared the row of identical-looking condos. She began counting the numbers as they steadily ticked upward. Then she spotted it: 63. There was nothing suspicious about the building, nothing to suggest it housed a serial murderer. It was plain and nondescript, with nothing memorable at all except the flag of Saint Zita College hanging out front, showing a golden key on a white background.

"Zita," Callaway murmured, staring fixedly at the flag. "I don't believe it."

"What?" Harley said, not making the connection.

"Ballard and Collington went to Saint Zita."

"Wait. I thought Daisy went to Columbia?"

"She did," Callaway said. "After a single semester at Saint Zita. Apparently, she wanted to go there with her friends, and then her dad convinced her there was an opening for her at Columbia and it was too much to pass up—that's how she described it on social media, anyway."

Harley considered this new information. "It could be a coincidence," she said. "What about the other three victims?"

"Shao, Whyte, and Reyes all went to UNM."

Harley peered through the windshield, searching for a place to park. "So he's hunting college girls," she said. "Didn't we know that already?"

Callaway turned toward her, his face growing more animated now. "Ferrill transferred to Zita about a year ago. Guess where he was before that?"

166

"The University of Claxton," Harley murmured, finally understanding. "*That's* how he's been finding his victims."

Callaway nodded. "He's been brushing elbows with them every day."

It was yet one more confirmation that they had found the right guy, and it sent a current of electricity through Harley's body as she parked the vehicle. At one time or another, Ferrill had gone to college with all five of his victims. Had he been personally rejected by each of them? Harley did not know for sure, but she had a gut feeling the answer was yes.

Without a word, both agents got out. Harley felt a tiny droplet of rain brush her cheek, a harbinger of things to come.

As they entered the foyer, the concierge—a young woman dolled up in so much foundation that Harley couldn't have said what her natural skin color was—half rose from her seat. Then, seeing the badge in Harley's hand, she sat down again, a puzzled expression on her face.

"We're here to speak with Tyler Ferrill," Harley said as she approached. "Which floor is he on?"

The concierge's long lashes swept the air as she regarded the two agents. "I'm sorry, may I ask what this is about?"

Harley did her best to downplay their presence. "Just clearing up a small issue," she said. "You can call security about it, if you're uncertain."

The woman hesitated, her hand close to the phone. She looked too embarrassed to make the call.

"No, don't be ridiculous," she said, smiling. "Floor three. Shall I let him know you're coming?" Now her hand did steal toward the phone, hovering there like a vulture over its prey.

"He already knows," Callaway said quickly. "No need to bother him twice."

The concierge appeared satisfied by this explanation. "Very well," she said, flashing a practiced smile. "Let me know if you need anything else."

Breathing a sigh of relief, Harley joined Callaway in the elevator. The door closed with painful slowness, as if reluctant to help them in their mission.

Neither spoke as the elevator rose. There was nothing to say. They both knew what could be waiting for them in the next few minutes: a shootout, a hostage situation, or a chase down the fire escape. Harley could only hope Ferrill had no idea they were coming.

As the elevator doors opened, they heard the beat of pounding music. The sound grew louder as they approached the door marked 63. The two agents looked at one another. Callaway's eyes were hard as marbles, his jaw set like stone. The cords on his forearm stood out as he drew his weapon.

Harley took several calming breaths. She could not tell where the excitement ended and the fear began. Both were inextricably wrapped together.

Finally, she gave Callaway the nod he had been waiting for. Callaway planted his left foot, then kicked the door with his right.

Several things happened at once: first came an explosion of sound as the door shattered inward, shards of wood blasting in all directions. At the same time, the volume of the music doubled.

Without pausing for her senses to catch up with this new information, Harley rushed into the room, gun drawn, shouting at the trio of young men seated on the couch, eating slices of pizza as they watched a movie. Their faces were frozen in identical expressions of panic, as if they had just stepped into a dark stairwell only to discover the stairs were missing.

"FBI!" Callaway bellowed beside her. "Show me your hands!"

For a split second, nobody moved. Then, as if finally registering the words, three pairs of hands shot toward the ceiling, one still holding a slice of pizza. Grease ran toward the point of the triangle and dripped on the man's head, but he didn't seem to notice.

"What'd we do?" he said in a quivering voice, his lower lip trembling as if he were about to burst into tears.

Harley scrutinized their faces, comparing each to the mental picture she had of Ferrill. None of them, however, matched the image.

"Where's Ferrill?" she demanded.

The young men looked at one another, dumb as newborn infants. She could see their minds scrambling to make sense of what was happening.

Finally, one of them—a redhead with a hooked nose and a t-shirt that, fittingly enough, read "I CAN'T BELIEVE I PAUSED MY GAME FOR THIS"—blinked, squinting at Harley as if to better understand what she was saying. "Herb? What d'you want with him?"

"Who's Herb?" Callaway said.

"That's Ferrill," the young man answered. "'Herb' is a nickname he got in high school when he went through his vegetarian stage. He was already interested in dinosaurs and ancient cultures and shit like that, so we called him 'Herb' for 'herbivore.' Genius, right?"

Harley heard a door creak. "Stay with them," she said to Callaway as she moved down the hallway, gun drawn. The first two doors—a bedroom on one side, a bathroom on the other—were open, allowing Harley to quickly clear the rooms. The third door at the end, however, was closed.

Unlike the bedroom she had passed, which showed the name "GUNNER SCHWARTZ" above a sign reading "BEER PONG ZONE," this door had no decorations at all. It was plain and nondescript.

Forgettable.

Harley kicked the door open. The room inside was dark. She flicked the light switch, which turned on a shaded desk lamp that left most of the room in shadows. Shrunken heads gawked at her from the bookshelf, serving as bookends for tomes with titles such as *Spirituality for Scientists*, *Religion in the Ancient World*, and *Ancient Incans, Primitive Pueblos*.

Another book, a novel with a cover that showed a grave opening like a pair of doors to reveal a starless darkness beneath, lay on the desk, its pages dark with water stains, the picture peppered with grains of sand. Harley had the sense that this was the book Ferrill liked to read the most.

"Callaway!" Harley called. "You need to take a look at this."

"Nobody move," Callaway said to the three young men before joining Harley in the bedroom. He looked around, a look of fierce concentration on his face. "Well, I'll be damned. He's not hiding under the bed, is he?"

Harley swept the blanket back and looked under the bed. Ferrill wasn't there, but there *was* a plastic bag tucked in the corner where the two walls met.

Holstering her pistol, Harley lay flat on her belly and crawled toward the bag, pushing past cobwebs, candy wrappers, and balled tissues whose use she did not wish to know. She grabbed the bag with her hand and dragged it backward into the light.

"What is it, old clothes?" Callaway said.

Harley reached inside and pulled out a red bra trimmed with lace. "Not *his* clothes," she remarked, feeling a chill. She thought of the bodies wrapped in gold foil. Now she knew what he had done with the clothing—he had kept it, rather than burning it or tossing it into a storm drain. She wondered if he ever pulled the bag out just so he could smell what was inside and remind himself of the thrill of the hunt.

"Okay," Callaway admitted. "Maybe you were right about Poletov."

Harley took no pleasure in her partner's admission. "Won't be worth much unless we catch this guy," she said.

"Then we'd better go ask these knuckleheads where we can find him."

As they returned to the main room, they discovered their redheaded friend was now on his phone, his back turned as if to shield the phone from the agents' view.

With several long strides, Callaway crossed the room and ripped the phone from the redhead's hand. "Calling your friend, huh?" he growled, ending the call.

Harley's heart rate spiked. "Did it go through?" she said. If it did, there was a distinct possibility their best chance of catching Ferrill had just gone the way of the dodo.

"It connected," Callaway said, "but I don't know if this punk had time to say anything." He glowered at the kid. "Where is he?"

The redhead shrugged, sinking deeper into the cushions of the couch. With that posture, he could have illustrated the letter C in a children's book.

"Not here," he said in a sullen tone. "If you're so curious, why don't you call him yourself and find out?"

Callaway lost his patience. He seized the kid by the collar, lifting him off the couch.

"Listen, you little punk," he said, "I don't have time for your games. Your friend is a murderer, and he's going away for a long time—he and anyone who helped him. That little phone call to warn him? That's aiding and abetting. So unless you want to go to prison, too—"

The redhead, whose eyes had begun to bulge as soon as Callaway grabbed him, suddenly squeezed his eyes shut like a child who didn't want to face an unpleasant reality. "Okay!" he cried, his voice cracking. "Okay! We didn't have any idea what he was doing!"

Harley was not interested in hearing him defend himself. "Where'd he go?" she demanded.

"Said he was going to visit his girlfriend, alright?"

"His girlfriend?" Harley repeated, not sure she believed the story.

170

"Look," the redhead said, cracking open his eyes now, "can we all just relax for a second?"

In answer, Callaway twisted the kid's shirt around his fist, tightening his grip. "Talk," he said.

The redhead squealed and went on in a frantic voice: "Okay, okay! We were surprised too when he said he had a girlfriend, but everyone gets lucky eventually, right?" He paused, as if thinking of something new. "Then again, I'm not sure a girl like that even has time for a boyfriend. She's a real workaholic. Always working at the lab."

"The lab?" Harley said.

"Yeah. Over at Saint Zita's. She's a scientist of some kind or so Herb said." He grunted, as if to say it was impossible to tell what to believe when Herb was talking.

"Does this girlfriend have a name?" Callaway said.

The redhead snorted and shook his head. "Not sure I can pronounce it. It's in my phone, though—we did a humanities project together last semester. 'Maka' something or other."

Harley picked up the discarded phone, which was still unlocked, and navigated to the contacts. She scrolled down to the M section.

"First name or last?" she said.

"First. I think. Last name starts with an N."

Harley continued down to N. Sandwiched between "NADER" and "NOEL" was the name "NAKAI, MAKAWEE." She read it aloud.

The kid snapped his fingers. "That's the one."

"Navajo," Callaway murmured. "Any idea where this Makawee lives?"

The redhead shrugged. "Beats me, man."

Harley glanced at the other two teenagers. The one with the pizza grease on his forehead held up his hands, as if afraid he'd be shot for not giving them the answers they wanted. The third one, a round-faced youth who was balding prematurely, rubbed thoughtfully at his hairless chin.

"What do you know?" Harley said to him.

They all looked at him. His hands wrestled uncomfortably in his lap like a pair of snakes.

"Herb and I were driving around a few days ago," he said, "and we went past her place. Herb pointed at it and said to me, 'She's going to be mine someday.'"

"I never heard about this," the redhead said.

171

The balding one shrugged. "You know Herb. He's always saying weird shit like that. I just smiled and nodded and pretended I was texting someone."

"What's the address?" Harley said.

"It's over on Billet Ave. Blue house, like navy blue. I don't remember the number."

"It'll have to do," Callaway said.

The two agents hurried toward the elevator.

"So that's it?" the redhead called. "You're leaving, just like that?"

Callaway stopped. "Thanks for reminding me." He went back and gathered the three cell phones. Then, as if for good measure, he snagged the set of car keys from the coffee table as well.

"What the hell, man?" the redhead protested.

"Just in case you had any ideas about trying to warn your friend again," Callaway said over his shoulder. "Don't worry—you'll get these back eventually."

The redhead shouted something in response, but Harley did not hear it. She was already in the elevator with Callaway.

As the door shuddered to a close, Harley found herself wondering how many times Ferrill had ridden in that elevator, just another college kid in a town full of them, heading off to stalk his unknowing prey or returning from doing the same.

It didn't really matter, she supposed, because she knew one thing for certain: He was never going to ride it again, not if she had any say in the matter.

She only hoped he wouldn't see them coming.

CHAPTER THIRTY

The storm finally broke as the agents raced outside, fat droplets of rain that burst on the pavement and sent up wisps of steam. An overpowering sense of urgency filled Harley as they hurried toward their vehicles.

"You know your way to Billet Ave?" Callaway shouted. The wide brim of his Stetson kept the rain off his face. Harley, on the other hand, had nothing to cover her head, and the rain was running down her face and getting into the corners of her eyes.

She hesitated just a fraction of a second. "I remember."

Callaway, however, had noticed her hesitation. "I'll drive," he said.

As they jogged to the Jeep, however, something else occurred to Harley.

"They said she's a workaholic!" she shouted above the rain.

Callaway turned back. "So?"

"So what if she's working late? Ferrill might already be with her at the lab, and if we both go to the apartment..."

Callaway stared at her, rivulets of water cascading off the brim of his hat. The whole world had turned gray.

"You take the lab, then," he said.

"What are you going to do? We drove here together, remember?"

Grinning, Callaway lifted the set of keys he had swiped from the condo. "I think I'll take a rental."

Harley knew he wanted the apartment because he thought the girl would be at home, and he would rather be the one to confront the killer than leave the task to Harley. She felt a strange thrill go through her body, knowing there was a good chance one of them would meet the killer on their own. It was not the way they had been trained to confront suspects, but under the circumstances, throwing their own lives into danger might be the only way to save an innocent victim.

"Be careful," she said, staring into his eyes and hoping it was not for the last time. "Whatever you find, you let me know as soon as you can."

His jaw clenched and he nodded. "See you on the other side?"

"See you on the other side."

She got into her car, then watched Callaway move along a row of parked cars, clicking the unlock button on the remote in his hand. The brake lights of a white sedan flashed. Callaway climbed inside, escaping the cascade of gray rain.

"Don't be a hero, Callaway," Harley murmured as she buckled her seat belt. "The world needs decent living people, not dead heroes."

She turned on her headlights, shifted into drive, and pulled onto the main road, heading for the lab.

Meanwhile, the gray rain drowned the world.

*

The rain hammered against the vehicle, entombing Harley in her thoughts. A sign emerged from the gloom, and Harley crouched over the steering wheel as she strained to read the letters.

"ST. ZITA CAMPUS."

The lots were deserted—it was approaching midnight on a summer's eve, after all—and the tall, sharply-built structures were as still as perched gargoyles in the gray. A steady wind rolled leaves along the gutters, occasionally growing to bursts that howled against Harley's window.

"Where is it?" she muttered to herself, looking left and right as she searched for the lab. In such poor visibility, she might wander the campus for fifteen or twenty minutes before identifying the right building.

Then she spotted a sign reading "LINDEN LAB" with an arrow pointing to the right. Harley followed the turn and entered a small parking lot fronting a long, one-story brick building.

A cherry-red sedan was parked close to the front door. Farther back in the corner of the lot, blending in with the night so as to be almost invisible, was a second car, this one gray. It could have been anyone's car, but for some reason, Harley felt certain it was Ferrill's.

A shudder passed through her entire body. A goose had just walked over her grave, her father would have said.

She turned off her headlights as she parked beside the Fiesta, not wishing the light to shine through the pair of glass doors leading into the lab. Stepping out into the rain, she hurried around to the car and peered in through the windows.

No Nakai. So she was still in the lab, then.

Harley glanced at the gray car, wondering if Ferrill was sitting in there, watching her. She did not have time to check. She needed to find Nakai.

The rain pelted her scalp as she hurried to the front doors. She pulled the handle, but the doors were locked. She cursed silently and took a step back, considering her options. She looked around for something she could throw to break the glass...

And that was when she saw the footprint in the flower bed. Squeezing between the boxwood bushes and the brick wall of the building, she followed the tracks through the flower bed. The coffee-colored mulch had been put in recently, and whoever had done the job had heaped it high, creating a thick pillow of material that captured every impression. A few clippings from the boxwoods, missed by the gardeners, lay tucked against the wall.

Harley reached the corner of the building. As she rounded the corner, she discovered a series of impressions overlaid with shards of glass. She looked to her right and saw the sash of the window beside her had been opened, the glass broken. The room inside—an office, by the look of the cluttered desk—was empty and dark, the door at the end open just a crack. The curtains stirred fitfully in the wind, restless as ghosts.

There was no question now where Ferrill had gone. The only question that remained was whether he had yet succeeded in what he'd set out to do.

Pressing her back to the wall, Harley dug out her phone and called Callaway.

"Pick up, pick up," she muttered as it rang. She could hear the rain falling in sheets on the roof, and the hollow rush of water coursing through the aluminum downspout beside her. Leaves caught in the boxwood writhed like spiders under a candle and tore free again.

The phone rang for several interminable, heart-pounding moments before her partner's voice came through.

"What's the story, Cole?" he said. "I was about to call and say the apartment's clear—no sign Ferrill was ever here."

"I've got a broken window here," she whispered, afraid to speak too loudly next to the open window, even though the rain was probably loud enough to drown out an orchestra. "And there was a second car in the parking lot when I arrived." She paused. "I think he's still here, Callaway."

Callaway's voice was firm. "Stay put, you understand me? Do *not* confront him on your own. I'll be there in just a few minutes."

She heard the squeak of a spring door through the phone, then the roar of the storm. She heard him open his truck door and climb inside, and the rain fell to a metallic drumming.

"I need to hear you say it," he added, his words interrupted by the sound of the truck's engine turning over. "Say you'll wait for me to get there."

The grit of the brick wall pressed into her back. She felt the darkness of the window beside her, a darkness so thick it might flow free like oil from a barrel. Her arms were beginning to shake from the cold, and her teeth clicked together.

"I'll wait for you," she answered. "Just get here as soon as you can."

"Good. Hang tight, Harley. We'll get him."

Harley ended the call and pressed her head against the wall. Her heart was bouncing like a basketball in her chest.

And what if he takes too long? she thought. *What if, by the time we get in there, Ferrill's work is already done?*

She saw an image of Ferrill bent over Daisy's body in the cavern, dipping his brush in a cup of gold paint and carefully brushing her cheeks, her lips, and her eyelids, her clothes bundled in a bag at his elbow, no privacy respected, no stolen intimacy spared. She saw the unconscious smile on his face—not a full-blown grin, but a mere stretching of the mouth, a twinkle in the eyes.

The secret pleasure of a man who takes what he wants, when he wants, knowing nobody can stop him.

How many more women had he marked? How many more names were on his waiting list, innocently going about their lives without any idea they were being stalked, obsessed over?

Drawn as if by an irresistible force, she turned back to the window and peered inside. As she stared into the dark office, a scream ripped down the hallway.

Without thinking, without pausing to consider her promise to Callaway, Harley planted both hands on the sill and lifted herself up.

CHAPTER THIRTY ONE

A sharp pain dug into Harley's hand as she lifted herself into the room. With two fingers, she plucked the sliver of glass from the side of her hand and tossed it aside. Then, careful to avoid any glass fragments on the tiled floor below, she dropped to the ground and paused, listening.

The building, battered and beaten by the raging storm, gave no protest. All was silent.

Unclasping her holster, Harley drew her Glock and held it low in both hands, ignoring the thin stream of blood now running from her hand to the trigger guard. Water dripped from her hair as she rounded the desk and approached the door at the end.

There was just enough gray light washing in through the windows for her to see the outlines of shapes: the closed door opposite her, the water cooler hulking in the hallway, the posters—a human anatomy chart, an ad for a campus concert, and an announcement for a movie produced by the school's drama team—tacked to the walls. Down one end, a red EXIT sign glared like a car's brake light. Down the other, a silvery light outlined a closed door.

Where are you? she thought. *Where'd you take her?*

It was a vast building, and even though she knew Makawee worked in the lab, there was more than one lab in the school. And what if Ferrill had ambushed her elsewhere—in the bathroom, for instance, or a dark hallway? The building was full of potential places for an attack.

Thunder growled, causing the lights to flicker. As they did, Harley noticed light gleaming off the tiles at her feet. Wet footprints, faint but visible. There was even a tiny piece of mulch, as if she needed further evidence.

Confident now she was heading in the right direction, she moved at a brisk walk down the hallway, past classroom doors with handmade signs. As she pressed deeper into the building, the sounds of the storm faded and her breathing grew louder. Her sodden clothes clung stiffly to her body, and her wet shoes squeaked on the tiled floor.

Then she heard a sound, like something metallic clattering to the floor.

177

She moved down the hallway in the direction of the sound, pausing to glance into each room along the way. She felt the tension in her body ratcheting higher with every passing second. She heard the ticking of a clock in the back of her head, but she was not sure if it was the time remaining until Callaway arrived or the last seconds of Nakai's life dripping away.

I'm coming for you, Makawee, Harley thought, holding desperately to the hope that she might still be alive. *Don't give up. I just need a little time to find you.*

She clicked on her flashlight, muting the beam with her hand.

The first thing she noticed was the row of skeletons perched on the tables like cats with their backs arched. There were wooden trays too, covered with an assortment of rocks that might have been fossils, but it was the framed picture on the wall that really drew her eye. It showed a group of smiling college students in bucket hats and safety glasses, some leaning on shovels while others held smaller tools of the trade: toothbrushes, picks, chisels, trowels.

In the middle row, the only one in the entire picture without a smile, was none other than Tyler Ferrill. He was holding, of all things, a wood-handled brush.

Was Nakai in that picture, too? Harley didn't know what Nakai looked like, so she couldn't say for sure, but she had a pretty good idea that Nakai was there.

That's how he knew she would be working late, Harley thought as a sense of dread welled up inside her. *Because he* works *with her.*

It made sense. The college gave him access to attractive women, and the lab dovetailed perfectly with his interest in all things past and dead. How Ferrill saw murder as an act of love was still a mystery, but Harley nevertheless felt she was one step closer to understanding the young man who had killed five women and dressed them up in foil and face paint.

Harley was startled from her reverie by another scream, this one much closer than the last. Wasting no time, she sprinted toward the door at the back of the room, her thoughts now focused exclusively on what was on the other side.

She reached for the handle, thinking it would be locked and she would have to find a way to break through, but to her surprise, it turned easily. She shoved the door open, revealing tables, rows of beakers…

And the startled, gaping face of Tyler Ferrill, staring at Harley over his shoulder while he clamped a rag down over the mouth of a dark-haired woman, his other hand pinning her wrist to the tiled floor. He looked even more youthful than his picture.

"FBI!" Harley shouted, both hands on her gun as she pointed it at him. "Get your hands off her!"

Nakai bucked against Ferrill like a turtle stuck on its back, but he held her down with his hips. Even though both were clothed, even though there was no evidence Ferrill had sexually assaulted any of his victims, there was something undeniably violating in the way he pinned her with his body, his buttocks smashed against her groin, his legs pressed against her sides as if he were fighting to keep his balance on an unruly horse.

Harley's finger moved to the blood-slick trigger. Just as she started to pull, however, Ferrill lifted the cloth from Nakai's face and raised both hands. Nakai's eyes fluttered, then closed, as if she were slipping into a deep slumber.

"Down on the ground!" Harley shouted at Ferrill, every cell in her body screaming at her to pull the trigger and spare the world his existence. Somehow, she found the resolve to resist the urge.

Ferrill stared at her, his eyes as wide and innocent as those of a newborn lamb. With agonizing slowness, he rose to his feet, still straddling Nakai.

"I said get down!" Harley shouted again. "Right now!"

With that same chilling look of innocence, as if he could not understand why she would ever want to harm him, he turned his back toward her and, as if moving through water, reached toward the wall.

What is he reaching for? Harley thought feverishly, tightening her finger on the trigger. She prepared herself for him to spin around, gun in hand.

Then, suddenly, the lights went out.

CHAPTER THIRTY TWO

The lab, situated deep in the bowels of the building, had no external windows, and so the room was plunged into utter darkness. Harley's eyes retained an after-image of the girl prone on the cold, tiled floor, arms limp at her sides with the elbows slightly bent, hair swept out beside her in a dark wave...

And looming over her, back turned so that Harley could not see his face, the killer who was Tyler Ferrill.

On instinct, Harley squeezed the trigger as soon as the lights went out. Immediately, she both smelled and tasted the sulfur of the gunpowder. There was a hard impact that suggested the bullet had buried itself in the drywall on the far side of the room—not the worst outcome, since a ricochet would have endangered not only her life but Nakai's as well.

She took an instinctive step back, wanting to find the wall, and bumped into the open door instead. She threw it closed, trapping Ferrill in the room with her. The blinds bounced as the door clicked shut behind her, rattling against the glass. Then the room was silent except for an industrial hum that might have been a refrigerator.

Her heart hammered inside her chest. It was like climbing into a cage with a leopard. The darkness was his domain, the cloak under which he hunted.

I'm a hunter too, Harley thought grimly.

The question was...were there other doors? She did not know—she had been too focused on the killer to look around the room. Unfortunately for her, he probably knew the layout very well. He had broken in, after all.

As Harley's eyes adjusted to the darkness, she discovered the room wasn't completely without light. Tiny colored dots, like the kind on her laptop charger that showed it was charging, interrupted the blackness. As she stared at them, she saw several of them blink out and come back on.

The killer was moving, circling the room in a counterclockwise pattern. The only problem was that she didn't know how close he might be.

"You shouldn't have interfered," a voice hissed from the darkness. "It's none of your business what I do with them. They're mine, don't you understand?"

She heard a metallic rasp, like a spoon drawn across the edge of a mug.

She sidled away, moving clockwise around the room. She needed to get to the girl and see if she was alright—that, and stall until help arrived.

Suddenly she remembered the flashlight on her phone. Careful not to make a sound, she passed the Glock to her left hand and pulled out the phone with her right. The screen glowed dimly for a moment, revealing a background of the horses that roamed next to her new house, and then she turned on the flashlight, shining it toward where she had heard the killer's voice.

A gleaming object cut through the darkness. She ducked, and the weapon—a ceremonial sword with a hilt encrusted with jewels—glanced off the metal shelf behind her, harmlessly striking her shoulder on the rebound. She turned the pistol toward her attacker, but the back of his hand knocked it aside just as she fired. There was a shatter of glass as the window of the front door exploded.

Harley's phone fell to the floor, the upturned flashlight casting dancing shadows on the ceiling.

"They're mine!" Ferrill hissed, his face ghoulish in the glare of the flashlight. His eyes were pools of glinting shadow, his chin a jutting fleshy shelf. "They belong to me!"

He brought the sword down with surprising swiftness, catching the gun. On another day, the sword might have slid harmlessly off. Harley's hands, however, were slick with blood and throbbing with pain from where she had cut herself on the broken window, and before she realized what was happening, the gun had been twisted from her grasp. It struck the floor, slid, and disappeared beneath a workbench.

Ferrill grinned, his face—one half in glaring light, the other in shadow—twisted with triumph. His eyes were impossibly bright, almost feverish.

"Do you like it?" he said, lofting the sword. "I stole it from a museum in South America. It was quite a challenge getting it back to the States, believe me. But it was worth it. You want to know why?"

Harley swallowed hard, not answering. She took a step back and nearly tripped on a power cord.

"The natives used it to make human sacrifices to their gods," he continued, advancing slowly toward her. "I thought it would make a fitting tool to send me on to the next world, once I've finished my work here."

"Why don't you just go ahead and fall on it now, if you're so eager to die?"

He chuckled. "I admire your fight—not everyone has such courage. I just might let you join Makawee."

"And be your victim?" Harley said, wanting to keep him talking as her hands scoured the darkness, frantically searching for something to use as a weapon.

Ferrill grimaced, looking genuinely pained. "My *bride*. Did you think I was some psychopath, killing these women just for the sport?" He shook his head, disgusted. "I'm sending them on ahead of me. When the time is right, I will join them."

It all made sense, from a twisted point of view—the loving way Ferrill had arranged the bodies, wrapped them, painted them. He really did love them—or believed he did, anyway—and somehow, perhaps through reading those dusty old tomes Harley had seen in his bedroom, he had convinced himself that this was his surefire way of being united with them. Why try to win them over when he could bind them to himself without their consent?

Harley's fingers closed around a beaker. "That time just might be sooner than you think," she said, chucking the object at Ferrill's face. He shielded himself, and the beaker bounced off his arm before shattering on the floor.

Ferrill laughed. "You just don't quit, do you?"

Harley took a quick backward glance—and realized with a sense of dread she had nearly reached the corner. She was almost out of real estate.

"I don't want to cut you up," Ferrill said, advancing at a slow, teasing pace. "The truth is, I don't like blood. The Mongols didn't like blood either, did you know that? That's why they put their prisoners in sacks and beat them to death. I prefer chloroform—a lot less messy and a lot less work. Besides, it wouldn't make much sense to traumatize the very women I'm going to be spending eternity with, would it?"

"You're sick," Harley said. "You need help."

"You want to throw me into a mental institution so you can study me, is that it? Try to find some rational explanation for my behavior?" He laughed. "You want to hear that I was abused by my parents, so you have an excuse to dismiss me. The idea that a rational, *normal* human being could do what I'm doing—you just can't stomach that, can you? It would ruin your idea of a perfect little society where everyone thinks the same way."

Harley bumped into a counter. *End of the line,* she thought. *Time to put up or shut up.*

But how was she supposed to fight Ferrill? He had a freaking sword, for goodness' sake!

With her hands behind her, she felt for something to grab hold of. Her fingertips brushed a steel thermos. Would it be enough to stop a blade?

"There is no such thing as true love," Ferrill continued, only a few paces from her now, "not in this life. It's something for the next part of the journey."

"You expect they'll love you after you murdered them?"

Ferrill made a *tsk* sound, as if Harley were a naive child. "You just don't understand," he said. "There is no bond in life as strong as the bond of death. To be with someone in their last hour—that moment is more powerful than a couple's wedding night, or a mother holding her baby for the first time. It binds you together as nothing else can."

"How would you know?" Harley countered, pulling the thermos closer. She wasn't sure how much Ferrill could see, and she didn't want to alert him.

"You haven't experienced either of those," she said. "That's the whole point, isn't it? This is just your desperate attempt to make women love you because you couldn't win them the way everyone else does. You had to cheat. Who hurt you, Tyler? Who made you what you are?"

"You have no idea what you're talking about!" he roared, advancing toward her. "You have no idea what I've been through, the rejection I've suffered! To be laughed at for not being like everyone else, not thinking like everyone else! To be treated like a...like a *freak* because I can't play the little flirting game the way everyone else does!"

Harley heard a sound come from the other side of the door she had used to enter the room; it sounded very much like glass crunching underfoot. Ferrill did not seem to hear it as he was so wrapped up in his speech.

"But I'm done playing their games," Ferrill said in a low, dangerous voice. "I have something more important to do, and I'm not going to let anyone get in my way."

He raised the sword. The jewel-encrusted hilt—a relic of the Conquistador days, Harley supposed—glittered in the harsh light from her cell phone. Ferrill's eyes, however, did the opposite of glittering. They seemed to swallow the light, a pair of black holes consuming everything around them. For how many women had those heartless, deep-space eyes been their last sight in this world?

The sword arched back like a spring-loaded mechanism. An expression that was half grin and half snarl remained frozen on Ferrill's face. Harley's fingers closed around the thermos.

Just as the sword started to descend, Harley raised the thermos. Had the sword been sharper, or had Harley waited for Ferrill to really get behind the swing, the blade would almost certainly have cut right through the steel and buried itself in her sternum. But instead, the sword cut through most of the thermos and then stopped, caught in the steel.

In that moment of surprise as Harley and Ferrill registered what had just happened, the lights came on. Ferrill flinched back, trying to block the glare from the light over Harley's head. Making the most of her opportunity, Harley advanced, ripping the sword from Ferrill's relaxed hands and tossing it aside.

Ferrill took a desperate glance over his shoulder and saw Callaway standing in the doorway, aiming a pistol at him.

"Hands up!" Callaway shouted. "Get on the ground!"

It only took Harley one glance at Ferrill's face, however, to know he wasn't about to go down easily. With a snarl, he lunged for her throat. Harley brushed his arm aside and then threw a jab at his nose. His head rocked back, blood trickling from his nostrils. She struck again, not giving him time to recover, a boxer driving her opponent across the ring with a series of swift, accurate punches.

After several blows, Ferrill finally lifted his hands to defend himself. Then, with a scream of rage, he threw himself at Harley. As he hurtled toward her, she threw the strongest right hook of her life and watched his head twist to the side. He stumbled past her for one or two steps, paused, and then crumpled to the ground.

Callaway crouched over Ferrill's body, checking his neck for a pulse. "Still alive," he said. "But he's out cold. Shit, Harley, that was some punch!"

184

Harley, however, was not interested in accolades at the moment. She dropped to the ground beside Nakai, hoping desperately that the girl was still alive. She could smell the chloroform coming in waves off the discarded rag, and she tossed it across the room.

"Wake up!" she pleaded, shaking the girl's shoulder. "Please wake up!"

She held her fingers to the girl's mouth, feeling for a breath.

"Anything?" Callaway said, crouched beside her now.

"I'm not sure!" she answered, her voice raw with emotion. "Where's the ambulance?"

"A few minutes out. They'll be here as soon as they can."

Suddenly Nakai's eyes began to flutter. She coughed weakly, grimacing.

"Where is he?" she said in a small, tired voice.

A sense of joy bloomed in Harley's chest at the sound of the girl's voice. "Don't worry about him," she said, brushing the girl's hair from her face. "He can't harm you anymore—you're safe now. I'm right here with you, and I promise everything is going to be alright."

She squeezed Nakai's hand, and Nakai squeezed hers back.

"You're safe," Harley kept repeating as they waited for the ambulance. She glanced at Callaway. He was standing close to Ferrill now, but his eyes were on Harley.

He was smiling.

CHAPTER THIRTY THREE

The storm had broken, the clouds rolling up and moving on, pushed by a brisk wind. Harley and Callaway sat on one of the bumper stops in the lab parking lot, watching Officer Bullock put his hand on Ferrill's head as he guided him into the police car.

"Wouldn't want him to bump his head," Harley mused with a wry sense of humor. It was strange, the way they fought their opponents with great violence up until the point of resistance. Then, like wrestlers practicing a fight, they would ease off so as to cause no harm.

The door clapped shut with a note of finality—as final as the sentence that would put Ferrill away for life, Harley hoped.

She sighed, relaxing the tension in her muscles as she realized Ferrill was no longer her responsibility. He was now the DA's problem and considering the personal stake Governor Ballard had in the case, Harley had no doubt the DA would have plenty of incentive to lock Ferrill away for good.

Callaway shook his head as he watched the squad car pull away. "I still don't get why he did it," he said.

"Unlucky in love," Harley said. "Or incompetent, you might say. He couldn't win them, so he decided to take them by force. Somehow, through all those old texts he was reading, he became convinced he could make them his death brides."

"I get all that. I just don't get the *way* he did it—the foil, the face paint, the locations."

Harley was silent, considering how to answer. It was still something of a mystery to her as well, though she was not sure how much more of the twisted mind of Tyler Ferrill she wanted to understand.

"He might have believed those sites brought him closer to the spiritual world," she said. "And the foil and paint—those were just his version of a bride's wedding day attire."

"You know," Callaway said, "most guys would just work on their pick-up lines."

Harley offered no response as she brushed a lock of hair from her eyes. The cool air, still soft and smelling of rain, felt pleasant on her skin. Her gaze shifted to a nearby stretcher as Nakai was loaded into an ambulance, groggy but conscious. The medic had assured the agents her vitals were all good and she would survive the attack unscathed, at least physically. It might take some time to heal the emotional wounds, but she was young and had her whole life ahead of her. She would be just fine.

"I have to admit," Callaway said, "that's the first time I've ever seen someone bring a sword to a gunfight. You did well, not getting your head cut off, though I'm a little disappointed you didn't pick up a sword of your own. You could have gone at it like gladiators."

Harley would have laughed if she hadn't been so tired. "Sorry to disappoint."

Callaway grew serious. "Honestly, though, I'm still a little pissed you broke your promise by going in there."

The words stung. "If I'd waited any longer—" Harley began to protest, but Callaway cut her off.

"I know, I know. Nakai might be dead. I guess I just don't like the idea that I might have lost you too." He shook his head, as if he didn't know what to do with her. "You have a way of throwing yourself into danger, almost as if you have a death wish."

She considered this, then shook her head back at him. "Not a death wish. I'm just not the kind of person who can stand on the sidelines. I'm a fighter, not a cheerleader."

Callaway grunted. "I'd drink to that if I had something to drink."

"How's coffee sound?" Officer Bullock said, approaching with a pair of steaming, styrofoam cups.

"Like the elixir of the gods," Callaway answered, accepting one of the cups and inhaling deeply. "Much obliged, my friend, much obliged."

Bullock smiled. "Pleasure's all mine." He handed the second cup to Harley, then stood there, lingering. She waited, sensing he had something more to say.

"Is it worth it?" he said.

Harley did not understand the question. "Worth it?"

"The job. All the stress, all the uncertainty. Is it worth it?"

"When we get the guy, absolutely," Callaway said.

"And when you don't?"

Harley thought about it. "Sometimes you do things because you want to do them, and sometimes because you have to do them. For me, this is the latter."

The officer nodded, growing thoughtful again. "Anyway," he finally said, "hell of a job, tracking him down. I think we'll all sleep a little better tonight knowing he's off the streets."

Harley nodded her acknowledgment and watched Bullock walk away. He was a fine officer, and she thought there was a good chance he would make homicide detective someday.

"You never know where you're going to make a friend," Callaway observed.

Harley sipped her coffee, thinking of that glint of admiration she had seen in Bullock's eyes. "He looked at us like we're heroes."

"We are, from a certain point of view."

"Is that what you think?"

He shrugged. "Hero, villain—with a job like this, you're balanced on the edge of a knife, and a few pounds of pressure on a trigger can determine whether you fall one way or the other. You do everything right, you'll get a few attaboys but otherwise be forgotten. You do things wrong, on the other hand, and you'll be immortalized for all the wrong reasons."

Harley arched an eyebrow, surprised by this sudden speech. "You sure that's coffee you're drinking?"

Callaway ignored the joke. "All I'm saying is, it only takes a single action to be branded a hero or a villain. If you kick the winning field goal in the championship game, they're practically ready to build you a statue, even if you kicked under seventy percent the entire season. If you miss it, on the other hand…"

"It doesn't matter how great your season was," Harley finished.

"Exactly. You fell short at the most crucial moment, and that's what history judges you by."

Harley couldn't help wondering where all this was coming from. "You ever worry about that?" she said. "How history will judge you?"

He thought about it for a moment, then shrugged. "If by 'history,' you mean 'posterity,' then yes. I care a lot about what my kids think of me. But the rest of the world?" He waved his hand. "Who needs 'em?"

Harley smiled, appreciating Callaway's down-to-earth attitude. She leaned back and closed her eyes, enjoying the smell of the night air. She was tired and knew she should probably get home soon, but she wanted more than anything else to just stop thinking, if only for a few minutes.

Callaway laughed abruptly.

"What's so funny?" Harley said, not opening her eyes.

"I asked Ray to look into those missing artifacts?"

"Yeah?"

"Turns out our good friend Boris was selling them on Ebay. That's why he didn't want to talk about it."

"So close, yet so far away," Harley said, thinking of the ceremonial sword Ferrill had nearly killed her with. Like Poletov, Ferrill seemed to have a great deal of interest in artifacts of historical and cultural significance, but they had not been an essential part of his ritual. The gold foil, the face paint, his ability to be with his victims in the moment of their death—those were the things he had really cared about. The missing artifacts had been no more than a distraction.

"You needed to hear that to realize Poletov wasn't the killer?" Harley said.

"No, but it makes me feel a little better. He's still in custody, pending a hearing for the assault charge. Now we can slap him with another charge as well. Justice is served."

Harley thought of the five women whose lives had ended because of one man's psychotic obsession with the afterlife. Had they gotten justice? Was it possible for the dead to receive justice, or was justice only for the families and friends who were left behind?

"I'll feel better when I hear the judge read Ferrill's sentencing," she said. She cracked one eye open to peer at him. "Thank you for getting here when you did, by the way. I don't like my chances with Ferrill if you didn't enter the picture."

"Ah, you would've been fine," he answered. While she knew this was possible, there was also a decent chance Ferrill would have hacked her to pieces if Callaway hadn't shown up. It was sobering, knowing how close she'd come to death. Then again, that was the nature of the job.

"What do you say we get something to eat?" Callaway said.

Harley sat up, thinking it sounded like a good idea. Before she could answer, however, her phone came to life with a text message from Bryce.

Sorry i lost touch. Crazy busy here. Dinner tonight

Harley stared at it a few seconds before realizing it was a question. She texted back: *YES. My place, one hour. Just have to make a stop first.*

She was thinking of her brother. Whatever he needed to talk about, she hoped they could deal with it soon so that she could go home, have

189

dinner with Bryce, and forget all about petroglyphs, gold foil, and the twisted reasoning of serial killers.

As she sent the message to Bryce, she realized Callaway was watching her, waiting for a response.

"Sorry," she said with an apologetic smile. "Bryce has been really busy lately, and after everything that's happened the past few days—"

Callaway waved his hand to stop her from finishing. "Another time, then," he said. He smiled, but she thought she detected a note of disappointment in his voice.

She rose. "Rain check?"

"Sure," he answered. "Rain check."

She started to leave, but Callaway stayed where he was. "You'd better get out of here before the press show up," she said.

Callaway leaned back and took a slow, thoughtful look around the parking lot, which was nearly empty now. "Nah," he said. "I'm gonna stick around a little bit. That way, if they show up, I can tell it the way I want."

She smiled and turned toward her car.

"Hey," he said when she was several paces away. She turned around, suspecting he must have forgotten something. His emerald eyes gazed at her steadily, as if seeing right through her.

"Get some rest," he said. "I need my partner at her best when the next case comes along."

She smiled. "I'll do what I can. See you tomorrow, Callaway."

"See you tomorrow, Cole."

EPILOGUE

A heavy fog seemed to envelop Harley as she climbed the steps to her brother's house, one hand gripping the painted railing. Her body ached from her fight with Ferrill. She felt like a soldier fresh off the battlefield, and she desperately hoped she was not about to walk into a new battle.

She paused at the top of the steps, her gaze drawn to the rocker parked at the end of the porch. The oil of many hands had worn down the varnish on the arms of the chair, making the wood appear dull and yellowish. Staring at it, she pictured her father sitting there and watching the traffic go by, his mind turning idly over old thoughts like a dog digging up buried chew-toys in the yard.

For years he had held onto Kelly, refusing to accept that he might never know what had happened to her. Now that he had passed the torch to Harley, however, what would happen to him? What did he have to live for?

I'm still here, she thought, *and so is Greg. Can't he go on living for us?*

Something touched her leg, and she looked down to see a tabby cat brushing against her. He stretched full-length, kneading the porch boards, and Harley noticed that the end of his tail turned at an odd angle, as if it had been broken and never healed.

The cat finished his kneading and paused by the screen door, looking expectantly up at Harley with greenish eyes that reminded her just a bit of Callaway's.

"Hey, buddy," she murmured, stooping and picking up the cat. She held one arm across her belly, supporting his feet, while she scratched his neck with the opposite hand.

When she was confident the cat was not about to jump from her arms, she pressed the doorbell. A faint jingle came from inside the house. Harley waited, trying to dredge up the energy she needed for this conversation, but she was scraping the bottom of the barrel.

The door swung open, and Greg stood in the dim hallway blinking at her, an expression of surprise written in capital letters across his face.

"Holy shit, Harley," he said. "What happened to you?"

191

She managed a weak smile. "Just the job. Sometimes it hits you like a wrecking ball."

The cat, spotting its opportunity, wriggled free from her grasp and tumbled to the floor, demonstrating that uncanny feline knack for landing on its feet. Harley watched it trot into the kitchen and settle down beside a stainless-steel bowl, crunching pieces of cat food with the side of its mouth one by one.

"How long have you had him?" Harley said, trying to break the ice. It was like chipping away at an iceberg with a spoon.

"Comstock? Found him curled up beneath the porch three or four months ago. No collar, so skinny he looked more like an oven mitt than an animal. He's doing better now, though."

Harley couldn't help smiling. "Comstock? As in Henry Comstock, the one who discovered that lode in Nevada?"

Greg shrugged. "Might as well give him a name to live up to."

Same old Greg, Harley thought.

"Is Dad here?" she said.

It seemed a silly question, given that their father was dying of cancer. The hospital had discharged him, so where else would he be?

Greg jabbed his thumb over his shoulder. "Asleep at the wheel, so to speak."

Harley could hear the voice of a gameshow host announcing a list of categories to the contestants. She had a memory of her father rolling the TV up to the kitchen table so they could watch while sharing a giant bowl of macaroni and cheese mixed with cut-up hotdogs, a staple in their family after Mom's passing. She wondered if it would ever be possible to experience that innocence again.

"I don't want to disturb him," she said, thinking Greg would tell her it was no big deal, Dad would want her to wake him up. Instead, however, Greg merely nodded.

A few beats passed in silence. Comstock continued to crunch away at his food, a sound not unlike the clattering of keys on an old typewriter.

"Sorry I wasn't able to come by sooner," Harley said. "It's just this case I was working on—"

Greg waved a dismissive hand. "I get it. If you've told me once, you've told me a thousand times." He smiled sadly, as if to let her know he wasn't holding it against her.

Harley nodded, waiting for him to continue. It occurred to her that, as much as she wanted to believe Greg was the same man she had known seventeen years earlier, the truth was he had changed too—not as dramatically as she had, perhaps, but enough that she could no longer predict his behavior as she once had.

She needed to start fresh, get to know him all over again instead of relying on what she thought she knew. But that was okay. She had time, now that she was back in New Mexico. She intended to stick around for a good while.

"How's Dad doing?" she said.

"Oh, hanging in there. Not much has changed since you last saw him." He paused. "He said he gave something to you?"

Harley hesitated, unable to read Greg. "Yeah. Did he tell you what it was?"

"Said he'd been taking notes about Kelly—talking to people, trying to piece it together. For a while, it seemed like it was the only thing keeping him alive. Now that he's passed it on to you, though…" He fell silent.

Harley was not sure how to feel. A sense of dread hung in the air.

"He talked with me about it a few times," Greg said. "It's funny, thinking back to what he told you in the hospital before you moved here. How you were living in the past." He rubbed his left forearm with his right hand and shook his head ruefully. "He was, too. He just didn't see it that way."

A clock chimed somewhere deeper in the house. The TV switched to an ad for the latest kitchen item every household in America suddenly needed to have.

"I guess I'm just wondering what chance there is," Greg said cautiously, "of learning what happened to her." He frowned, not looking at Harley, and Harley had the sense he was not sure he wanted to hear the answer.

"I'm not sure," Harley said softly. "There's always a possibility, but you know it's a long shot."

Greg nodded, looking somewhat relieved. "But if there's any way you can piece together what happened—before Dad passes, I mean—any way you can give him that peace…"

"I'll try," Harley said. "But knowing the truth doesn't always bring peace. Sometimes it just reopens the wound."

Greg was silent. Comstock paused his chewing to stretch out his paw and begin licking the fur between his toes.

"Maybe it won't bring peace," Greg agreed. "One way or the other, though, he wants to know. Don't worry about what the truth might do to him—he's tougher than you realize."

Harley nodded, but inside she doubted. Their father's mind might still be as tough as a chestnut, but his body was failing him. He could not hold onto life by sheer willpower alone, not forever, and if Greg was right that Kelly's investigation had been the only thing keeping him alive at times, what would happen now?

Suddenly she found herself thinking of Ferrill. He had failed at finding true love, and so he had tried to make it himself, like an alchemist seeking to create gold. His efforts had been doomed from the start, however. Harley, on the other hand, was already surrounded by people who loved her: her father, her brother, her boyfriend, and even her partner. Their love might be imperfect, certainly, but that didn't make it any less genuine.

She felt a surge of gratitude at this realization. She smiled gently at Greg.

"I don't know if I ever thanked you for sticking around," she said.

Greg's eyes flicked toward her, waiting for her to continue.

"For staying here, I mean," she said. "If you'd left, too—joined the Navy, like you were planning at one time—what would have happened to Dad?"

"It doesn't do any good to dwell on that."

She sensed there was something he needed to hear—something he had needed to hear for a long time.

She reached out and took his hand. "I don't regret leaving, and I couldn't change it even if I did…but I'm sorry I didn't do more to stay in touch, to repair things between Dad and me. I left you to deal with everything—his sickness, his grief. And I guess now…"

She paused, searching her heart. She hadn't planned to say any of this, but now that it was coming out, she wanted to make sure she really meant what she was saying.

She straightened her back. "What I'm trying to say is, I'm here now—for both of you. I know it's awfully late to be hearing this, and I understand if you can't forgive me—"

Greg grabbed her arm and pulled her toward himself. Harley felt the tears coming—tears for the years with family she had lost, for the burden Greg had carried out here on his own, for the father slowly dying in the next room.

She sensed she had needed this cry for a long time.

Neither spoke as they cried in one another's arms. Comstock came over, brushed tentatively against Harley's legs, and then decided he had better things to do elsewhere and wandered away, his crimped tail waving.

After a few moments, they pulled apart. Greg gave a satisfied nod, as if they had just accomplished something important together, and rose to grab a box of tissues.

"So what's next?" he said, pausing to blow his nose. "I have to admit…you were gone for so many years that I don't really remember what it's like to have a sister."

The words stung, but Harley understood what Greg meant.

"One day at a time," she said. "Do you remember what Dad used to say?"

He nodded, staring soberly at her, and repeated the phrase. "You can't live tomorrow."

Harley smiled. "That's right. You can't live tomorrow."

*

Harley closed the door and leaned against it, letting out a deep sigh. The silence of the house seemed cavernous, and when she closed her eyes, she saw Ferrill's grinning face lit by the upturned flashlight. Then, with a smile, she saw Nakai laid out on the stretcher, one hand reaching toward them.

The fear passed.

Bryce was running late, so she had some time to kill. She went to the stereo and turned on a soft rock station. She moved through the house, letting her thoughts wander. Finally, she found herself back in the office.

The papers were still spread out across the floor, awaiting her return, like a scene frozen in time. It was strange to think that just a few days earlier she had been sitting here, searching these papers. It seemed like a lifetime ago.

What chance is there really of figuring this out? she wondered. *It's been so long. The case went cold years ago.*

Staring down at her father's handwritten scribbles, she couldn't deny the fact that more than likely she would never know what had happened to Kelly. The world was full of unsolved mysteries, even ones much better documented than her sister's case, and many of them would never be solved.

Harley knew in her heart there was a good chance Kelly's disappearance would never be solved...but she had to try. Her father had gone on searching for nearly twenty years, and he had passed that responsibility on to her. She couldn't just give up, not without exhausting every option.

She picked up the pages one by one, searching for common threads, things she might have missed before. She had read through every word in the file several times already, but it was always possible there was a connection she had failed to make.

She came across the witness statement from the homeless man found sleeping in his car not far from where Kelly had disappeared. Idly scanning the officer's notes for the tenth time, Harley poured herself a glass of wine and wandered outside. Fireflies winked in the darkness, and she could smell the scent of the horses who were her neighbors, a scent she was slowly beginning to enjoy.

She stood beneath the porch light, letting her eyes scan the document as the shadows of moths drew dark zigzags across the page. The wine felt good in her throat, and it helped her mind relax—something she desperately needed after the past few days.

As she read, more as a way of unwinding than a deliberate effort to puzzle over the case, a lone coyote howled in the distance. This struck Harley as particularly fitting, since each of Kelly's friends had mentioned hearing coyotes that night so long ago.

Then, as the cry of the coyote rose to a single, high shriek, Harley's heart seemed to freeze inside her chest. Her fingers tightened on the page.

Setting her glass down so quickly that the wine sloshed over the edge and spilled into the grass, Harley placed her finger on the document and read the homeless man's statement again: *Ain't heard nothing all night but them crickets.*

The call of a coyote could travel a long distance, especially in the night air of the desert, and Kelly's friends had all mentioned hearing coyotes. So why had this man lied to the police?

And, more importantly, if he had lied about the coyotes, what *else* might he have lied about?

NOWHERE LIKE THIS
(A Harley Cole FBI Suspense Thriller—Book 4)

"This is an excellent book… When you start reading, be sure you don't have to wake up early!"
—Reader review for The Killing Game

When a young woman goes missing at a music festival in the desert, FBI special agent Harley Cole is assigned to the case. With one dead end leading to another, and with the clock ticking, Harley must crack this elusive killer's pattern—before it's too late.

Nowhere Like This (A Harley Cole FBI Suspense Thriller—Book 4) is the fourth book in a new series by #1 bestselling mystery and suspense author Kate Bold, that begins with Nowhere Safe (book #1).

When a body turns up after a drug and booze-fueled party, no one is surprised. Until they realize the person is dead.

But what is the connection to the festival?

And is Harley hunting this killer? Or being hunted herself?

A page-turning and harrowing crime thriller featuring a brilliant and tortured FBI agent, the HARLEY COLE series is a riveting mystery, packed with non-stop action, suspense, twists and turns, revelations, and driven by a breakneck pace that will keep you flipping pages late into the night. Fans of Rachel Caine, Teresa Driscoll, and Robert Dugoni are sure to fall in love.

Book #5 in the series—NOWHERE GIRL—is also available.

"This book moved very fast and every page was exciting. Plenty of dialogue, you absolutely love the characters, and you were rooting for the good guy throughout the whole story… I look forward to reading the next in the series."
—Reader review for The Killing Game

"Kate did an amazing job on this book and I was hooked from the first chapter!"
—Reader review for The Killing Game

"I really enjoyed this book. The characters were authentic, and I see the bad guys as something we hear about daily on the news... Looking forward to book 2."
—Reader review for The Killing Game

"This was a really good book. The main characters were real, flawed and human. The story went along quickly and wasn't mired in too many unnecessary details. I really enjoyed it."
—Reader review for The Killing Game

"Alexa Chase is headstrong, impatient, but most of all brave with a capital B. She never, repeat never, backs down until the bad guys are put where they belong. Clearly five stars!"
—Reader review for The Killing Game

"Captivating and riveting serial murder with a twist of the macabre… Very well done."
—Reader review for The Killing Game

"WOW what a great read! Talk about a diabolical killer! Really enjoyed this book. Looking forward to reading others by this author as well."
—Reader review for The Killing Game

"Page turner for sure. Great characters and relationships. I got into the middle of this story and couldn't put it down. Looking forward to more from Kate Bold."
—Reader review for The Killing Game

"Hard to put down. It has an excellent plot and has the right amount of suspense. I really enjoyed this book."
—Reader review for The Killing Game

"Extremely well written, and well worth buying and reading. I can't wait to read book two!"
—Reader review for The Killing Game

Kate Bold

Bestselling author Kate Bold is author of the ALEXA CHASE SUSPENSE THRILLER series, comprising six books (and counting); the ASHLEY HOPE SUSPENSE THRILLER series, comprising six books (and counting); the CAMILLE GRACE FBI SUSPENSE THRILLER series, comprising five books (and counting); and the HARLEY COLE FBI SUSPENSE THRILLER series, comprising five books (and counting).

An avid reader and lifelong fan of the mystery and thriller genres, Kate loves to hear from you, so please feel free to visit www.kateboldauthor.com to learn more and stay in touch.

BOOKS BY KATE BOLD

ALEXA CHASE SUSPENSE THRILLER
THE KILLING GAME (Book #1)
THE KILLING TIDE (Book #2)
THE KILLING HOUR (Book #3)
THE KILLING POINT (Book #4)
THE KILLING FOG (Book #5)
THE KILLING PLACE (Book #6)

ASHLEY HOPE SUSPENSE THRILLER
LET ME GO (Book #1)
LET ME OUT (Book #2)
LET ME LIVE (Book #3)
LET ME BREATHE (Book #4)
LET ME FORGET (Book #5)
LET ME ESCAPE (Book #6)

CAMILLE GRACE FBI SUSPENSE THRILLER
NOT ME (Book #1)
NOT NOW (Book #2)
NOT WELL (Book #3)
NOT HER (Book #4)
NOT NORMAL (Book #5)

HARLEY COLE FBI SUSPENSE THRILLER
NOWHERE SAFE (Book #1)
NOWHERE LEFT (Book #2)
NOWHERE TO RUN (Book #3)
NOWHERE LIKE THIS (Book #4)
NOWHERE GIRL (Book #5)

Made in the USA
Monee, IL
12 October 2022

15738085R00121